Advance Praise for
The Women of Bandit Bend

"C. C. Harrison's *The Women of Bandit Bend* is a gripping, heart-pounding tale of resilience and courage, where every page crackles with tension, richly drawn characters, and a frontier as wild and untamed as the women who dare to claim it—an absolute must-read."
—Clay Stafford, author, filmmaker, educator, and founder of Killer Nashville International Writers' Conference and The Balanced Writer.

"Gold, greed and grievous wrongdoings propel a robber and determined women to forge a new life in 1800s Colorado—no matter what it takes. This tale of hardship and resolve proves all a woman needs to prevail is a strong will and wit, matched with a determined challenge in order to conquer any challenge that gets in the way."
—Deborah J. Ledford, Award Winning author of *Redemption* and *Havoc*

"Suspense, romance and historical accuracy weave a story of girl power in the old west. Harrison's attention to detail and the masterful way she paints her characters and settings make for a page turner. *The Women of Bandit Bend* is a book you won't be able to put down!"
—Lena Jo McCoy, author of *Special Run*.

"A remarkable foray into the lives of two adventuresome women—strong-willed Tally Tisdale and her younger sister, Ivy. Harrison knows her history and it shows in the near flawless details of her story. You'll care about these two women; you'll root for their success and happiness, and you'll feel like you're a part of their family.

You can't ask for more than that from a novel."
—Michael Zimmer, award winning author of *The Poacher's Daughter*

"In 1863 Colorado, sisters Tally and Ivy inherit a perilous homestead. Facing outlaws and kidnappers, they outsmart danger, reclaim hidden gold, and unravel family secrets in a gripping tale. C. C. Harrison's book has heart, adventure, and just enough unpredictability to hook readers! With limited room on my bookshelves, I'm happy to make a space for this engaging Western adventure."
—Michael R. Ritt, award winning author of *The Sons of Philo Gaines*

"A wild horse romp of an adventure. C. C. Harrison's terrific tale of homesteading against all odds is filled with heart, determination, and a huge dose of sisterly grit. In the event of catastrophe, I'd want Tally and Ivy on my side."
—Scott Graham, National Book Award-winning author of *Grand Canyon Sacrifice*

Other Books by C. C. Harrison

The Charmstone

Running from Strangers

Sage Cane's House of Grace and Favor
(written as Christy Hubbard)

Picture of Lies

Death by G-String, a Coyote Canyon Ladies Ukulele Club Mystery

THE WOMEN *of* BANDIT BEND

by
C. C. Harrison

Artemesia
Publishing

ISBN: 978-1-963832-16-7 (paperback)
ISBN: 978-1-963832-29-7 (ebook)
LCCN: 2025933503
Copyright © 2025 by C.C. Harrison
Cover Illustration and Design © 2025 Hannah Linder

Printed in the United States

Names, characters, and incidents depicted in this book are products of the author's imagination or are used fictitiously. Any resemblance to actual events, locales, organizations, or persons, living or dead, is entirely coincidental and beyond the intent of the author or the publisher.

All rights reserved. No part of this book may be reproduced or transmitted in any form or by any means, electronic or mechanical, including photocopying, recording, or by any information storage or retrieval system without written permission of the publisher, except for the inclusion of brief quotations in a review.

NO AI TRAINING: Without in any way limiting the author's [and publisher's] exclusive rights under copyright, any use of this publication to "train" generative artificial intelligence (AI) technologies to generate text is expressly prohibited. The author reserves all rights to license uses of this work for generative AI training and development of machine learning language models.

Artemesia Publishing
9 Mockingbird Hill Rd
Tijeras, New Mexico 87059
www.apbooks.net
info@artemesiapublishing.com

PROLOGUE

April 1863 Colorado

THE THREE HORSEMEN HID in the trees, tense, expectant, crackling with nervous energy. The jittery horses, sensing the edginess of the men in the saddles, snorted loudly, stomped their hooves and tossed their heads. Leather squeaked, metal rattled.

"Whoa!" Boss soothed his horse with soft words and a touch, then scowled at the other two men and gave a harsh command. "Settle your horses."

The two men tugged the reins and muttered at their horses. They stopped fidgeting and quieted down, but swished their tails to chase off the flies that were making their skin twitch.

Satisfied, Boss turned back to look with narrowed eyes through the newly leafed trees. But there was no need to keep watch. He'd know when the stagecoach was approaching. The hooves of the galloping six-horse team would beat the ground in a rapid staccato then slow as the driver hauled up on the reins and applied his boot to the brake before entering the bend in the road.

All the stage drivers knew they'd have to slow their teams when they got to this spot or the stage could heave over onto its side spilling passengers or payroll or mail or gold all over the rutted roadway. Boss knew it, too, which is why he'd chosen that exact spot.

Omaha Jones shifted in his saddle easing the pressure on his generous backside, and yanked out his pocket watch to look at the time.

"How much longer you think, Boss?"

Boss didn't answer, just kept staring through the branches. He was a handsome man, well-spoken when he chose to be, and smart. If it hadn't been for him, those picks and shovels wouldn't be shored up against the nearby tree trunks. He knew they'd be needed later, but the other two wouldn't have planned that far ahead. It had been up to him. It was always up to him. That's why they called him Boss.

Edgar Rico, the Mexican, stretched his back and shoulders, then sent tobacco colored spittle onto the ground. Rico didn't talk much and he had a reputation for meanness, but was a dependable sort when motivated by money, so Boss brought him along.

Omaha Jones, a saddle bum on the drift picking up jobs at whatever trail town he found himself in or on the dodge two steps ahead of the law was also there only for the money.

Boss would be hard pressed to call those two men his friends or even companions. He liked to play a lone hand, though he did tolerate them when there was whiskey to be shared, cards to be played, or a job to be done. Like now.

A wind came up. Leaves rustled, branches creaked and scraped against each other until the gust died off. And that's when Boss heard it.

The other men heard it, too. They exchanged a look. Boss nodded, then all three pulled up the bandanas tied loosely under their chins.

A rolling dust cloud pulled by a stagecoach appeared in the distance. It wasn't a fancy long distance Concord, but rather a mud wagon open on both sides with only canvas flaps between passengers and the weather. It was built for speed on short hauls in the mountains over rough terrain. This one carried a monthly payroll down to a bank in Denver along with a stash of gold.

As it neared the onside of the turn, the driver, seated on the right with a shotgun by his side, expertly slowed the horses to negotiate the sharp curve. The Wells Fargo guard, a mountain of a man in a canvas duster seated to the driver's left, tightened his grip on the sawed-off shotgun in his lap and came alert, looking right and left, front and back.

Though Boss could see them, he and his men were well hidden. He raised his arm signaling his men to stand back. When the time was right, he thrust his arm downward signaling *now*. Revolvers drawn, they positioned their horses in the middle of the road and pointed their guns in the direction of the approaching stagecoach.

At the sight of the bandits as the stage came around the bend, the driver, a mustachioed dandy in a cutaway coat and striped trousers, pulled up on the reins, and put his boot to the brake. Before the Wells Fargo guard finished raising his sawed-off shotgun, Boss sent a bullet whizzing past his ear. The man ducked and the shotgun slipped out of his hands coming to rest under the driver's seat.

When the team came to a full stop, Boss waved his revolver and spoke to the driver, his tone conversational. "How about tossing those shotguns over the side. And your other weapons, too, whatever you're both carrying."

There was no use resisting, the bandits had the drop on them, so the men did as they were told, then sat with their hands raised, looking daggers at Boss. Four frightened passengers, three of them women, stared out the windows at Rico who was ordering them to disembark one by one.

"I'll have that payroll pouch," Boss said to the driver. "Hand it over, easy like."

Without a word, the driver picked up the leather money bag and dropped it over the side.

"That's all there is, mister." The driver glanced over his shoulder at the passengers handing Rico their valuables. "I just got these innocent souls wanting to get to their loved ones in Denver. So if you don't mind, we'd like to be on our way."

"Not so fast," Boss said. "How about that strongbox under your seat? I'd like that, too." The timbre of his voice suggested a request, but everyone knew it was no such thing.

The driver and the guard conferred with their eyes, silently debating their next move.

Boss and Omaha raised their guns with both hands and took aim. "Don't even think about it, sirs," said Boss. "All we want is that gold you got and no one gets hurt."

Reluctantly, the driver and the guard reached for the strongbox. It was heavy just as Boss knew it would be. Filled with gold, coins, and bank notes, it made for a hefty load. Breathing hard and grunting with effort, the driver and the guard dragged the bulky metal box out and together heaved it over the side. It hit the ground with a thud throwing up dirt.

The passengers, stiff with fright, watched it all with jumpy eyes. The lone male passenger, using his good sense, stood with hands in the air, his face grim. The three women huddled together. The younger one, a girl about eighteen, was sobbing into a crunched up handkerchief, her wet shining eyes riveted on Boss. She lowered her shaking hands. "Don't hurt us," she pleaded.

Boss took in her curly hair and pretty mouth, then slid his eyes over to Rico who was stashing the valuables in a leather pouch attached to his saddle with one hand and pointing a revolver at the passengers with the other. Boss dipped his head in the girl's direction.

"What did she give us?"

The Mexican stopped what he was doing, but held his gun steady while he pulled a gold ring from the pouch and held it up for Boss to see.

"Give it back to her," Boss said.

Rico balked, shaking his head. "But Boss, it looks like a real diamond."

"Give it back."

Clearly not happy about it, Rico tossed the ring in the girl's direction where it landed at her feet. She looked at Boss and moved her lips in a silent thank you, then quickly bent down and picked it up. She closed her fingers tightly around it.

Boss touched the brim of his hat with his fingertips. "Sorry to inconvenience you, ma'am."

With the payroll satchel and the strongbox now in their possession, Boss motioned with his revolver sending the passengers back into the coach. "You can be on your way. Enjoy your trip. Sorry to detain you."

The bandits reined their horses off the roadway to make room for the stage to pass unimpeded.

When the passengers were safely back inside, the driver released the brake lever with one foot and took up the lines, but didn't move. His eyes darted uncertainly, unsure if Boss meant what he said.

"Go on, git," Omaha shouted, and shot a bullet into the air. The horses reared slightly, then whinnied and bolted forward. Once past, the Wells Fargo guard turned around in his seat aiming a revolver. But Boss was faster and fired first. The guard slumped over as the driver cracked a bullwhip, setting the team to a steady gallop.

When the stage was out of sight, the highwaymen dismounted and tied their horses. Boss hoisted the strap of the payroll pouch over his shoulder, then picked up the digging tools. Omaha and Rico took the weapons from the roadbed, then grabbed a handle on each side of the metal box. Following behind Boss, they lugged it through the trees to a ramshackle cabin a good distance off the road.

Omaha and Rico set the strongbox and the shotguns on the ground and cast an eye at the woebegone dwelling. Rico swiped off his hat, wiped his forehead with his sleeve. He slapped his hat on his thigh a few times to shake off the dust, then plopped it back on his head.

Omaha did the same, then still catching his breath from the weight of the heavy load, he asked, "Who lives here?"

Boss shook his head. He'd planned this job carefully, had tracked the route and scouted out the area well in advance. The only thing he'd seen was a black bear in the berry patch beyond.

"No one. It's abandoned." He leaned the shovels and picks against a stack of roughcut logs, then shouldered off the payroll pouch and opened the flap. "We'll split up the payroll money now, then bury the gold and come back for it later. The next swing station is only ten miles away. If that Wells Fargo agent is dead, they'll be riding out here looking for us in a couple of hours, so start digging."

Rico and Omaha exchanged a doubtful glance. Omaha spoke up. "Well, I don't know, Boss. When are we coming back to get it?"

"When it's safe. When the Wells Fargo investigators stop riding the trail looking for us."

"But that could be—"

"Yeah," Boss interrupted and locked eyes with Omaha daring him to argue the point. "It could. I'll let you know when it's time."

Omaha scowled but said nothing.

Rico spoke up. "How did you even know there was

gold on that stage?"

Boss smiled as he emptied the pouch. "I met a Wells Fargo driver at the Diamond Rio. They'd just fired him. All it took was a few dollars and a bottle of whiskey to loosen his tongue."

He finished counting out the payroll money and gave each man his share. While they recounted their take, Boss pointed out a burial spot.

"There," he said. "That old crooked tree yonder next to that pile of boulders. We'll bury the strongbox there and come back for it when things quiet down."

Still unsure, but giving in anyway, Rico and Omaha cast their eyes where Boss indicated, then looked around taking in the long view.

"How we gonna remember where we dug?" asked Rico. "That cabin looks like a good wind would blow it away."

Boss unbuckled the pockets on the now empty payroll pouch and dug around until he found a stubby pencil and a crumbled up receipt. He handed both to Omaha. "Here. You start making a map. Draw the pile of tumbled rocks. That'll be our landmark."

Rico and Boss picked up shovels and began digging as Omaha sketched out the lay of the land. After a few minutes, his hand stilled and he studied the rock pile. "Don't the shape of those big rocks look like a nun kneelin' there prayin'?" he said. "What do you think, Rico? You go to church, don't ya?"

Rico nodded, and Boss said, "Put it on the map. But hurry. That stagecoach driver is going to report the robbery at his next stop. We have to get out of here or we're going to end up dangling from the end of a hanging rope."

CHAPTER ONE

A month or so later

THE HIRED DRIVER, A beanpole of a man with scraggly hair under a gambler hat that had lost its will to live stopped the buckboard on Bandit Bend two miles outside the burgeoning new settlement of Sutton Creek. It had been a bumpy, dusty ride, and his passengers recently arrived from Denver were still wearing their traveling clothes. The two women on the bench seat brushed away road grime from their garments, and scanned the raw, wild and sparsely inhabited landscape.

"Are you sure this is where it is?" Ivy asked.

Tally looked at her much folded and unfolded hand drawn map, and held it so her sister could see it, too. She studied it a moment, then placed the tip of her finger on it.

"Well, Father's map shows the mountain range to the north and there it is in front of us."

Soaring peaks in the near distance poking the big bowl of blue sky drew three sets of eyes. "That's the Mosquito Range," pointed out the driver who said his name was Buster Morton. "Part of the Colorado Rockies."

"And the map shows the river west of Father's homestead. I can hear it from here." Tally looked to the left. "There, on the other side of the road through the trees."

She rested her eyes on the map again. "He drew a line of evergreens running north to south, and beyond that a two humped hill. His letter said it reminded him of a camel." She shrugged and raised her eyebrows. "This has got to be it."

She turned to the driver. "Mr. Morton, can we go a little farther around this curve?"

Buster clucked his tongue and flicked the reins lightly. The horse moved into a slow walk. They hadn't gone very far when Tally asked the driver to stop again.

"Look there." She pointed. "Father's letter said he cleared some trees at the road for an entry gate. I don't see a gate, but there's a wagon track heading off that way."

Ivy shaded her eyes from the sun with a flat hand. "Yes, I see it."

Tally folded the map and put it back in her drawstring bag. "Turn in here, Mr. Morton. We'd like to take a closer look."

"Surely, ma'am. Hold on, though. It looks rough."

Buster reined the horse and wagon off the roadway and onto a track that was nothing more than a narrow, deeply rutted swath cut through the trees.

"Hyah!" he hollered, urging the horse forward. The buckboard bumped and swayed as it proceeded, and the sisters braced their legs and held on to keep from bouncing off the seat. The track widened onto a broad, scrub dotted front yard.

"Whoa!"

Buster stopped the horse in front of a sorrowful looking log cabin with a board roof. Two windows without glass were cut into the logs on either side of a front door hanging from a single hinge. Exterior shutters meant for privacy and protection from the elements did little to perform those functions. Most of the slats were broken or missing.

The women stared at the dwelling and the sad assembly of broken down and partially constructed outbuildings. A chicken coop without chickens, a sheep pen without sheep, and a partially built corral. Most of the posts were tamped solid, but the rails were strewn haphazardly on the ground next to the skeletal framework awaiting hammer and nails.

Ivy's face drooped with disappointment. "This is it?" she said miserably.

Buster brushed his black, round-crowned hat back, and gave his head a couple of shakes. "Doesn't look like anybody's been here for some time. You sure we didn't make a wrong turn somewhere?"

Tally, travel worn and now disheartened, let out a long, exhausted breath. "No. This is it. The map matches the landmarks exactly. It's in my father's own handwriting. Everything is here just like he drew it on the map and wrote in his letters."

Ivy, stricken, pressed her hands to her mouth under crestfallen eyes. "I thought he would have proved it up more than this."

"Excuse me, ladies," Buster said. "None o' my business, but when's the last time you heard from your father?"

Tally sighed. "Not since last summer."

The three of them sat motionless, letting the silence hold their thoughts. The horse snorted and shifted his weight, as if it was bored to death and ready to go back to the livery for food and a snooze.

Tally stood and straightened her shoulders stoically. "Let's go in," she said, lifting her skirts and making an effort to lift her spirits, as well. "I want to see the inside."

Buster frowned. "Might want to reconsider that, ma'am. Homestead empty this long, animals might have moved in. Never know what you're going to find in there."

"We'll be quite all right, Mr. Morton, I assure you. Would you mind helping me down?"

Ivy held her lips in a stubborn pout. "Maybe we should go back to Denver."

Tally edged a narrow eyed gaze at her recalcitrant sister. Sixteen years old and already headstrong, which Tally feared would turn into bullheadedness as she got older.

"We're not going back," Tally said. "We came here to see father, and that's what we're going to do. I don't know where he is, but I intend to find him."

Buster climbed down from the buckboard and tied the horse to a rickety hitch rail. Taking his outstretched hand, Tally got off and then turned to Ivy, who still hadn't moved and was sitting with her arms folded tight.

"I'm not going in there," she said. "I'm wearing new shoes."

Ivy's tone and cadence warned Tally that her sister might be working up to a godawful fuss fit of the kind her mother favored before she died. Ivy had a deep-seated abundance of their mother's most irritating qualities.

Tally pinned her with a sharp look. Her voice was soft, but it held a push. "Come along Ivy, or do you want to wait out here alone? God knows what's lurking in those trees yonder. Remember what we saw on the ride out here?"

The ride to Bandit Bend had been hard and tedious with nothing much to see once they left the broad main street of Sutton Creek proper. Until they came upon a hanging tree.

It had been an extremely unpleasant sight, but not an unusual one for folks who lived in this rough country. Buster had explained the law on the frontier was frequently taken into the hands of locals, and necktie party justice was often administered by men more lawless than those that got hanged. The sisters had gasped at the sight of three headless bodies sprawled on the ground, their detached heads still stuck in the nooses slung over a thick tree branch.

Buster hadn't stopped or slowed, but instead cut a wide berth for the sake of the sisters' sensitivities. "When I get back to town," he'd mumbled, "I'll have someone come out take care of that." It wasn't spoken of again.

Remembrance froze the features of Ivy's face after which she shuddered. She sat a moment, stubborn, then released a sharp breath, and reluctantly held out her hand to Buster standing beside the buckboard patiently waiting for her to decide what she was going to do.

"All right," she said, stepping down. "But I want new shoes if these get ruined."

Tally led the way, skirts lifted so they wouldn't drag in the interminable dirt. Clearly, she was going to need new shoes, too.

Three planked steps led up to a split log porch under a slumping low pitched overhang. "Well, these steps are new," Tally said making a feeble effort at lightheartedness and giving what she hoped looked like a reassuring smile.

She pushed the door open. Two dark and chilly rooms of hard living greeted her. Ashes on the hearth of an unlit fireplace, the dominant feature inside the cabin, was evidence that someone had lived there through a harsh Colorado winter. Doorless cupboards held tins of coffee and other packaged food items. Knives and forks and cooking utensils stood upright in a tall metal mug on a shelf that held matching tin plates and more mugs. There was a sink with a catch basin underneath, and beside it a two-burner wood stove. Cast iron fry pans hung on hooks within reach.

Rope used for drying laundry, some still hanging, was attached to a wall. Lengths of rope from the same coil had been used to support a skinny mattress on a crude bed frame. Several tattered blankets were folded on top of it along with a thin pillow.

The only light source besides the two uncovered windows was a burned out candle on top of a barrel in the corner next to a rope bottomed rocking chair. A small eating table stood in the middle of the room surrounded by four chairs that wobbled on uneven legs when Tally put her hands on them.

A second room meant to be a bedroom was being used for storage pending the completion of the half-built barn outside. Digging tools, buckets, axes, coils of rope, bags of animal feed, and a variety of tools and other items usually stored in a barn took up most of the space. A small two drawer chest against the wall next to bags of chicken feed held two shirts and two pairs of denim trousers neatly folded, underwear, and several pairs of mismatched socks all of them darned and patched to cover the worn places.

Tally stared, demoralized. She didn't feel good about this. Two worries seesawed foremost in her mind. First, the harshness of her father's life as a homesteader. How had he managed? And second, a thought too terrible to ponder—was he alive? She gave specific thought to dismissing the worst possible answers.

Ivy was on the verge of weeping. "Where do you suppose he is?" she said, fighting tears.

Tally wiped the frown off her face and fought to hold back her own tears. *The strong have to be strong for those who are less so.*

"I don't know," she said, forcing the words through a tightness in her throat.

"But do you think he's all right?" Ivy's question was full of hope.

Tally's answer was quick and optimistic if falsely so. "I'm sure he is. He's done enough work around here to make himself somewhat comfortable." She paused, feeling uneasiness spreading through her stomach, then had to admit, "But it's not like him to leave chores unfinished."

She tilted her head toward the outside. "The corral and the barn and such."

Buster, clearly ill at ease over the women's obvious distress removed his hat and held it in front of him, his jittery fingers dancing on the brim.

A long stretch of silence followed during which Tally came to a decision. "Mr. Morton, could you please tell me where I can find the closest Land Office?"

Buster bobbed his head eagerly. "Yes, ma'am. Right across from the sheriff's office a block from the livery where you hired me and the buckboard. Land Agent's name is Foster Goodnight Pettyjohn."

"Thank you. We should be getting back now. Come along, Ivy." She turned and with long strides went out the door and down the steps.

This time Ivy followed without argument, quickening her pace to keep up with her fast-walking sister whose determined steps took her to the buckboard before Buster reached it.

Once they were settled in their seats and Buster had picked up the reins, Ivy took Tally's hand and held on. "What are we going to do?"

"First, we're going to get a room at the hotel or at one of the nicer boarding houses in town. I'm sure Mr. Morton can direct us to a clean and safe establishment."

"Yes, ma'am, I can."

"Then we're going to talk to Mr. Pettyjohn about Father's homestead. If he can't see us today, we'll meet with him first thing in the morning. He may know where Father is and why we haven't heard from him." Tally silently prayed such information would be forthcoming.

Buster made a sound to the horse and slapped the reins guiding the horse into a full circle around the yard stopping to peer at the barn.

"That barn needs a lot of work," he told them as if they

couldn't see that for themselves.

Tally sharpened her gaze and raised a finger suddenly remembering something important. "And, oh, yes. We're going to need new shoes."

They started off again, but before they reached the wagon track that led to the road, Ivy squeezed Tally's hand and exclaimed, "Oh, look! Over there. That rock pile. It looks like a nun kneeling in prayer, don't you think?"

Tally, busy running through a plan newly forming in her mind, absently noted the perceived likeness and agreed that it did.

CHAPTER TWO

***T**HE TOP OF FOSTER* Goodnight Pettyjohn's otherwise shiny bald head was plastered with scant strands of fair-colored hair darkened with pomade. Though portly around the middle, he cut a fashionable figure in a well-cut frock coat and vest. A gleaming watch chain draped across his paunch hung with a little gold fob in the shape of a dollar sign. His white shirt buttoned to the neck, the symbol of a man who does not work with his hands, was impeccable, and Tally couldn't help wondering if such a fine shirt would still be pristine at the end of a day in a dusty, often windy town like this one.

He stood and greeted the women with a smile when they entered the Land Office the next morning. After he executed a chivalrous little bow, hardly more than a dip of his head, really, he gave Tally's hand a light shake, released it, then repeated the gesture with Ivy.

"How are you this fine day?" he said, and Tally could tell right off that he fortified his morning coffee with whiskey. But never mind. She sometimes did the same though no one knew and she would have denied it if asked.

The office was clean and bright, decorated in the popular Western style with Navajo rugs on a floor made of old wood planks. Maps covered the walls, and bookshelves filled with ledgers behind an oak desk nearly as big as a billiard table took up most of the floor space. A row of chairs just inside the front door provided seating for anyone waiting their turn during busy times.

Pettyjohn took his seat behind the oversized desk and motioned Tally and Ivy into the chairs facing him on the other side. When they were seated, they introduced themselves, and Tally explained that they had come to Sutton Creek after not hearing from their father.

"He's not at his homestead and it appears he hasn't been there for some time. My sister and I are worried about him, and hoped you might have some information that would help us find him."

"Oh, my." Pettyjohn frowned. "I'm sorry to hear that. I don't know how I can help, but I'll do what I can. What is your father's name?"

"Carl Henry Tisdale. People call him Hank."

Pettyjohn stepped over to one of the bookshelves and ran his finger along their spines. He finally grasped and a thick ledger and sat back down at his desk.

He removed his gold wire rimmed spectacles, dragged a handkerchief from an inside pocket, and wiped the lenses clean. Then he held them up to the light, gazed through them to check their clarity.

"Well," he said in exaggerated accommodation, "this is his ledger. Let's take a look." He opened it flat on his desk, and leafed through pages one by one muttering the name of each under his breath—*proof of citizenship, proof of age, receipt for filing fee*—before moving on to the next. Finally he stopped turning pages and removed a document. Tally caught sight of her father's name on the signature line at the bottom.

"Yes, here it is," said Pettyjohn. "His patent application. It seems it was approved with no difficulties. He provided all the required documentation. All that's needed now is proof that he's proved up the claim and a deed will be issued forthwith."

He looked up and tilted his head. "But you say he's not there and you haven't heard from him?"

"Not since last summer," Ivy said. "We were hoping you'd have some information. Or perhaps know friends of his, or someone with whom he'd made acquaintance that could tell us where he might have gone." She finished on a note of dejection, and the corners of Pettyjohn's mouth turned down in a show of empathy.

"I'm sorry, my dear, but I don't. Did you ask any of his neighbors?"

"We didn't see any neighboring homesteads. His land borders the road, and the boy from the livery told us it was the same road used by the stage line. But there were no nearby cabins."

The Land Agent replied with buoyancy. "I wouldn't worry too much. Homesteaders often take leave temporarily to, say, take a job in a nearby town to acquire additional funds so they can continue proving up their claim. It's a common occurrence. Or perhaps he left to purchase equipment, something not available here. Sutton Creek is still growing and expanding. Not all supplies are available locally and deliveries of necessities are erratic."

Tally hadn't thought of that, and his words ignited a small spark of optimism. She exchanged a hopeful smile with Ivy. Perhaps they were worrying needlessly.

Pettyjohn turned his eyes back to Hank Tisdale's application. He took a moment before asking, "Has the homestead been proved up at all?"

"Oh, yes," Tally replied. She filled him in on the condition of the rest of the land. "Until our father comes back, my sister and I would like to move into the cabin and take over the responsibility of the claim."

He frowned and his mouth fell open a little. "Proving up a homestead is not an easy undertaking. Even the hardest working homesteaders have a tough go of it, and not everyone succeeds. It involves a lot of hard, dirty work and a good deal of money. Do you have the wherewithal to purchase the necessary supplies? Hammers and nails and axes and lumber? You'll need a wagon. And a plow and a team of horses or oxen or mules to pull it. Do you and your sister have the funds for that, Miss Tisdale?" The tone of his voice suggested he expected the answer would be no.

"Rest assured, Mr. Pettyjohn, we're adequately situated with financial resources." She smiled to cover up her lie, but had felt she was losing ground and needed to say something in order to strengthen her position. "I meet the financial requirements handily."

Beside her, Ivy stirred and Tally prayed she'd keep her mouth shut for once.

After a polite pause, Pettyjohn folded his blue veined hands on the desk, leaned forward a little and looked Tally directly in the eye. "Tell me. How old are you?"

"Twenty-two." She uttered a silent prayer that he wouldn't contact anyone in Denver and discover this lie. This one or any other.

Without appearing quizzical, he shifted his gaze to Ivy. "And you?"

Ivy lifted her chin and spoke up before her sister could answer for her. "I'm twenty." She skittered a side glance at Tally who lowered her lids to her lap so as not to give away that this, too, was a lie.

Pettyjohn let out a long breath, and cleared his throat, his eyes sliding from one sister to the other and back again. He had the look of a man pondering a weighty decision.

"Forgive me for saying so, ladies, but I'm not so sure women, uh, fine ladies like the two of you," he paused, letting the implied compliment sink in, "would be able to complete the job of proving up a homestead." He referred to the piece of paper on the desk in front of him and shifted uneasily in his seat.

"These claims need to be proved up within five years. There's just under four more years remaining on your father's application. From what you've told me, there's a lot of work yet to be done. There's no livestock, no crops. As I explained, you'll need lumber and saws..."

He started to repeat himself, then sat back in his chair and chuckled as if certain he'd convinced them that their idea was so fanciful and farfetched it should have been obvious to both of them that only an idiot would have considered it.

Tally swallowed the retort on the tip of her tongue, letting him get away with what she felt was a slight to her gender. Pride straightened her spine and she replied in a voice slightly brassier than what was considered ladylike. "It's my understanding that women are eligible under the Homestead Act, Mr. Pettyjohn, and my sister and I are quite capable of putting a home together. I did so quite successfully after our mother died and again after I got married."

The condescending smile on Pettyjohn's face was wiped away with a scowl. "Oh. You're married then. Is your husband with you?"

Tally wished she hadn't said that, wished she could breathe those words back into her mouth. Now that they were out, she hurried to cover up.

"No. I'm... I'm a widow. Jacob is no longer with us." Then to forestall further questioning, she hurried on. "Four years is a very long time, and I'm sure there are any number of good, strong, iron muscled men around town who would be happy to earn a few extra dollars helping us with the *really hard* work."

Holding on to his scowl Pettyjohn nodded slowly, but said nothing as Tally went on.

"There are tools and equipment in my father's cabin and surely some in the barn. Whatever materials needed that aren't there will be provided in a timely manner."

Pettyjohn touched each sister with a penetrating look, and in the silence Tally could hear his agitated breath going in and out of his nostrils. Then his face softened.

"I'm only concerned for your welfare," he said kindly. "Women alone are sometimes bothered by outlaws."

She could have assured him that she was perfectly capable of taking care of herself, and of Ivy, too, but she bit her tongue. It wouldn't do to tell him too much. She'd been prepared to push hard for what she was asking if she had to. But now she turned her lips into her sweetest smile as a way of smoothing things over in case she had come across as a harpy. That would surely make her a target of gossip and call attention to herself in all the wrong ways inviting unwanted scrutiny. She wasn't overly given to talking about the past. *Her* past.

After taking in a calming breath through her nose, she gentled her voice. "So if my sister and I could sign whatever paperwork is necessary to make this official, we'd like to take over the claim today."

His voice was cheery, but his smile was definitely an effort. "Certainly. By all means."

He opened his desk drawer and removed a printed sheet of paper with blank spaces needing to be filled in. He picked up a pen, dipped it in ink, and began by writing in the date. After that he asked them some questions and filled in the other blanks with their answers. When he was finished, he pushed it across the desktop and handed over a pen for their signatures. The sisters each signed where indicated, and Tally slid it back to him.

Pettyjohn examined the signatures, then put the sheet of paper in the stack with the others. "This will prove that the property has been temporarily transferred to you and your sister."

"I assume I can get a copy of that paper we just signed?" Tally asked.

"I'm afraid not today. All paperwork is the property of the government. Colorado is not a state as of yet, so we're beholden to the Department of the Interior for all matters of homesteading. But they have a staff of copyists there. I'll be happy to put in a request for them to send you one," Pettyjohn said, his manner demurringly accommodating.

"And I'd like a copy of everything in my father's file, as well," Tally said returning his pen. She held faint hope he'd actually comply with her request, but asked anyway keeping her smile as dazzling as she could manage.

Pettyjohn stood, ending the meeting, and the sisters stood, too.

"Would you kindly point the way to the sheriff's office, Mr. Pettyjohn? He or his deputies may have some information about my father."

He chuckled indulgently. "Unfortunately, the sheriff and his men won't be much help to you in that regard today."

"Why not?"

"Workers at the edge of town preparing to build a new harness shop dug up some bones yesterday. Human bones. The sheriff and his men have their hands full trying to figure out whose they are."

Ivy gasped and Tally shuddered.

"Oh, dear," Tally replied. "Well, I suppose I won't bother him right now, then. Thank you for your help, Mr. Pettyjohn. Have a good day."

"You as well," he said. "And good luck."

CHAPTER THREE

TALLY THOUGHT BACK ON the entirety of the conversation with the land agent, and decided it was mostly positive even though he was unable to provide any information about their father's whereabouts. That's what caused her unease.

But the somber look on Ivy's face told another story. They walked half a block along the boardwalk running parallel to a main street half as wide as a pasture before she spoke up.

"I was hoping he'd know something about Father," she said, crestfallen.

Tally's reply came on a breathy sigh. "Me, as well."

"Do you think Father's all right?"

"I'm certain of it. Mr. Pettyjohn was probably right. Father ran out of money and had to take a temporary job somewhere. There's nothing to worry about. He'll be back when he's ready." Lacking any news to the contrary, she very much wanted to believe that and felt it was imperative that Ivy believe it, too. Tally hoped her own restive thoughts couldn't be read on her face.

"Why did you say we were going to prove up father's claim?" Ivy's question was laden with anxiety. "We don't know anything about homesteading."

Tally exhaled softly. "We have no choice. We can't afford to live in the hotel while we wait for him to return. And abandoned homesteads are either patented to someone else or taken over by squatters. We don't want Father to come home to find he's lost his property. As long as we're living there no one can take it away. At least not for another four years, and surely Father will have returned before then." Despite her valiant show of optimism, she was quickly becoming dispirited.

"But can we afford to do it?" Ivy asked. "Do we have the money?"

Tally did some quick calculations in her head. There was still some of the money their mother left them when she died. Then, when Jacob passed away, he left a little, too. By living frugally in Denver, she'd managed to save almost half of what she earned from her job dressmaking and altering ball gowns for society ladies while Ivy attended school. It wasn't a substantial amount and wouldn't last forever, but they would no longer be paying rent when they moved into the cabin so they should be all right for a while.

She did her best to wipe the apprehension off her face and out of her voice when she answered Ivy's questions. "We're going to be fine. Please don't worry. I know there's a lot to learn about homesteading, but there are all kinds of ways to cut corners and bring in extra money. I read that some families earn income by breeding their livestock."

Ivy lifted her brows to underscore her cynicism. "Do we *know how* to breed livestock?"

"Well, no, but… we'll learn," Tally finished, flustered. "And besides. It's a sound investment. Once Father has the deed, he can sell the spread at a nice profit."

Ivy's expression indicated she was still not overly convinced.

Tally continued persuading. "And you heard what Mr. Pettyjohn said. There may come a time when one of us might have to take a job in town to build up our reserves."

She swung her hand palm up indicating the street and gesturing to the commercial establishments on either side. "And look. There are plenty of places where we might find work if we have to."

Ivy's eyes drifted to the many businesses lining the thoroughfare, and Tally was relieved to see Ivy looked mildly interested. Restaurants, saloons, candle makers, booteries, haberdashers, cobblers, dressmakers, tailors, and two stores selling men's, women's and children's readymade clothing. In the short time they'd been in town, Tally had counted three general stores, the largest of which was called Gallagher's. They all featured shelves stocked with flour, sugar, coffee and an untold number of other foodstuffs as well as dry goods.

Several shops sold mining supplies exclusively while others had expanded their offerings to include items on the list the Land Agent had rattled off. Tally slowed her pace, motioned Ivy to follow, and pressed their way through the crowd to browse the equipment offered for sale in front of one such retail establishment.

She blinked and her heart seized up a little when she saw the price tag on a hay rake. Next to that was a steel plow and harrow combination marked down to fifteen dollars from the original price. Ivy noticed, too, and shot her a dubious glance. Without comment, they made their way back to the boardwalk and continued on.

In their father's letters that had arrived fairly regularly until they didn't, he'd told them that Sutton Creek had become a boomtown in the four years since gold was first discovered in the surrounding mountains, and miners had begun pouring in. Though not a metropolis now, the town was certainly thriving. A small ragtag collection of tents and huts clustered together in the older part of town were being replaced by more solid structures. Further down the street sturdy wood and adobe buildings were on the rise as far as Tally could see.

A sign attached to a three-legged stanchion on a side street announced in big hand painted letters, FUTURE RAILROAD STATION. Construction had already begun on another hotel adjacent to the site, and around the corner an opera theater marquee declared GRAND OPENING NEXT WEEK. Newly built homes climbed the side of the mountain almost to the upper reaches of the mining camps.

It was noisy as all get-out and the streets were swarming with people and horses and horse drawn wagons of all kinds. Men in business suits and boots that looked custom made. Men with the grime of work lining their fingernails. A few fashionably dressed women stepping out in the company of smartly dressed men. Tosspots who had overstayed their welcome at the saloons—Tally and Ivy gave *them* wide berth—and miners! There were hundreds of them. Peddlers with pushcarts in the street and hawkers on the boardwalk shouted out their wares, everything from pins and needles to baskets, bowls and silver spoons. The walkway was so crowded, they sometimes had to turn sideways to squeeze past a rowdy bunch.

Faint tinkling of piano music came from the interior of a saloon. Intrigued, Ivy stopped and raised up on tip toes to peer in over the batwing doors. Tally joined her. Animal heads decorated the back wall, and a six foot painting of a belly dancer was framed behind the bar. Though it was not yet noon, all the tables were occupied, and beer and whiskey flowed freely. A ravishing red haired beauty with generously applied makeup wearing a provocative décolleté gown stood on a small stage. She was singing a song in a seductive, bewitching voice, but most of the men at the tables ignored her preferring to play cards or billiards, or flirt lewdly with the saloon girls.

The girl on the stage kept singing anyway.

A man in a well-cut suit carrying a gold tipped walking stick pushed open the doors. The sisters had to step aside to avoid a collision. He briefly tipped his hat, directed a nod and a full bright smile at Ivy, then walked away swinging his stick in a most cavalier manner. He carried the air of a man of some standing, and Ivy followed his progress down the boardwalk with her eyes until he was out of sight.

"Come along, Ivy."

When Ivy didn't budge, Tally tugged on her arm until she reluctantly fell in step.

Tally feared it was going to take some doing to keep Ivy in check and focused in this wild, not yet completely civilized frontier town. Ivy was the pretty one of the two having inherited the delicate stature and fine features of their mother. Her high cheek bones, pert nose, glossy hair and thick lashed blue eyes commanded more than a mere passing glance from men and boys of all ages. Women, too, who truth be told couldn't hide their slant eyed envy when Ivy entered a room, never mind she was hardly more than a child.

Back in Denver, Ivy had many suitors, mostly fitting and proper, but some unquestionably not. Unfortunately, those were the companions Ivy preferred, saying they were ever so much more fun. And of course they were. But still.

Tally admittedly took after her father. Tall, wide shouldered and broad backed, not unattractive, but plain faced without a touch of makeup though the church ladies always complimented her smile. Tough would be the wrong word to describe her. Pragmatic would be more apt. Her own suitors had been few and far between, their relationships short-lived. When Jacob came along and asked for her hand in marriage, she immediately accepted fearing there would be no more chances. There hadn't been anyone else since he died.

Peevishly, Ivy shook Tally's hand off her arm. "Where are we going now? I'm hungry."

"So am I. Let's go back to the hotel and pay for another night. The hotel dining room looked lovely. Would you like to have lunch there before we do our other errands? We have lots to do in the next two days."

Ivy's face brightened a little and she nodded.

"Then after lunch we'll find the telegraph office and arrange to have our furniture and belongings packed up and shipped to the homestead. And I'm pretty sure I saw a newspaper office somewhere close by. I want to place an ad in the help wanted. We're going to need a hired hand, the sooner the better."

They walked on as Tally talked, making plans and thinking out loud.

"We're going to need a solid work wagon and a good strong horse to pull it. We'll go to the livery and ask Buster if he can outfit us and have it ready by tomorrow. I saw at least a dozen horses in the stalls and corral when we hired him. And the wagon yard was full, too. They're bound to have something suitable for us. And maybe they can help us find a hired hand."

Tally decided to disregard Pettyjohn's counsel to skip the sheriff's office. It was on the way to the livery, just a few doors down, so she might as well stop in tomorrow on the off chance someone there might know something about their father. In a town like this, no one knew more about the townsfolk and what's going on than the sheriff and his men.

Tally kept walking, but halted and turned when Ivy stopped midstride.

Ivy stood with her hands folded on her hips, her head tilted indignantly. "But what about shoes? You said we could get new shoes."

"Oh, yes. We'll get shoes."

Ivy's smile went all the way to her eyes. "Honest?"

"Yes. I promise."

"Really? You mean today?"

"No. Let's put that on our list for tomorrow. We probably won't have time today, but I saw a nice looking outfitter shop right across from the livery. We'll go there before we head back to the homestead."

CHAPTER FOUR

*T**HE MORNING DAWNED BRIGHT* and clear. Tally woke eager to meet the challenges of the upcoming days. Lord knows she'd been through worse. Much worse.

Fortunately, unlike many women who had been born and raised in a city setting, the transition to homesteading and life in the rugged West would not be an insurmountable undertaking. Hank Tisdale made sure his daughters could take care of themselves.

He taught them both to ride, drive a team, and use a gun. He was a man of the earth, raised in the mountains, transplanted to the city when he married their mother. But he knew how to hunt, grow, shoot and ride, and by God the Tisdale girls would know, too. City life never set well with him, and after their mother died, he yearned to go back to the life he knew. He decided to stake a claim in Sutton Creek, because he felt homesteading was filled with opportunities, a way to build a new home and life for himself, his girls, and future Tisdale generations.

Tally's greatest misgiving, beside the fact that she didn't know where he was at the moment, was Ivy. She wasn't sure how her sister would take to the demands of life on the frontier, or if she could adapt to a completely self-sufficient way of life. People still rushed around in an all-fired hurry like they did in the city, but the people were different. Here they accepted that hard work was a way of life, that there were few luxuries, and leisure time was at a premium.

Tally had a gift for making do. Ivy fell short. When difficulties arose, Tally coped. Ivy, less intrepid, fussed. Her displeasure often took the form of temper and inflexibility. Other times, it showed up as impulsive poor decision making. Though she had come along willingly to Sutton Creek seeking information about their father, homesteading hadn't been in the plan. That had been a last-minute course correction, a spontaneous but ultimately beneficial decision made by Tally on the spur of the moment.

Tally's quick mind had immediately realized that it would serve two purposes. They had a better chance of finding out what happened to their father if they were living in the place where he was last known to be. And, it was an opportunity for her to throw away her old life and put the past good and well behind her.

After a delicious breakfast of eggs, fruit, sweet cakes and tea in the hotel dining room, the Tisdale sisters set out on foot for the livery.

At this early hour of the day, the boisterous activity of the night before had morphed into a busyness of a different kind. Most noticeably, there were more women and children about, shopping, strolling, visiting. Indian mothers wearing copiously quill-beaded buckskin dresses carried their babies in cradle boards while they set up tables to display handmade baskets, blankets, rugs and jewelry for sale or barter.

Supply wagons pulled by shaggy, mud-caked oxen bellowing throaty, ear-splitting roars lined up on the street. Burly bullwhackers unloaded cargo and delivered goods to storekeepers. Shopping, socializing and commerce had taken the place of riotous revelry. Which is not to say the nighttime merriment had been displaced altogether. Saloons and pleasure houses were still open for business.

A crowd gathered around a public sign board in front of the bank. A painted sign called it a Shouting Post, a place where townsfolk posted news and announcements of interest in between weekly editions of the newspaper. There were several reports of recent gold strikes, bulletins announcing new businesses, Sunday church times, and stagecoach schedules, as well as listings of meetings, and social functions. There was an abundance of buy, rent, or sell notices, death notifications, and a good many job openings. Even though Tally had already purchased an ad in the newspaper for hired help, she made a mental note to post a notice there, as well.

A deputy was using a hammer to nail up a Wanted Poster, and right next to that was a broadsheet with news of what everyone in town had been talking about. The bones dug up by a construction crew. The sheriff was asking for information that would help them make an identification.

Ivy's face went white when she read it. She gripped Tally's upper arm, digging in her fingernails. "You don't think they're Father's, do you?"

The same thought had crossed Tally's mind, but not wanting to alarm Ivy she answered firmly and without hesitation.

"Of course not." Turning abruptly, she hurried off along the boardwalk in a go-getter stride. Ivy hurried to catch up.

Hodges Livery spread out over the better part of a quarter block on the main street at the edge of town. It was a huge two-story building with stables, barns, and in back, a pasture extending to the street behind. A painted sign stretched across the whole front of the building.

**HATHAWAY HODGES TRANSPORTATION
LIVERY — WAGONS AND HORSES
FOR SALE OR RENT
SPECIAL RATES FOR LOCALS
OF GOOD STANDING**

A smaller sign in the dusty front window offered overnight accommodations to bullwhackers upstairs in the hayloft at twenty-five cents a night.

Fenced off along the right side of the building was a corral with a dozen fine looking horses. Some of them frolicked, neighing and kicking up, but others stood at the rail looking lost and forlorn like orphaned children waiting to be adopted. Beyond that, a large wagon yard fenced off a variety of carriages and wagons including a fancy hitch wagon like the ones used in parades.

Liveries were mostly a men's domain, but out of necessity now that women were beginning to seek independent lives, a few could be found browsing or bargaining for livestock and wagons. That was, if the women could abide raw language, spitting, cigar smoke, and the pungent horsey odor of grass, hay and manure, the latter being a hearty olfactory stew some people liked, some didn't notice, and others called a stench.

Buster was busy talking to a customer, a woman wearing a dress of cambric, cut simply and closed at the throat with an amber brooch set in rose gold. Ivy recognized her immediately.

"Look." Ivy leaned into Tally and with a delicacy of manners spoke behind her hand. "It's the woman we saw singing in the saloon last night." Tally slid the woman a curious side glance, but Ivy openly stared at her on their way to the corral.

Ivy loved animals and was immediately drawn to a spirited sorrel with a light coppery coat and creamy mane and tail. She stepped up on the bottom rail and held out her hand. The horse sidled over and whickered as she reached for his muzzle. She spoke softly to the horse as she stroked his head and neck. "I like this one. Can we get it?"

Before Tally could answer, a man approached.

"Good morning, ladies. I'm Hathaway Hodges, but my friends call me Hath and I'd be obliged if you did, too." He was six feet tall and had a sturdy frame topped off by big shoulders. Dark hair wisped in soft curls around his neck. High cheekbones spoke of Indian somewhere in his ancestral lineage. His large, lustrous brown eyes, deep and observant, widened and fixed on Tally in a most charming way. His broad smile landed hard, and she almost smiled back but caught herself in time and didn't react. She'd learned not to be so quick to trust smiles like that.

"I'm Tallulah. Everyone calls me Tally." She put her business face on and kept it there. "And this is my sister Ivy. We were here yesterday."

Ivy acknowledged Hath with a nod, then turned back to the horse who was gently nudging her arm asking for more loving touches.

"Buster was going to outfit us with a horse and wagon," Tally continued. "He said he could rig up something for us this morning."

Hath nodded. "Oh. You're Hank Tisdale's daughters."

"Goodness, word travels fast as a freight train in Sutton Creek, doesn't it? Do you know our father?"

"No, I don't, but Buster said he took you both out to his place. Only he wasn't there, so you're both moving in."

"Yes, we are. We're going to work the claim until he returns."

"Uh huh."

Hath adjusted his hat and squinted against the sun as he studied Tally's face. She didn't know what he was thinking, but he looked and sounded as skeptical as Pettyjohn had. Unwilling to be seen as one of those women who took offense easily, she forced a grin and hurried to correct his misapprehension if that's what it was.

"I realize it's a lot of hard work," she said anxious to clarify that she was not letting naiveté get them in over their heads. "And it will take a while. We're going to need hired help, of course." A slight edge tinged her voice, so she took a breath and softened her tone. "But we're going to be fine. In fact, we're looking forward to it. You wouldn't happen to know anyone I could hire to come out and help us, would you?"

"Not off hand, but I'll be happy to ask around and send them your way. Your cabin's out on Bandit Bend, isn't it?"

"Bandit Bend?"

He made an immediate apology. "Oh, beg your pardon, ma'am. I mean Dunbeaton Bend."

She looked at him quizzically. "Why did you call it Bandit Bend?"

"Not my doing," he said with a smile and a half shrug. "That's what folks around here call it because of the number of stagecoach robberies there. Someone once called it Bandit Bend and the name stuck. Nothing for you to worry about, though. Highwaymen don't bother any of the people living out there." He paused a moment and again his smile lit his face. "Anyway, congratulations. You got yourself some prime land."

"Really?"

"Oh, yes, ma'am. Land out that way is much in demand. The government gave the railroad a huge land grant near there. Rumor has it they're going to build a railroad spur, and if they do, cattle companies will want to come in and set up nearby. They'll pay big prices for land."

A thought jolted. Tally wondered if that was the reason her father had chosen that particular claim two miles from town instead of one closer in. He had a good head for business, so would have taken that into consideration when he made his selection. She couldn't imagine he'd simply abandon it later.

"Well, our documents are safe in the Land Office. Mr. Pettyjohn showed them to us yesterday." She gave her head a quick shake. "We don't intend to give up our father's claim and I'm quite sure he doesn't, either."

Hath nodded and got down to business. "Let's go take a look at the rig Buster picked out for you. He said you were looking for a farm wagon, something economical, and I have a used one in good condition that I can sell you for a fair price. Why don't you come out back with me and I'll show it to you. Then we can find a horse you like."

She looked over his shoulder to where Ivy was still speaking softly to the sorrel. The horse was now resting his head on her shoulder while she stroked his neck. Tally gave a little nod.

"I think we've already found one, if he's not too expensive."

Tally followed Hath into the wagon yard. The wagon he showed her was well used, but serviceable, and after a little haggling, they agreed on the price. Hath went inside to prepare the bill of sale. While Tally waited outside, she walked around the wagon giving it a final assessment. The two axle assembly appeared to be in good condition, and the wagon tongue looked new. She was glad to see the sturdy wooden wheels were rimmed with iron. It helped reduce wear. A couple of coats of hunter green oil base paint and linseed oil for protection would freshen it up. Maybe even some bolder colors on the gears and wheels, red or yellow or orange, the way she'd seen some of the wagons in town brightened up.

She felt a tap on her shoulder, and turned to see the

saloon singer standing there.

"Excuse me." The woman's smile was cordial, her expression apologetic. "I didn't mean to eavesdrop, but I happened to overhear your conversation with Hath about Bandit Bend. You're going to be working your father's claim out there?"

Tally returned her smile. "Yes, just until he returns."

"Oh, I see. Well, I wanted to welcome you and offer my congratulations, too."

Tally gazed at the woman. She was small, fine boned and moved her hands gracefully when she spoke. Hands that were so delicate they looked breakable.

"Thank you," said Tally. "We signed the papers yesterday. This will be our first night in our new place."

"Well then, good luck. By the way, my name's Mimi. Mimi Merchant. If you ever need help of any kind—advice, company, a cup of tea, a book, someone to talk to…" She let her words drift but her eyebrows popped and her smile remained. "A loan to get you through a rough spot if things get tight. I can arrange that for you, too."

Tally laughed lightly as if Mimi were joking, and was touched by the sincerity underscored in her voice. It sounded like she meant it.

She considered Mimi with curiosity and sensed in her a nimble, dynamic energy that Tally herself hadn't felt for some time. But there was something else, too. Something in her eyes that said she'd buried a lingering pain in some deep, safe place. Tally recognized it. She saw the same reflected in her own eyes.

The woman rearranged a strand of her fiery red hair that had been shifted by the breeze across her face. "Please let me know. I'd be happy to help. We women have to stick together."

Tally chuckled. "Yes. We do." Then, "Thank you," she said, acknowledging Mimi's generous officer. "It's very kind of you. I'm sure it won't come to that, but I appreciate the offer nonetheless."

"Truly. It would be my pleasure. More women should be independent, have money and land of their own. You can find me at Gold Star Saloon. I have a room upstairs in back. And I sing there three nights a week."

"Yes. We heard you when we walked by last night on our way back to the hotel. You have a lovely voice."

Mimi's eyes sparkled. "Thank you. It gets me by." Her thick mane of red hair piled and twisted and curled beautifully on top of her head was her most outstanding feature. She was probably a few years older than Tally, the faint lines around her eyes gave that away, and Tally began to feel they could be friends.

Mimi said goodbye, and Hath came back with papers. Ivy was right beside him radiating excitement over the horse. It looked like her feet were barely touching the ground as she walked beside him. Tally haggled a bit over the price of the sorrel, but in the end, they came to a meeting of the mind on the horse, too. She signed the ownership papers and paid him in cash.

"It's a pleasure doing business with you," Hath said touching his fingers to the brim of his hat. "If you'll give me about twenty minutes while we finish grooming the horse, I'll harness him up and bring the rig around to the front."

"That will be fine. Thank you."

That settled, the sisters started across the street to shop for the necessities they'd need to set up life in the cabin. Ivy chattered away about what to name the horse.

"Red? Rusty?" Her brow puckered in thought. "No. Too common. He needs something with gumption. Something with mettle. Stormy? Trooper? Trooper! Yes, that's it. Let's name him Trooper."

They stopped to let a couple of freight wagons go by,

the drivers cracking their whips and shouting profanities at their teams. While waiting for the street to clear, Ivy said, "Who's that man?"

"What man?"

Ivy didn't point, but gave her head a subtle tip in his direction. "That one. Over there. He's staring at you."

Tally slowly slid her gaze where Ivy indicated. He was heavily mustached, and the shadow cast by the brim of his hat almost but not quite hid his eyes. His fringed buckskin jacket hung to his knees. He stood outside the Hombre Café next to the barber shop, one shoulder braced against the door frame. The man didn't flinch when Tally caught his eye, just stood there stone-faced and intense, his gaze so penetrating she felt the thrust of it in her middle.

Another freighter rumbled by and she lost sight of him for a moment. When the wagon passed, she saw him open the door of the cafe. He tossed a quick glance over his shoulder, casually flung one side of his jacket open so that it caught on the gun in his gaudy leather holster, and went inside.

Tally's heart dipped into her stomach.

Ivy lifted her eyebrows in question. "Do you know who that man is?"

"No," Tally said which was the truth, but she had a bad feeling. His look was not casual. It held a meaning she could not decipher, and a disconcerting flush burned through her.

She squeezed Ivy's fingers in her hand and they hurried across the street into the mercantile.

***

Foster Goodnight Pettyjohn had a late breakfast at the Hombre Café most days of the week. He had finished eating but kept his seat at a table facing the door and the front window. A pretty Mexican waitress came over.

"More coffee, Señor Pettyjohn?"

"Yes, thank you, Clementine." She poured until he signaled her to stop. When she turned to walk away, he reached out and gave her a little smack on her bottom. She hitched a half-step and giggled, but kept walking. When she wasn't looking, he took out a flask and filled his mug to the top.

He should have said no to the coffee. He didn't need more. He was jumpy enough. He hadn't stopped thinking about the Tisdale sisters since they showed up unexpectedly at his office saying they were taking over Hank Tisdale's claim. He'd tried to dissuade them. But now to his chagrin, it looked like they were going through with it.

He'd doubted it at first, thought the older one would come to her senses, city girl like her taking up homesteading. No man to lean on with her husband dead and her father gone. And the young one, the sister, Ivy. He suspected she'd lied about her age. To his eye, she looked more like a child than a full grown woman. She wouldn't last long in a town like this. She didn't look up to it. Pale skin, pale blue eyes, skittish as a colt. He was sure that after a good night's sleep, they'd be on the morning stage out of Sutton Creek and back to Denver.

But no. They'd already sent for their belongings in Denver, ordered chickens and a flock of sheep from a farmer in South Park. And now it looked like she'd bought a horse and wagon from Hath.

He exhaled a frustrated breath through his nose. Tally was going to be a handful, that one. Ivy was sure to be a pushover, but Tally had pluck. Though maybe later with their father not around she might be persuaded to change her mind especially if things got too difficult out there. Two woman proving up a claim. It wasn't going to be easy for them. And Pettyjohn knew there were ways to make it more difficult, if not downright impossible.

The man in the fringed buckskin jacket came through

the door, his narrowed eyes moving from table to table. When he spotted Pettyjohn, he walked directly over, pulled out a chair across from him, and sat down like it was a hugely painful inconvenience to be there.

"We have a little problem," Pettyjohn said. "Tisdale's daughters showed up."

"I heard."

"Before the new paperwork was ready."

"Uh huh. And do you have a solution to that little problem?"

"I was hoping you would," answered Pettyjohn.

The man locked his unsmiling stare on Pettyjohn. "Well, I might be able to come up with something. But remember. There's no profit in weakness." He stood up, pushed his chair back with his boot and stomped out the door.

CHAPTER FIVE

Three months later

IVY STOOD IN THE doorway of the cabin squinting against the sun, exhausted, dirty, and fed up. Work reddened hands gripped the doorframe on each side as if it were needed to hold her upright on her feet. Her fingernails were jagged and broken, the surrounding skin cracked and sore. Her face and arms were brown as tanned leather and felt like leather, too.

What a raw frontier woman I have become.

The promised new shoes turned out to be thick-soled work boots that squeaked when she walked and rubbed painfully. She'd worked out the squeak, but they still rubbed.

Her cotton dress was torn and mended and so horribly stained it would never look clean again. But it was all she had. Crisply pressed and Sunday Best was a thing of the past. The freighter Tally hired to bring their belongings up the mountain didn't make it over the treacherous pass. Their furniture, clothes, bed linens, books and papers were at the bottom of a canyon. Rains had washed out the trail. It caved in when the freighter started across taking everything with it including the wagon, the bullwhacker driving it and the oxen pulling it.

She looked down at her skirt, mud caked and frayed at the hem. When it finally disintegrated into shreds, she

would have to wear a pair of her father's pants. Tally would, too. They had nothing else.
    They had cleaned the cabin the best they could to make it livable. Swept out the dirt and dust and insects, shooed away the rodents, a task that was an everyday chore. They nailed a few boards together from the stack in the yard to make crude bunks with rope and padding so they wouldn't have to sleep on the split log floor. The second room meant to be a bedroom was still being used for storage. So far, daily chores took up all their time. They'd get to the second room when they finished the barn.
    Sheets of newspaper clung for dear life to the inside walls. Canvas nailed above the windows was rolled up during the daytime to let in dusty light, but the breeze barely freshened the air inside. After dark, they rolled the canvas down to keep out nights that were heavy with strange sounds and wild animals.
    From where she stood she could see in the near distance veins of tiny creeks formed on the mountainside after the frenzied rain of the previous night. The moaning of the wind and the sound of whipping tree branches woke her in the night. Rain pounded the ground as silver lightning bounced from peak to peak in the mountains.
    When she woke, she discovered the rain had flooded the gardens, washing away the beans and potatoes and carrots and corn she'd spent a week planting. She and Tally had used pitchforks and spades to break up the earth enough to drop the seeds in. Now they would have to do it all over again.
    Shreds of clouds remained, but the sun burned hot. A broad winged hawk soared above the treetops against a backdrop of long vistas and a big bowl of sky rimmed by the frosted tops of the Rockies.
    Early that morning, Tally had hitched Trooper to the wagon and gone into town to learn how to preserve veg-

etables in a class being held at the Sutton Creek Social Center. Ivy had never heard of a Social Center in such an isolated out of the way town like Sutton Creek, but saw it as a sign of enlightened advancement. Unfortunately, she wouldn't be able to spend any time there. She wasn't here for that. Neither was Tally. So far, every minute of their time had been spent on the homestead and almost none on a search for their father.

She hoped Tally would bring back supplies from the general store. They were low on everything—lard, butter, sugar, dried fruits, desiccated vegetables, corn meal. They had to sift out the worms in the last of theirs. She didn't know when they would be able to get pigs of their own, but when they did they wouldn't have to buy bacon and ham. Tally kept a ledger of every penny spent. Only so much allowed each week. No room for extras or unexpected expenses. They rather quickly realized the need for another wagon. Another horse, too, and a dairy cow. Before next winter, they'd need to chink and plaster the logs in the cabin to stop up the cracks. It seemed there were a million things that needed to be attended to.

As for Tally, she was handling the hard times well enough. One couldn't ask for a better older sister. She never complained, but something else was bothering her, Ivy was sure of it. She wondered if it had something to do with the man they saw staring at her as they left the livery that day. Tally said she didn't know the man, and it wasn't spoken of again. But Tally had a sixth sense about her and could tell the goodness in people, and the badness, too. Maybe he was a bad man, but Ivy felt it was better not to press her about it. But still, she worried.

She let out a robust sigh, wiped strands of hair off her face with the back of her hand and headed for the barn where a dozen sheep waited in a woven wire pen they continually knocked down. She loaded the hay and grain feeders for the sheep, then filled a bucket with chicken feed and emptied it in the feedbox in the coop. After spreading some scratch feed around the yard to give the chickens some exercise, she checked the nest boxes and collected the eggs.

The lays were good. She marked each egg to indicate which hen laid the biggest ones. There was a contest in town for the best layer. First prize was a pedigreed White Leghorn cockerel. If she won, she would use the cock for stud to increase the flock and sell the best breeders to new homesteaders. For now, she collected the eggs for meals. Overages would go to town to one of the general stores along with a half dozen loaves of bread Tally had baked. For now it was their only source of income.

Tally usually took the goods to the stores and collected the money. Ivy hadn't been back to town since they moved into the cabin, but she wanted to go next time. Tally told her she'd seen some men pushing a gallows on wheels behind one of the saloons. Ivy thought she'd like to get a look at that. Tally said when she nailed up a sign asking for information about their father, she noticed that cowboys advertised on the signpost for wives.

Ivy wanted to get a look at that, too.

It was well past noon now, and Tally said she'd be back before suppertime. Ivy hoped she would. She didn't like being out there alone, especially when it started to get dark. Lately, she thought she heard noises at night, like someone was outside the cabin walking around, boots padding softly on the dusty ground. Trooper must have thought so too. He'd snort and carry on, kicking the sides of his stable in the barn. But when she tweaked the canvas window covering to look outside she saw no one.

Now, cabin swept and aired out, livestock fed, Trooper's stable cleaned, afternoon chores completed except for the laundry, Ivy stared longingly down the long tree-shaded two track leading to the road and the river on the other side. Perspiration ran down her face and dripped off her chin. Tendrils of hair stuck to the back of her neck. Wood still needed to be chopped, but what she needed was a walk and a cooling dip in the river. A bath. And surely even this high in the mountains there would be blueberries ready to be picked from the berry patch near the shore. She gathered tooth powder, harsh smelling yellow soap, and a threadbare towel from the cabin, then grabbed a bucket from the barn for the berries.

 She crossed the road and headed down the path to the river, but after a few moments had to stop to catch her breath. She wondered if she would ever get used to the high altitude, or be comfortable in the desolation.

 The bushes were indeed laden with sweet, ripe, juicy blueberries. She picked a few for taste, then walked to the water's edge. After the storm the air was fresher and smelled of earth, wet leaves and pine needles. The river, broad and still, was as smooth as if the wind of the night before had never disturbed it. Aspens, regal pines and snow-covered summits were mirrored on its glassy surface.

 She undressed and waded into the water. At first, it was so cold she gasped and shivered, but it didn't take long for her to feel refreshed. She waded out waist high, then lowered herself up to her neck, and vigorously soaped up her body and her hair. She dipped her head back and combed her fingers through her locks to rinse out the suds. Staying close to shore, she floated on her back a while watching big fluffy clouds curl over the tips of the mountains like giant crashing waves. Before long she felt her shoulders relax as though relieved of a great load. She let out a huge breath, all her nerves loosening. Back on shore, she dressed, dried off, and picked up the berry bucket.

Most of the berries went into her mouth. She felt guilty for taking this leisure, but the sun, the fresh air, the sound of the river and the birds, all of it filled her with delight. Quite the opposite of her usual sourpuss way of getting through the days of her new life.

Her bucket was almost full, but she continued to reach for the most luscious looking berries when a sound sent her heart pounding against her chest. She knew instantly what it was and held her breath trying to hear past the rush of panic flooding through her.

Her eyes drifted to the sight of a black bear and her cub partially hidden in the trees. They were slowly making their way toward her, drawn to the same clump of berry bushes where she stood frozen. The wind blew from behind and the mother bear had not yet picked up her scent.

Fear gripped her as the bears drew closer. Her bottom lip quaked. Should she scream? Who would hear her? She was two miles from town, all alone in the middle of this unpeopled land. No one would hear and she dared not run.

The bears kept coming. Ivy's knees buckled and she straightened them by sheer force of will, but couldn't stop shaking. The bear stopped to root at something in the dirt still unaware of Ivy's presence. Ivy's mind flashed through a dozen retreats, but she rejected them all. She would never be able to outrun a bear. The bucket slipped out of her trembling hands and clattered to the ground scattering berries.

The bear raised its head, and looked toward the sound, confused, its poor eyesight preventing it from locking on to the intruder. But then she caught Ivy's scent on a shift of the wind. The huge animal stood up on hind legs, sniffing the air. The frightened cub climbed a nearby pine tree. The mother bear roared and dropped to all four feet in a charging posture.

Shaking uncontrollably, Ivy managed to grab a fallen branch with a pointed end, but it wasn't much of a weapon and she was afraid to brandish it. Instead, she yelled.

"NO! GO AWAY! NO! NO! NO!"

Nose in the air, the bear started forward, but paused, perhaps startled by Ivy's skirt and petticoats billowing and flapping in the wind.

Emboldened by the beast's hesitation, Ivy continued yelling.

"NO. GO AWAY. GO BACK. NO!" Her voice was frantic.

She gripped the branch with both hands prepared to use it as a bludgeon if the bear charged. The bear could kill her, but she wasn't going down without a fight.

The wind let up a little and in those long silent seconds, she stared at the befuddled bear. All she heard was the bear's panting and her own thudding heart.

Then the cub cried out from its perch in the tree. The mother bear looked back at it, and Ivy considered making a run for it, but there wasn't enough time. In an instant, the bear gathered itself and charged through the bushes as if they didn't exist. Its powerful muscles rippled under black fur, eyes glared, mouth hung open showing sharp, pointed teeth.

The cub cried out a second time and briefly caught the mother's attention again, but only for a second before turning back toward Ivy. The mother bear rose up to her full height and roared. She was closer now, close enough for Ivy to smell its musky odor wafting through the air. She was paralyzed, unable to move, tears burning the back of her throat. Suddenly the bear dropped to all fours and charged.

Using all her strength, Ivy thrust the pointed stick into the bear's wide open mouth. The force of the impact when it connected threw Ivy backward off her feet and she hit the ground. The bear stopped and gagged, making strangling sounds. Ivy began to belly crawl away while the bear pawed at the branch wedged in its bloody mouth all the while making ghastly sounds.

The bear dislodged the makeshift spear and went after Ivy again. Ivy got to her feet, but before she could take a step to run, a gunshot boomed like thunder. A bullet thudded into the animal's hip. It faltered and stumbled. The hind legs gave out momentarily, but the bear didn't go down. It was only wounded.

A man stood on the rocky embankment where the path fed onto the shore. An ammunition belt slung slantwise across his chest. Moving swiftly, he worked the repeating rifle's lever, sighted on the bear and took aim. The second shot missed, and the bear stumbled toward Ivy again, slower, but no less determined.

It was almost on her, but paralyzed by fear, Ivy stood frozen in place. The man pulled down on the lever, slammed home the action and took aim a third time. Roaring in pain and anger, the bear swiped at Ivy with a huge front paw just as a third shot hit the mark. The huge animal crashed to the ground, its claws catching on Ivy's skirt ripping a tear from waist to hem. For a split second her muddled brain thought she'd been mauled and she felt a ghost pain surge down the front of her body. She screamed and collapsed.

A distant sound merged with the rushing wind. A voice calling to her. Only half conscious, she saw a man, rifle in hand, running toward her. He swooped her up in his arms and carried her back to the cabin. Gently, he laid her on one of the bunks.

"I don't see any blood," he told her as he placed a wet cloth on her forehead. "Except for where you fell, but I don't think the bear touched you."

Ivy managed to open her eyes. She stared at him unable to speak. He was short and stout, but broad in the shoulders. He had dark hair under a slouch hat and cinnamon colored skin. A shriveled ear hung from a leather cord around his neck. A big pistol was strapped to his leg.

"Who are you?"

"My name is Wren Touwee." He spoke softly with the distinct tonal accent of an Indian. "When I heard you yell, I ran down to the river. You're lucky I came by when I did."

"Are you a homesteader? Do you have a claim around here?" Ivy managed to ask through parched lips.

Wren filled a metal cup with water and held it so she could drink. "Saw a notice on the Shouting Post that you needed hired help. I rode out to ask for the job."

Ivy drank greedily, then handed back the cup and stared at him. "You've got the job," she said.

CHAPTER SIX

THE TWICE WEEKLY STAGECOACH carrying mail had just pulled into Sutton Creek when Tally arrived. Townsfolk, eager for their mail order packages, Denver newspapers, and letters from loved ones, besieged the stage making the street near impassable. There was no room at the hitchrack in front of the Gold Star Saloon, so Tally gave the reins a shake and directed Trooper through the narrow, muddy passageway between buildings. The wagon groaned to a stop behind the saloon next to the steps leading to Mimi Merchant's upstairs quarters.

She sat a moment, looking up at the windows on the second floor. Taking a deep breath, she readied herself for what she was about to do. What she *had* to do. For all her bravado of a few months ago, she now had to admit there was no other choice.

She took a moment to order her thoughts. When the words she wanted to say came together in her mind, she ran her palms over her skirt in a vain attempt at smoothing out the wrinkles. Nothing could be done about the dirt stains that remained after washing or the stitches holding the rips together. She climbed down from the wagon, tied Trooper to the handrail and went up the steps.

A window with lacy curtains on the inside covered the top half of the door. She raised her hand to knock, and caught her reflection. Was that her haggard face staring back at her? Dull hair pulled back severely, pinned every which way. Strands that looked like saddle strings hung loose and unruly. Stress had carved a permanent line on her forehead. Nothing could be done about that, either. She pasted on a smile and rapped lightly.

Mimi opened the door and greeted Tally with a huge friendly smile.

"Tally! It's so good to see you. Come in."

She was wearing a stylish dress of fine cambric, light grey in color with a bit of a gloss to it where the sun's rays touched it. Her coppery hair was swooped up into a bun, but a few tendrils fell. A gold nugget on a chain around her neck added a certain elegance to her graceful bearing. When she backed away and widened the door in gracious welcome, Tally caught a glimpse of a crimson petticoat beneath the hem of her skirt and couldn't help feeling a bit of envy. She managed to hold her smile as she stepped over the threshold even though she was perilously close to tears.

Mimi's home was moderate. Two rooms and a small kitchen, moderately furnished and *clean*. Smooth pine walls gave off an amber hue. There was a wood stove for heat, a sofa upholstered in velvet, a rocking chair, and a lamp with a cowhide lampshade. Colorful Navajo rugs covered the floor. Not much of a kitchen. Tally thought Mimi must take her meals downstairs in the saloon, but there was a dining table with four ladder-back chairs. A hanging shawl covered the bedroom door. It was draped open allowing a glimpse of a real brass bed with extravagantly ruffled bedding and a pile of fluffy pillows. An elaborate lavender shade topped a lamp on a table next to the bed. It brought to mind what Tally supposed a soiled dove's room might look like, though she'd never seen one.

She spoke hesitantly. "I'm sorry to show up uninvited. I hope I'm not intruding."

Mimi's sapphire eyes were steady and earnest. "Not

at all. Please sit down and join me for tea." Mimi motioned Tally into a chair at the dining table and put the kettle on. Waiting for the water to boil, she chatted amiably about the weather, the heat, the chance of a cooling rain by week's end.

"Hath Hodges was asking about you," Mimi said, pouring from the teapot for both of them. "Wondering how you and your sister were doing out there. Why don't you stop at the livery while you're in town and say hello? He'd love to see you." She slid Tally a slow side glance full of meaning.

Tally returned a polite grin. Hath was a door best left closed for now. "I will if I have time."

After that, conversation dwindled until Mimi picked it up again.

"So," she said sitting opposite Tally over steaming cups of tea. "What brings you to town today? Everything going all right on the homestead?"

"I... Well, I..." Tally's voice faltered, her carefully rehearsed words stuck in the tightness in her throat. Instead, tears flowed humiliating her even more.

Mimi's face collapsed in sympathy and her cup clattered back to its saucer as she reached across the table to put a solicitous hand on Tally's arm. Her voice took on a soothing tone. "What is it? Tell me. What happened? Is Ivy all right?"

There was no speaking through the sobs. Tally simply nodded, indicating Ivy was fine, except that wasn't the truth. Ivy wasn't fine. She was stick thin and hollow around the eyes. Unsuited for homesteading, she didn't belong in this rough and tumble place.

Try as she might, Tally couldn't stop the flow of tears.

Mimi shook her head sympathetically and *tsked*. "Things not going well? Harder than you thought?"

Tally nodded again, then plowed forward with what

she had come to say. Her words tumbled out caught up by pauses and hesitations.

"I wasn't prepared for the unexpected. We have to replant the gardens because of the rains. Coyotes killed two of the ewes, and they raid the chicken coop every night. Livestock feed costs more than I planned for, and the freighter bringing our belongings from Denver had an accident on the pass and never made it. We lost everything, all our belongings, everything we owned."

Again, the words got stuck on another sob. She detested the pleading sound of her voice, strangled and small, but she cleared her throat and went on.

"We need to fence our acreage so Trooper and the sheep can graze and get to the water holes. Chopping wood is an everyday task." She turned her cracked and calloused hands palm up as if to prove what she was saying was true. "The barn is caving in and that's where the sheep pen is and Trooper's stable. I think someone is creeping around outside at night. And… and still no word from our father. I don't know where he is. I'm afraid the worst has happened and we'll never see him again."

With that, Mimi left the table and came back with a fresh handkerchief. Tally took it and held it to her streaming eyes while Mimi patted her shoulder and shook her head at the trials of life as if she could relate to them. When the sobs subsided, Mimi took Tally's hands in both of hers to stop them from shaking.

"Look. Here's what you need to do right off. Two things. First, you need a hired man. You and Ivy cannot prove up that homestead all on your own especially weighed down as you are with worries about your father. You need a man to do jobs that require muscle, preferably one possessed of a selective lack of conscience in case the need arises. Someone with a tough reputation. A tough reputation carries a lot of weight in Colorado. Women alone in the wilderness cannot be too careful."

Tally filled her lungs with air and let it out slowly in an effort to regulate her breathing. She was deeply ashamed at exhibiting such fragility. She'd gotten along so far by keeping her chin up and making the best of things while suffering diversity. She prayed Mimi would not speak of this to anyone. She herself hadn't told anyone of her past hard times. Not even Ivy knew the truth about what happened back then.

"And you need money," Mimi said. "I can help you with that. A loan."

Tally dropped the hand holding the tear-soaked handkerchief to her lap. She wanted to object, wished she could decline the offer, but a loan was exactly what she'd come for.

"I'll pay you back. I've never had to turn to charity. I've never even had to borrow. I'll pay you back as soon as I can, I don't know when that will be, but—"

"Fine," Mimi interrupted. "I know you will, but let's not worry about that right now. Do you own weapons?"

"We did, but they're at the bottom of the canyon along with everything else we lost when the freight wagon went over. But both Ivy and I know how to use them."

"All right then. That's the third thing you need to do. You think someone is creeping around your cabin at night? You need to get some guns! If for no other reason than the coyotes. You have to protect your livestock as well as yourselves. Hath knows a lot of people. He could probably help you get guns at a good price."

She said all that in a tone of voice that wasn't meant to be argued with, so Tally sniffed and agreed, her anxiety uncoiling a little. She dabbed at the dampness under her eyes, strength beginning to flow back into her body and her brain.

"I'll make a deposit in an account at the bank in your

name today. Enough to cover what you've just told me."

Tally let out another long, slow breath, and her thank you came out a whisper.

"Now that's settled. What about a hired man?"

"I put an ad in the newspaper and a notice on the Shouting Post."

"Good. Desperate, hungry men straggle into town every day. You should find someone suitable before too long. Until then, you and Ivy only do the chores you can handle. Meanwhile, make a list of what you need right away, and I'll order it delivered to the livery. Hath can bring it out to your spread." Mimi took a sheet of paper and a pencil from a drawer in an end table and put them in front of Tally. A diamond ring on her little finger sparkled. "Here. Write down what you need."

Tally's grateful smile was unstable, but she managed to lock it in. "Thank you," she said out loud this time, and began writing. When she finished the list, she pushed it across the table to Mimi, who folded it in half and tucked it into her reticule. She sat back and regarded Tally.

"Now, I don't want you to worry, but I have something to tell you. It's about your father."

Tally sucked in a quick breath. "What?"

"Did you put up a notice on the Shouting Post asking for information about him?"

"Yes, I did. Why? Do you know something?" A pitch of hope lifted her voice.

"I overheard two men talking about him in the saloon last night during my intermission. I was going to ride out to your place to tell you about it."

Tally's heart began a dull thudding against her ribs. "What did they say?"

"I couldn't hear every word, the piano player was banging out a song that everyone knew the words to. But it was something about your father getting into an argument, a very public argument in the Diamond Rio. There was some pushing and shoving."

A deep thump of dread banged in Tally's chest and she frowned. An argument in a public place? She'd never known her father to get into fights, though he was a man who never failed to stand up for what he believed even if it wasn't a popular opinion.

"One of the cowboys said he saw your sign on the Shouting Post asking for information. Said he was going to ride out to tell you what he saw. The other man told him he should mind his own business. Told him to keep it to himself if he knew what was good for him."

The words passed through Tally like a chilly breeze. "A threat?"

Mimi nodded. "It sounded like it. But they'd been at the bar quite a while and were pretty roostered up by then. So, I can't really be sure. Then my break was over and I had to go back on stage. They left while I was singing."

"Who were they? Do you know their names?"

The corners of Mimi's mouth turned down. "No, sorry, I don't. I don't know where they're from or anything about them. I'll ask the bartender what he knows."

"What did they look like? Would you know them if you saw them again?"

"I might." She thought a minute. "I only saw one of them in profile. He was wearing a fringed deerskin jacket."

Tally frowned and began to get a sinking feeling in the pit of her stomach. Her mind tumbled over itself with possibilities, none of them good. Then she reined in her chaotic emotions. There were hundreds of men in Sutton Creek wearing fringed jackets, some of them passing through never to return. What Mimi told her wasn't much, but it was a start. If this man saw her father arguing in the saloon there must have been others who saw and heard it, too. If only she could find them.

Her earlier relief at the promise of a loan to keep the homestead going was tarnished with disappointment by this unspecific news about her father.

She took a deep breath and exhaled. "Thank you, Mimi. I can't thank you enough. For *everything*." She stood to leave.

Mimi stood, too. "My pleasure. As I said at the livery, women need to stick up for each other. Help each other out if they can. Thankfully, I'm able to."

At the door, she put her hand on Tally's arm and grinned. "Stop at the livery and see Hath on your way back home. He's a good man."

CHAPTER SEVEN

*T*ALLY RETURNED TO THE homestead elated after having secured the promise of funds necessary to keep the spread going, and considered the unexpected information about her father a bonus.

Ivy, jittery and excited, came running fairly bursting with the story of the bear attack, and her rescue by Wren Touwee as Tally drove Trooper to the barn.

Tally agreed to hire him on the spot. Ivy had insisted on it, and in truth Tally didn't object even though he didn't look like the muscled hired help she'd envisioned. Nor did he appear to be a man of rough reputation as Mimi had suggested she needed. He did have the look of someone who might have a compromised conscience when warranted, though. A big revolver rested on his thigh, a bowie knife in a belt full of cartridges hung from his hips, and a Spencer and a Henry rifle were tied to his saddle. She decided he'd do for now until someone bigger and tougher came along and took the job.

Wren was soft spoken, polite, didn't talk much. That first night at the homestead he set up his bedroll in a corner of the barn, and by the next day had cleared enough space to transform it into sleeping quarters and a meager living area for himself. Ivy took candles out to him for light and extra blankets for warmth.

Wren said he'd worked at other homesteads, and seemed to know what needed to be done. In short order, he finished the corral and enlarged the sheep pen, then cleared space in the barn in anticipation of the supplies that were due to arrive. With his help and guidance, they used the rough boards laying on the ground to build a rudimentary supply shack in case extra storage was needed.

Location of the shack had been a subject of some discussion. Tally thought it should be built closer to the cabin for easy accessibility. Wren thought it should be closer to the barn. Ivy didn't care where it was built just as long as it didn't disrupt the praying nun in the rock pile where she'd set up a cross and a prayer bench nearby. Wren won that argument and promised not to disturb Ivy's improvised shrine before setting to work.

Tally thought Wren was a strange one. She sensed something off about him, but couldn't put her finger on it. She was curious about his heritage though he didn't mention his family. Maybe it was because he didn't have one that he was close to. Or maybe it was because he didn't like prying questions, so she didn't disrespect him by asking any. He made her think of the long ago housekeeper her mother had come in to help in Denver, a kind and loving Navajo woman by the name of Lorraine. She'd been with the Tisdales for years, but almost never talked about her family, and got stone faced and suspicious if anyone asked.

The supplies arrived under blinding blue skies and lemony sunlight. A wagon driven by Hath and pulled by a big dun colored quarter horse clattered into the yard. Hath's horse followed on a lead tied to the back of the wagon. Board lumber, fence posts, rails and many spools of barb wire filled the wagon bed along with buckets of paint, tin cans filled with nails, bags of stock feed, and a plow.

Ivy was sweeping the front porch and saw him turn

in. "Tally," she called, excitement in her voice. "The supplies are here!"

Delighted, Tally hurried outside. "I didn't expect the shipment so soon," she said.

Hath tightened the reins and brought the horse to a stop. His boots hit the ground and he flashed a smile.

"It arrived at the livery late yesterday, so I thought I'd bring it out first thing this morning. I knew you were anxious to start getting proved up. It came by mule, so it got here sooner. Oxen take longer because they graze along the way." He pushed his hat off his forehead. "Looks like your hired man has already helped with a lot of the work around here."

"Yes. I'm grateful to have him."

Wren sauntered out of the barn carrying a shovel and stood with his hand on the top rail of the corral. Tally introduced them, and Ivy told Hath how Wren had saved her from a bear attack. The bear skin was draped over the porch railing drying in the sun. More of Wren's work.

Hands on hips, Tally walked around the wagon mentally taking inventory. Hath followed.

"You brought your horse?"

Hath nodded. "Yes, ma'am. That way you don't have to take me all the way back to town, because the wagon and the quarter horse belong to you, too."

Tally's mouth widened into a grin. "Really? I didn't expect them for another two weeks."

Ivy, wearing her father's pants cinched up with a rope though the belt loops, already had her hands on the horse, stroking and patting his neck. The horse looked at her with big liquid eyes.

"He's so handsome. What's his name?"

"Champion," Hath replied. "But you can name him something else if you want."

"No. Champion is perfect," Ivy said. Tally nodded

agreement.

Wren's admiring smile as he studied the horse confirmed it was a good one. Looking pleased, he said, "I'll start unloading the supplies."

Ivy grasped Champion's bridle and led the way walking the horse to the barn, its hooves throwing up little puffs of dirt.

Tally watched their progress admiring the horse and the rig, then turned to Hath. "What do I owe you for bringing that all the way out here?"

Hath shook his head. "No charge."

"Well, at least let me make you a cup of coffee before you head back." She motioned him to come inside the cabin.

Hath carried his rangy frame up the steps, and wiped his feet at the door. He set his leather rucksack on the table.

"What's that?" she asked.

He opened it, removed a deer hide folder tied with twine and handed it to her. "This is for you."

Tally had asked that loan papers be drawn up by the new lawyer in town. Mimi had been willing to make the loan on a handshake, but Tally wouldn't hear of it, insisting on making it official as well as confidential. She glanced at the pages, saw that Mimi had affixed her signature to them all. Tally set them aside to read and sign later.

Hath reached into the rucksack and pulled out a bottle of whiskey. "This is for you, too. From Mimi. She thought you could use it."

Tally turned a half smile and accepted the bottle and looked at the label. This was no rotgut. It was good stuff. Mimi probably got it from the saloon stock.

"Thank Mimi for me, would you?" She put the bottle in the cupboard and got busy with the coffee.

Hath sat down, took off his hat, and hooked it on the

ear of the ladderback chair next to him.

From the corner of her eye Tally saw his gaze fall on her and follow her movements. A warm, little tug just below her breast bone surprised her. She set her chin in a stubborn line and tried to ignore it. His eyes were saying more than she wanted to hear. A memory of such eyes rose up from the past. Eyes that had promised safety and happiness and security, but had delivered nothing but torment.

She shoved those thoughts from her mind, and met his gaze. No doubt he had an easy time with the women in town. Was Mimi one of them? Mimi with the lustrous hair and ivory skin, the modish dress, clean and crisp fresh from the seamstress.

Tally's cheeks and chest burned with embarrassment. Her own dress was faded and frayed. Her hair dull and drab and falling out of its pins. She swiped her fingers under her eyes as if to wipe away the ever present ash grey shadows.

Shoulders straight, chest lifted, she affected a proud stance as she placed steaming cups of coffee on the table between them and smiled. Perhaps a little wanly because he narrowed his eyes and asked, "So, how have you and Ivy been out here?" He wrapped his hands around his cup and looked at her directly. "Everything going all right?"

Before answering, she brought her cup to her lips and looked at his face to see if there was a hint of scorn or mocking in the question. Perhaps a glint of ridicule in his eyes behind which were the words *I knew you couldn't do it, women weren't meant for this.* Perhaps a flicker of amusement, or worse, disappointment. But she honestly didn't see any of that. His look was inquisitive, genuine. He really wanted to know.

So, she told him what she'd told Mimi. Her voice tight with anxiety, she described the trampled garden, the turned over chicken coop, the dead coyote she found propped up against the door so when she opened it in the morning the bloody carcass fell in on her feet. She told him about the night she heard a scrape and a thump on the cabin door, and slipped out of bed, took a knife from the kitchen drawer and turned to the window knife in hand. She couldn't see out into the ebony night, but knew whoever was out there could see her in a ray of silver moonlight. Hooves clattered as a horse galloped away out of the yard toward the road.

His eyes darkened and his brows bunched into a frown. His gaze was intent and unblinking. "Does the sheriff know about all that?"

"Yes." She lifted her mug and took a sip. "I reported it when I went in to ask about my father."

"What's he going to do?"

"He said he'd come out and look around. Write up a report for his file and let his deputies know." She tilted her head and her shoulders came up in a shrug. "What else can he do? It's not his job to watch my spread twenty-four hours a day. He's got enough to do in town."

"I know, but..." Hath gave his head a shake, and frowned in thought, his eyes locked on hers.

"We have shotguns and a rifle coming in the next shipment of supplies," she said answering the unasked question in his eyes.

"When will that be?"

"Next week, I hope." She sighed and sipped her drink.

"Look," he began, "you'll need weapons for protection in the meantime, I can—"

"No," she broke in. "We'll be fine."

A stubbornness had crept into her voice and before the words were out of her mouth, she wanted to take them back. She could use all the help she could get, but here she was declining it from a nice man who was offering it up. She felt the heat on her cheeks, and she tried to think of a way to smooth over what must have sounded like ingratitude, but he changed the subject and asked another question.

"What did the sheriff say about your father? Does he know anything?"

She shook her head no, then went on to tell him what Mimi said about the men who heard her father arguing in the Diamond Rio. "The sheriff said he'd ask around. Keep his eyes open and let me know what he finds out."

Hath crinkled his eyes and mulled this over looking inward in remembrance. Then he nodded. "I believe I was there that night. What does your father look like?"

"He's tall, dark hair, big hands and wide shoulders… wait. I have a photograph." She left the table to retrieve it, and when she returned handed it to him. "He sent this to us last year. It's not very clear, but you can see his features."

Hath studied the picture and his lips parted. "Yeah. Now I remember. I've seen him around town."

"You have?"

"Yeah, and he's been at the livery a couple of times." He looked up at her. "I didn't know this is who you were looking for. Did you show this to the sheriff?"

"Yes."

He kept his eyes on the picture as he spoke. "Yeah. He got into a disagreement in the saloon. It started out with pushing and shoving and came to blows."

Awestruck, Tally wondered what could have possibly provoked her father into an argument like that in public?

Hank Tisdale was a gentle father and an affectionate husband, but it was true that he had strong opinions about many things and had no problem giving them voice. Politics, women, how to raise children, the place of the church in the family, the rewards of hard work, and the value of owning land. Growing up, both girls had been taught the importance of loyalty, patriotism, and putting money away for a rainy day. None of which, she thought, was a topic that would lead to pushing and shoving in a saloon.

Well, politics, maybe. Yes, most likely it was an argument about politics. She knew from his letters that he was strongly in favor of President Lincoln's Emancipation Proclamation which was a topic of much debate. He had often discussed the benefits of legitimizing the territories with legislatures, territorial governors, and judicial systems. Such advancements were slow in coming, but he felt it was best for the country over all and he was fully supportive. Colorado had been a recognized territory for two years. Arizona was currently being considered. Not everyone agreed with her father's stand on these issues, either. Maybe that's what the argument was about.

Hath looked up and handed back the picture. "It's the same man I saw. I'm sure of it. Ambrose Clarkson stepped in to break it up. This was months before you arrived."

"Who's Ambrose Clarkson?"

"He's a pretty important man in town. Owns real estate on main street and just outside of town on Seventh Street. He platted out a residential section up there behind the Social Center to build homes. He owns the hotel around the corner from the theater, too. He'll probably be elected mayor when the town gets around to drawing up a charter and organizing a governing body. Right now, we're just a settlement on its way to becoming a town. A citizen's council meets a couple of times a month, but we're far from officially organizing." Hath's eyebrows popped. "You'd know Ambrose Clarkson if you saw him."

"I would?"

"He's a hard one to miss. Very dapper. Always dresses in a suit. Every day of the year. Dark frock coat, matching vest with a gold watch chain across his front. Lately he's taken to carrying a fancy cane, but I don't think he's lame. He doesn't even limp. I think he thinks it's fashionable. Maybe it is, in the cities."

Something set in her brain like a hook and Tally thought back to the charming man she and Ivy saw coming out of a saloon their first night in town. The fancy dressed man with the jaunty mustache who swung his cane and propped it over his shoulder like a soldier marching into battle. He'd exchanged a smile with Ivy, and she'd looked eager to make his acquaintance, but Tally had put a stop to it. In the luxury of hindsight, she was sorry she hadn't let her so they could find out more about their father.

Hath studied her face. There were serious wrinkles around his eyes. "Does your hired man sleep on the property?"

She nodded. "In the barn."

"Have you considered hiring a second man?"

"Yes, but not yet. Wren is bringing in some men to help fence off a pasture. I'm hoping the necessary equipment will be on next week's delivery."

Hath's gaze fell to his coffee cup. He picked it up, threw his head back and finished it off. Then he stood and reached for his hat.

"I have to go now, but I'll ride out here and check in every few days. Make sure you have everything you need." He said it kindly, his tone sincere.

"Thank you, but I think Ivy and I and Wren can handle anything that comes up."

She cringed inside. There, she did it again. Declined his offer of help. What was wrong with her? Why did she continually spurn him when the mere sound of his voice soothed her apprehensions?

He ignored the rebuff and his vast smile returned.

Outside, he mounted up, touched the brim of his hat, then reined his horse around and galloped off. She watched until he was out of sight and wondered if he meant what he said about looking in on them. She stared at the spot where he'd disappeared, and even though she could no longer see him, the thought of him stayed in her mind's eye.

    Suddenly her dead husband's face superimposed over that spot where she'd last seen Hath, and she quaked inside.

CHAPTER EIGHT

***H**EAT WAS LOOPING OFF* the dirt street in waves when Boss entered San Miguel looking for Rico. It was time to dig up the gold. A few shovelfuls of dirt is all it would take to extricate it from its shallow grave.

He hadn't seen Rico since the holdup at Bandit Bend, but Clarita, Rico's wife or girlfriend, Boss wasn't sure which, worked at the trading post in Poncha Springs and told him she heard from a cowboy passing through from Antonito that Rico was in a San Miguel jail.

Boss was going to get him out.

He'd made good time traveling into the darkness before stopping to make camp. The landscape was barren and the full moon in the deep western sky had been so bright it made for easy passage on a dirt trail which wind, water, and many horse hooves had beaten smooth. Almost no miners ventured this far out of the gold fields, and it was tough going for travelers making their way along the route on their way to Denver. There were no hotels in which to enjoy even a modicum of comfort, but Boss didn't mind. He liked sleeping under the stars.

San Miguel wasn't much of a town. It provided the minimum of whatever necessities a body could need, but only that. Nothing more. The one-street town was like many others on the Colorado/New Mexico border. A livery. A tiny building with a faded sign over the door that spelled out PROVISIONS. A tinier chapel, a cantina, a makeshift café that served Mexican food out of a window in the side of a half-burned down structure that used to be a barbershop. A one-story adobe building served as a jailhouse.

No planked walkways bordered the buildings, no overhangs to cast shade, and no water troughs for the horses. No false fronts nailed up on the one story structures to make them look two storied. Boss didn't see any dance halls or houses of ill repute, but he had no doubt those activities carried on somewhere.

The street was mostly empty. Here and there long-skirted señoritas made their way with babies in shawl slings, older children toddling behind or racing ahead. A few high booted men lounged on wooden benches, their eyes probing the distance at the end of the rugged uneven track that ran away from the town.

Occasionally their eyes drifted to the passing señoritas and lingered a moment, then drifted away again. Skinny chickens and a few slump-headed dogs roamed the street in search of something to eat, but Boss could have shot a cannon from one end of town to the other and not hit man nor beast.

He reined his horse to a stop in front of the livery which was nothing more than a long three-sided shed with stalls. He dismounted and limped in under the roof, feigning a lame leg, using a cane brought for the purpose. If anyone bothered to look, all they'd remember later if anyone bothered to ask, was a man hobbling inside on a gimp leg. He found Rico's horse, paid the man the boarding fee, saddled it up, and with Rico's horse following on a lead behind, rode to the jailhouse.

It was across the street and a short distance away, a simple, square, squat, low roofed rundown affair with patches of adobe flaking off in places and falling into dust. A street-side window next to a front door that stood open to catch whatever breeze there was. Boss dismounted, tied the horses to the falling down hitchrack that didn't look strong enough to survive a nudge from a brisk breeze. He hobbled inside favoring his right leg, moving with exaggerated effort again in case someone was looking.

The jailer, young and muscled, couldn't have been much more than eighteen, was sitting behind a desk with one legless corner propped up by a stack of crumbling bricks. On the wall behind the desk was a narrow door with a narrow window. The glass in the window was smudged and dirty.

The jailer looked up when Boss entered.

"You speak English?" Boss asked.

"Yes, señor. My name is Alejandro. What is your mission today?"

"I'm here to speak to Edgar Rico. He's in your jail."

Alejandro nodded. "*Si*. He is. But sorry, señor, no visitors allowed. Mr. Rico is waiting for his trial. The circuit judge will be here in two weeks."

"What did Mr. Rico do?"

"Oye." The jailer gave a sad chuckle. "He was a bad man. He flirt with the mayor's daughter with lust in his eyes. She works at the cantina on weekends."

The flirting didn't surprise Boss, but the fact that this godforsaken town had a mayor did. "Oh, yeah? Is it a crime to flirt with a pretty girl?"

"It is in this town, señor. The mayor is also the *policia*."

"Where can I find him?"

"He went to Denver to visit his sister. He'll be back tomorrow, or the next day. Maybe the day after." Alejandro straightened his shoulders and swelled his chest. "He put me in charge until he returns, or until the judge arrives."

"Well, the judge sent me here to speak to Mr. Rico," Boss said, making it up as he went along. "I need to get the prisoner's side of the story."

This caught Alejandro by surprise. He twisted his lips doubtfully. "The judge no do that," he replied. "He takes care of those things himself. I'm just here to keep watch until the mayor returns. I can't say yes or no to nothing."

Boss impaled him with a hard stare, and the young jailer hurried to offer up a suggestion.

"Maybe you can wait for the mayor to return? No hotel or boardinghouse here, but Maria will let you stay in her room. She lives behind the jailhouse and comes in to clean the cells. She'll be here soon…"

His words died away at the sight of Boss' pistol pointed at his chest. He stared at the gun, then at Boss with deep observant eyes filled with fear.

Boss waved the gun. "Just get the keys and hand them over, if you don't mind."

Shoulders drooping in defeat, Alejandro turned and took the cell keys from the top drawer of a small chest. Before he could turn back, Boss brought the butt of his gun down hard on the back of the jailer's head. Alejandro slumped to the floor landing with a thud.

Tossing the cane aside, Boss picked up the keys, stepped over the jailer, and slipped through the narrow door leading to the cells. Two adjoining cells were separated by thick iron bars. Rico was in one of them, a tall, gangly kid with bad skin in the other. The handcuffs on the boy's wrists were so tight they cut into his flesh making his hands swell. His mouth fell open at the sight of Boss coming through the door with keys.

Boss opened the boy's cell, then found the right key for the handcuffs and unlocked them.

"Run!" he barked. "Go on! Before I change my mind!"

The prisoner shucked off the wrist shackles studying Boss with wary eyes, unsure if this stranger was going to shoot him in the back on his way out the door.

"Get outta here," Boss growled, and the kid's boots beat the floor as he took off running.

Rico's eyes glittered and he smiled big. "Hey, Boss." He grabbed his hat as Boss unlocked his cell. "Where's the jailer?"

"Out cold. We gotta move fast before he wakes up. Your horse is outside, saddle bags still packed."

"Thanks, partner."

The two men galloped out of town, Boss leading the way. After a hot, hard ride with a few stops for water they set up camp in a cleared spot next to the San Luis river. Boss took the horses to drink while Rico gathered wood for a fire.

While the horses grazed, Boss shared the food he'd brought along in a rawhide bag tied to his saddle. Smoked pork, boiled ham, bread and potatoes. Both men ate hungrily, especially Rico who set to the food with vigor saying his diet in jail had consisted of some unidentified gruel thrown together by the mayor's wife. He shoved a piece of pork in his mouth and talked while he chewed.

"Where we going, Boss?"

"Sutton Creek."

Rico lowered his hand, a piece of meat in his fingers, and his eyes gleamed. "For the strongbox?"

Boss nodded. "We'll stop for food before we get there. That way we won't have to eat in town where someone might see us."

Rico was silent for a moment, then said, "Thanks for coming to get me." Unlike his usual bluster, his tone was sincere. "I owe ya."

Boss shook out his bedroll. "Don't mention it."

After that, conversation fell off. The two men were not friends to speak of. They had little in common other than the matter at hand—the contents of the strongbox. Money and gold.

Darkness fell and without the sun, cool mountain air rushed in. Rico hunkered down in his clothes using his slicker as a ground cover and his saddle blanket as a quilt. He laid there staring at the fire and though his eyelids drooped, he didn't drift off. "How much money you think is in that box we buried? Countin' the gold and all?" he asked.

"About two hundred and fifty thousand dollars. Maybe more."

"So divided between you, me and Omaha that comes to…" Rico paused to calculate in his head what his share would be, but Boss spoke up.

"Forget Omaha."

Rico's eyes narrowed with cunning. "Really? Are we cuttin' him out or is he dead?"

"Cuttin' him out."

This left Rico with a mathematical problem he could easily solve, and he guffawed loudly. "One hundred and twenty-five thousand dollars! I'll be rich." After a moment of thought, he chuckled to himself. "First thing I'm gonna do is buy Clarita a nice little *casita* in Juarez."

"Yeah? What's the second thing you're gonna do?"

Rico huffed a breath through his nose. "I don't know. I'll have to think on that." Firelight danced in his eyes.

"We'll leave at dawn."

"Sure thing, Boss." Rico wrapped the saddle blanket around his body swaddling himself for the night. He fell into sleep, his smile still on his lips.

Boss stayed awake tending the fire. Except for a faint fluttering of leaves overhead when the wind came alive, there were no other sounds. He gazed across the campfire at Rico's bulk under the blanket. Flames threw dancing shadows over his sleeping form. His breathing came even and steady, his chest moving up and down in cadence with a soft snore. His gun poked out from the saddle bag he was using for a pillow.

Boss waited until the fire burned down to coals, then got to his feet taking great care not to make any noise. He moved slowly until he stood over Rico, revolver in hand.

"Sorry, Rico," he whispered. "I'll give Clarita a goodbye kiss for you." Then he fired, putting a bloody hole in the middle of Rico's chest.

He snatched up Rico's pistol and stuck it in his belt, then rolled Rico onto his side, and picked through the contents of his saddlebags. There wasn't much, but Boss took the extra picket pin, the spare horseshoe, and the extra ammunition. He shoved it all into his own saddlebag.

Thunder rumbled and he looked up at the sky. Mist was spinning, but he was relieved to see racing clouds uncovering the moon and illuminating the landscape.

He unhobbled Rico's horse, and with a smack on its rump sent it galloping into the night. Then he mounted up and started off. He had a long ride in front of him.

CHAPTER NINE

*J*UST BEFORE SUNRISE, *IVY* rose, lighted a lamp, and attended to her toiletry needs moving softly so as not to wake Tally who was still sleeping. For Ivy, restful sleep had not been forthcoming. It rarely was. She picked up her hairbrush breathing in the flowery citrus fragrance of the bergamot and vanilla shampoo Tally had purchased at Gallagher's Mercantile. Expensive, a splurge, but one they couldn't resist the last time they went into town.

The past drifted into the present and she thought with longing of the beauty products that had been lost when the freight wagon bringing their belongings went off the mountain. In Denver—back home, as Ivy still thought of it—both she and Tally had pampered themselves with an array of readily available sweet-scented lotions and oils and creams for skin and hair. Such niceties were sadly lacking here in the rough country. She missed them mightily, a feeling almost like mourning, but she forced herself to focus on the homestead and the uncertain future ahead of them.

This brought her to thoughts of her father. Enough time had gone by that the talons of reality had taken a firm hold. She'd begun to think of him in terms of missing instead of absent or away. Tally, too, had with reluctance admitted as much. Ivy attempted to put aside ruminations of what misfortune may have befallen him, but they were always there, mind pictures moldering and putrefying in the back of her consciousness the longer it went on with no word from or about him. When she tried to talk to Tally about it, her sister waved away the conversation like so many annoying winged insects. But it was always there, the burden of not knowing, the unanswered questions hanging around their necks like millstones.

The sheriff checked in regularly to assure them that he and his deputies continued to make inquiries about Hank Tisdale. So far, no one had come forward whether because they truly had no information or for whatever reason they chose not to speak out.

Tally was convinced that someone knew, but was afraid to tell. Ivy agreed.

She set aside thoughts of her father, and went back to preparing herself for the day. She dressed quickly, hastily pinning up her hair ignoring the messy loose strands. There was work to do. There was always work to do.

Moving quietly, mindful of her sleeping sister, she started a fire noticing the wood in the bin under the stove was low. She picked up several small sticks from the pile, tossed them in, and with an iron poker shifted them around until the wood caught fire. She then laid larger pieces of wood atop the flames. Within moments a roaring fire engulfed the logs. Outside the back door was a pile of kindling, and a stack of cut logs waiting to be split. More work. Always more work.

But coffee first. And biscuits, too. Might as well mix up a batch and get them baking. Through the window, the sky was preparing a velvety canvas upon which the sun would paint variable shades of orange, pink and yellow. It would be a while still before the day brightened enough that she could safely use the hatchet to replenish the wood supply. She didn't mind doing it, and some doctors were saying that the regular intake of fresh air into one's lungs had supreme health benefits. God forbid she or Tally came down sick.

She washed her hands at the pump, put the coffee on, then brought out the flour, the butter and the milk, enough to make a double batch. Wren usually stopped in for coffee and breakfast then carried it outside where he made himself comfortable on the boulder pile while he enjoyed his morning. Hath said he would be coming by later with some supplies that had been left out of the last shipment. Better make enough. Ivy stirred the ingredients in a mixing bowl, prepared the board for kneading, and pondered Hath Hodges.

It was obvious he was taken with Tally and had been since he laid eyes on her that first day at the livery. Not that Tally responded or encouraged him in any way. After her husband died, she steadfastly eschewed romantic gestures. Undiscouraged, Hath continued coming around even when he wasn't bringing supplies. Ivy noticed Tally preening whenever he showed up or when he was expected.

Tally would sit with him awhile at the table or on the front porch of an evening, just talking. Never more than that. Tally didn't seem to notice that he looked at her like he was trying to breathe her in. Either that, or she deliberately ignored it.

Ivy sighed as she kneaded the dough, using the heels of her hands to push downward and away. With her fingers, she sprinkled a bit of flour on the lump of dough, flipped it over, then pushed again.

She wished she had a man that looked at her that way. One day she asked if Tally thought Ivy would ever find someone to marry her. Tally had flavored her reply with a bit of wisdom, assuring Ivy that she would meet someone suitable, but adding that women needed to choose a life companion very carefully. Ivy wasn't certain, but it sounded more like a warning than sisterly advice.

When the biscuits were done, she put them on a rack to cool. Pale light was greying the sky, so she took a shawl from the hook next to the door. She wrapped it around herself against the morning chill, tying it securely in front to free up her hands and went outside to split enough wood to replenish the bin. She picked up the axe, but before her hand touched the first log, she froze, still and stiff as if she'd turned to stone. Predawn winds sounding like a chorus of voices as they made their way through tall pines eddied around her causing the fringe on the edge of her shawl to flutter.

She gazed at the sheep, their heads wrenched from their bodies and strewn in the dirt. For a heartbeat or more, she stared speechless, thinking she was dreaming, then glanced around in a frenzy. A scream began, but got stuck deep in her stricken throat. She heard a noise and raised her tormented eyes to see Tally standing in the doorway, her hand pulled to her mouth in shock.

The hatchet slipped from Ivy's hand as she continued to stare at the blood and gore. Her heart was beating too fast and her mind spun with questions competing to be answered. Full blown dread seized her. "Why didn't we hear this? The sheep would have wakened us."

Tally turned her eyes into the distance. She pointed to a trail of blood, mud and hoofprints leading to the cabin from the back pasture where the sheep had been moved the day before. "They were dragged here behind the horses after they were killed."

Then she yelled, "Wren! Wren! Come now!"

Wren came running out of the barn carrying a rifle, but he slowed and angled the barrel down when he saw the ghastly carnage on the ground. He stopped and gestured to the women waving them inside.

"I'll take care of this," he said softly, calmly. "You go on inside. I'll come in when I'm done."

A sudden thought struck Ivy. The chickens! She lifted her skirt and started for the chicken house. "No. I have to go check on my chickens."

"Don't," Wren said.

"But I need to go see if..."

"Don't!" he said and gave her a hard look. Then more softly added, "I'll take care of it."

Ivy started to cry. Tally's face darkened, overtaken with anger and determination.

CHAPTER TEN

*I*VY HASTENED INSIDE TO Tally's open arms, her breath labored by sobs. Tally embraced her until they subsided. When Ivy had settled enough, Tally sat her at the table and put a plate of biscuits in front of her.

"Here. Eat something. It will help you feel better."

Ivy sniffed and pushed the plate away, her eyes glued to the window. She couldn't seem to look away from the frightful sight.

While Ivy watched Wren, Tally reached to the top of the cupboard and took down a holstered pistol and a gun belt. She slipped the gun out of the holster, releasing the faintest smell of saddle soap. The gun's grip was wood, the barrel cool and blue. The only sound aside from Ivy's struggle to control her breath was the soft *click-click-click* of the cylinder when Tally turned it to check the load. She buckled the gun belt around her hips yanking it tight, then reached up and retrieved a second gun belt, this one also holding a pistol. She laid it on the table in front of Ivy with a *thunk*.

"You'd best start wearing yours, too." There was a snap in her voice she didn't mean to be there, but she did mean to make the point that maliciously decapitating livestock was a violent act, and whoever did it could easily take the next step. They had to protect themselves. "Wear it all day, and keep it next to you at night."

Ivy squeaked a reply, her voice still wrenched with

fear. "I will." A hiccup jumped up in her throat and caught on a sob. She looked at the gun belt on the table, but kept her fingers laced in her lap.

Tally filled two mugs with coffee, added a splash to each from the bottle of whiskey Mimi had sent with Hath. She put a mug in front of Ivy who reached for it with trembling hands. Then, not wanting to show Ivy her own fear she shored herself up and stood at the door gripping her mug, watching Wren.

Wren caught her eye and held it. His gaze was full of *told ya so* admonition. She knew what he was thinking. He'd been dropping hints for weeks, then recently breached the subject. The amount of work and daily chores had grown beyond what the three of them could manage even with the help of an occasional itinerant worker who stayed briefly before moving on. They needed more help. Someone who could help keep watch at night.

Tally agreed, but had deliberately dragged her feet before making the decision because of the money. Now she gusted a sigh, pressed her lips and lowered her chin in a slight nod signifying capitulation. Wren dipped his head in shared understanding, and resumed cleaning up.

Tally turned back to the kitchen. "We'll work inside today. Let's go through Father's things. Sort his papers. Launder his clothes and pack them in a box in case," she paused. "I mean, for when he comes back."

Ivy inclined her head. "All right."

"But eat something first. Please try." Tally slid the plate back to Ivy along with the butter dish and a knife. "It's imperative that we keep our strength and our spirits up. Father would want that."

Tally busied herself washing the mixing bowl and baking pan, then stone faced and silent, she ran a cleaning rag over the counters with wide overly purposeful swipes moving cups and cannisters and other items as she went.

At the table, Ivy broke off tiny pieces of a biscuit and put them in her mouth one by one with indolent savor. She finished chewing and asked again, her voice buckling under the weight of the question. "Who do you think did this?" Her bewilderment could not be more apparent.

Tally's jaw tightened, and the wash rag slowed to a stop as she pondered her sister's question. What Ivy had faced that morning at the woodpile was something no one could have anticipated, so her fear and agitation were understandable. In one smoldering moment Ivy's innocence had ignited and disappeared with a *whoosh*! From the day they'd arrived young Ivy had done her best to stand up against the hardships of homesteading, though not without complaint and sometimes argument.

But she was going to have to do better.

Tally slapped the cleaning cloth into the wash basin and spun around.

"I don't know who did it," she said, her voice full of fire. "But you're going to have to buck up. Whoever did it means business. So we have to mean business, too. And that means no more complaining. No more grumbling. No more wistful whining about going *back home. This* is our home and *this* is where we're staying. At least for now.

"So you can cry in the face of trouble if you have to, but then you've got to pull yourself together straightaway. I can't do this alone. I need you. I'm going to hire more men and we're going to fortify. We have no choice. We have to be prepared to fight back." She didn't add that she didn't know who exactly they would have to fight back against.

Ivy snuffled in a shaky breath and let it out, but didn't look up. Shoulders drooping, she placed her hand on the still holstered gun where it lay on the table, but she didn't pick it up. A long silence followed while she held herself in a position of uncertainty.

Tally crossed her arms and leaned her hip against the table, a charged silence pulsing between them. Minutes passed as she centered herself in the here and now, slowing her mind so she could order priorities. There were so many things that still needed to be done to make the cabin a decent place to live and the spread productive.

After Wren finished construction on the half-built barn, the bedroom had surrendered up all the tools and other farm equipment stored there and found a home within its newly built walls. The makeshift cots Tally and Ivy had been sleeping on were moved from the main room into the cleared out bedroom providing them with a modicum of privacy.

That done, Wren quickly built an extra room onto the back of the cabin originally intended for storage, but Ivy claimed the room for herself. Though small, she was happy to have her own private space whatever its size, and Tally conceded it would give Ivy comfort. Only the boxes containing their father's belongings remained. She had pushed them aside intending to deal with them another time.

Today was the time.

Hank Tisdale didn't own much in the way of garments, just a bare minimum of work clothes, good quality, but showing wear. Tally lifted his boxes of papers and files onto the kitchen table for sorting while Ivy filled the wash tub at the pump outside. She breathed a little easier seeing Ivy had relented and buckled on her gun belt. A good sign.

Tally opened a box and removed files labeled LAND OFFICE, PROOF OF IDENTIFICATION, PATENT APPLICATION, and PROVED UP WORK. A second box, smaller, contained letters, assorted magazine and newspaper clippings, a Bible, and prayer cards. At the bottom was a book.

A journal. It was Hank Tisdale's journal.

Curious and a little surprised, she picked it up. Though her father was educated and well read, she'd never known him to keep a diary or any written record of his private thoughts. She opened the cover and flipped through a few pages, but set it aside to read later. She wanted to tackle the bills first. Methodically, she organized the bills and receipts in sequence according to date. After she matched the receipts to the bills, she'd know which had been paid and which, if any, were still due.

Finishing that, she glanced through page after page of ledger sheets detailing in her father's cramped handwriting what appeared to be a notation of every single outgoing and incoming penny along with mentions of source and supplier. It was going to require long stretches of time to adequately analyze these records, so she set them aside along with the journal and the other files. She needed to tend to the bills first.

Time passed. She wasn't sure how much, but with the washing done and drying on the line, Ivy came inside and sat down at the table. Tally was relieved to see that the adrenaline had seeped out of her somewhat though she still seemed a bit unsteady.

Tally slid the journal across the table.

"Here," she said, her tone apologetic after her earlier outburst. "I found this. Do you want to read through it?"

Ivy pulled it closer. "What is it?"

"Father's journal."

She frowned and looked up. "He kept a journal?"

Tally nodded. "Looks that way. Maybe there's something in there that will tell us where he went and why."

Ivy began reading, slowly turning the pages.

When it was time for lunch, Tally lifted her arms overhead and stretched her spine to ease her aching back. She wasn't used to sitting for such long periods of time. She rose and put on a pot of leftover soup to heat.

"Anything helpful in his journal?"

"Not so far. He mostly wrote down what he did each day. Chores and such. Sometimes what he ate. He made notes documenting his compliance with the government's requirements aimed at acquiring full ownership of the homestead." She continued to turn the pages. "He had a cow at one time, and two dogs. Homer and Hector. One was an indoor dog. He called the other a barn dog." Ivy paused, her expression serious. "Maybe we should get some dogs, too. You know. The kind that bark at strangers."

"We will. What else is in there?"

"Weather—storms and daily temperatures. Planting schedules. Trips to town. Names of merchants he patronized. Which ones he didn't." She looked up and added, "Mostly because they wouldn't extend him any more credit."

Tally hummed a note.

Ivy read on. "Meetings with Pettyjohn at the Land Office. Seems like he did that a lot."

"That's funny," said Tally. "Pettyjohn gave us the impression he didn't know Father very well. How many times did they meet?"

Ivy looked back through the pages counting to herself in her head. "Ten times. At least, that's what he wrote down." She read silently a few minutes, turning pages. "Oh." She said it with surprise and so quietly it was almost a breath.

"What?"

"After his last meeting with Pettyjohn there was a long period of time when he didn't make any journal entries. He started up again five weeks later." She continued reading to herself.

When the silence had gone on uncomfortably long,

Tally turned from the counter where she was slicing a loaf of bread.

Ivy's lips were parted, her expression mystified as she turned a page.

Tally put the bread knife down. "What is it, Ivy?"

Ivy looked up from the journal, stunned. "He said men came to the door and told him he had to move out."

"Let me see that."

Ivy put her finger on the page and turned the journal so Tally could read it. "Right here. He said the man showed him a deed in someone else's name, and told him he had to leave."

Tally lifted the journal. A folded piece of paper fluttered to the floor from between the pages.

Ivy picked it up. "It's an eviction notice."

Distracted, Tally's eyes leaped across the page.

"He said someone shot his dogs... stole his cow... tore down the corral..." She read on silently, an onslaught of dread growing in the middle of her chest. "They threw a flaming torch on the front porch, and tried to burn down the cabin, but Father was able to put it out."

Ivy leaned forward in her chair, listening with a fretful expression.

A memory zinged back to Tally of the day Buster brought them out to see the place for the first time. "That explains why there were new planks on the porch steps when the rest of the cabin was in such disrepair." Quickly she turned the pages looking for more, but there were no more entries.

Tally exhaled a long breathe. It wasn't a sudden shock. It was more like a slow dawning. Realization seeped into her mind and suddenly she felt weightless, renewed, like she'd just dug herself out of her own grave.

Clarity expanded as her mind began fitting previously unexplained pieces together—the noises outside after dark, noises that had no place in the normal range of night sounds. The footprints in the dirt below the windows. The trampled garden. Trooper and Champion spooked in the night, stomping and carrying on in the stable. They—*someone*—sneaking around. Then this morning, the sheep.

"Someone ran Father off and now they're trying to run us off, too." It was almost a relief to know.

She pressed the open journal to her breast, her cheeks burning with anger.

"Well, it's not going to work," Tally said, her voice infused with resolve. She clapped the journal shut and slammed it on the table.

"We're not leaving!"

CHAPTER ELEVEN

*T*HE *SILVERTHORNE SALOON WAS* long, low, and dimly lighted, but not so dark Boss couldn't see the full display of saloon art on the walls. From where he stood elbows propped on the bar, boot heel hooked on the brass rail at its base, he studied the murals of undraped, sumptuously endowed women that decorated either side of an ornate, hand carved backbar. Through the thick fog of smoke from cigars and cigarettes, an elaborately framed mirror on the backbar allowed an unobstructed view of what was going on behind him.

What the saloon lacked in luminosity it made up for in noise. Talking, laughing, shouting, and swearing competed with an all-woman band playing fiddles, banjos, and a piano on a raised platform next to the bat-winged entrance. Chairs and tables ranged along the walls and bunched up in the center were crowded with both sexes talking all at once and at the top of their voices.

It was a mixed crowd. Stone-faced gents played cards, their weapons on the table close at hand. Flirtatious saloon girls circled the game tables drifting their fingers over the backs and shoulders of the players, trying to make solid eye contact with the winners.

Other women, horse faced, no longer young, no longer fair, wearing clumsy oversized boots peeking out from long calico skirts drank with the men. Ragged miners from the mountains, leather faced old geezers.

Ranchers, cowboys. Unshaved trail hands, some of them young and gawky, looking bewildered, as if it was their first time away from home. Sawdust covered the floor. Spittoons were strategically placed for ease of use.

A man sitting by the cash box was painting on an easel. Boss recognized him as Charles Russell. He'd heard the artist traded paintings for drinks. A sign above the cash drawer said, "In God we trust. Everyone else pays cash." But apparently that excluded Charles Russell.

Suddenly chairs scraped back and two men shot to their feet, hands hovering over their holsters. After a warning from a bouncer sporting holstered pistols on both hips, they settled down at their table and returned to their whispered argument. An old man, his wrinkled face cheek down on his table was sound asleep in the corner. Four vaqueros speaking Spanish and wearing broad brimmed sombreros and big jangly spurs attached to mud caked boots were celebrating something. Their conversation was jovial and animated, their laughter riotous.

Boss kept his eyes moving over the mirrored panorama.

The bartender, well-appointed and dapper in black and white with a glossy handlebar mustache and gartered sleeves that showed off his iron-muscled biceps, was busy pouring drinks at the far end of the long bar. When he finished, he hurried over to Boss.

"What'll you have?" he asked speaking up to be heard over the clamor.

"Taos Lightning."

The saloonkeeper's luxurious black mustache twitched and he gave Boss a dubious look, but said nothing. He poured from the keg into a glass so clean it sparkled.

Taos Lightning was no ordinary barrelhouse slop. The extra potent drink made from river water, grain alcohol, bitters, and ginger gave many a man the jimjams after only a few sips. With practice it went down easier. The bartender brought the drink and Boss slid some coins across the bar. The barkeep picked them up and started to walk away, but Boss stopped him and beckoned him to lean in close.

"I'm looking for a friend," Boss said. "His name's Omaha Jones. Been told I can find him here most days."

The barkeep nodded. "Most days, yeah." His gaze swept the room probing the gauzy haze. "He's not here yet. Haven't seen him today." He took out his pocket watch and glanced at it, then put it back. "But it's early. He usually takes a table over by the window. Either that or he goes upstairs with Trudy." He gestured with his chin. "That's her over there."

Boss lifted his gaze to the mirror so he could see behind him. Trudy was young, fine featured, light haired, and much too pretty to be interested in a snake like Omaha. At the moment, she was sitting on the lap of a cowboy.

Boss picked up his drink. "Thanks. I'll wait."

He kept his eyes glued to the mirror behind the glittering array of liquor bottles of various shapes and sizes. He could see the front door, the female band, and the whole expanse of the room including the stairway leading upstairs to the closed doors aligned along the balconied overlook.

Omaha eventually arrived, already at this early hour of the day glassy-eyed and unsteady on his feet from too much drink. Keeping his back turned, Boss watched Omaha's progress in the mirror. When Omaha spotted Trudy sitting next to one of the card players, he waved her over. She got up, led him up the steps and along the balconied walkway to one of the rooms. The door closed behind them and stayed closed. Boss ordered another drink to give them time to get their business done.

When his drink arrived, he tilted his head back and emptied it in one quick motion, then casually made his way over to the table where the vaqueros were still reveling. He tapped the shoulder of the biggest one.

The man looked up. *"Si, señor?"*

Boss lowered his voice so only the table could hear. "See that man over there in that big poker game? The one with the bushy beard, and the pile of chips?"

Four pairs of dark drunken eyes turned toward the poker table Boss indicated.

"Si?" said the vaquero. "What about him?"

Boss leaned in closer. "Well, I just heard him say he could take on all four of you without breaking a sweat."

In an instant, chairs were kicked back and tables turned over, fists flew and guns exited holsters. Onlookers scattered tripping over each other in an effort to get out of the line of fire. The bartender and the bouncer rushed to intervene. While everyone was so occupied, Boss went up the stairs taking them two at a time.

He stood a moment outside the door Trudy and Omaha had entered, then tried the handle. The door was locked, but gave way easily with a minimum of pressure on the latch mechanism. Boss opened the door a crack and peered in through the slit. The curtains were drawn casting the room into shadow, but a bit of late afternoon sunlight spilled in through a narrow space where they didn't quite meet. Omaha lay on the bed under a blanket snoring like a bugling elk.

Trudy lay next to him. Her eyes were open and she saw Boss come in. She sat up, grasped a loose corner of the blanket and held it in front of her. "Who are you?"

Boss put his finger to his lips.

"Shhh. He's my friend. I need to talk to him. That's all."

Trudy opened her mouth and cocked her tongue ready to argue, but changed her mind when Boss scooped up her clothes from a chair and tossed them to her.

"Please, ma'am. Just get dressed and leave. You can come back when me and him finish our business. It's about money. You won't be sorry."

At that, Trudy's eyes came alive and she gave him a sly look. She slid off the bed and hurriedly got dressed, noticing him watching her and not seeming to mind.

He smiled and tipped his bowler when she went out the door. "Much obliged," he said watching her head for the stairs. When she caught sight of the ruckus downstairs, she sent a curious backward glance over her shoulder, and went down the back stairway.

Boss closed the door and looked around the room. It was small, but neat and clean. A diamond dust mirror on the wall and a fine glass chimney on the kerosene lamp were feeble attempts to add elegance to the otherwise shoddy quarters.

Boss picked up Omaha's pants and went through the pockets one by one, then searched the shirt. Not finding what he was looking for, he turned Omaha's leather satchel upside down spilling papers and personal belongings onto the counterpane. Not there either.

Omaha stirred, snorted a honk through his nose, then heaved himself over onto his back and continued snoring. Boss stepped to the bed, touched Omaha's shoulder and shook it lightly.

"Omaha," he whispered.

When there was no response, Boss shook harder. "Wake up. Omaha, wake up. Where's the map?"

Omaha's eyes fluttered, but stayed closed. Boss kept shaking the big man trying to drag him out of his drunken torpor. "The map!" he hissed. "Where's the map?"

"Huh?" Omaha's eyes opened, but wouldn't focus.

Boss gripped Omaha's chin and squeezed his cheeks with his fingers. "Hey. It's me. Boss. Wake up. Where's the map? Remember? You drew a map."

Omaha groaned, but wouldn't rouse. His eyelids fluttered again, and this time Boss shook him so hard the mattress bounced, making the iron bed squeal.

"The map," Boss implored through his teeth in a harsh whisper. "Shows where we buried the gold. Where is it?"

This time a measure of understanding began to take hold. "The gold?" Omaha croaked. "We goin' for it?"

"Yeah," Boss answered. "Yeah. We're going to dig it up, but we need that map you drew. You still got it?"

"Ha…" Omaha mumbled, still foggy. "Hath." The word was slurred and he couldn't quite get it out, but Boss knew what he said.

He found the hat on the floor under the bed, and went down on one knee to retrieve it. He turned it over and removed a folded piece of paper from the sweatband. The crudely drawn map of the abandoned homestead, an X marking the burial spot. Boss refolded it, slipped it into his pocket and stood up.

Snoring loudly, Omaha sunk back into a deep sleep. The muffled noise from downstairs had changed from a clamor to bedlam. Boss stared at the man sprawled on top of the bed wondering if he was unconscious. After some thought, he picked up a pillow, shoved the full weight of his knee into Omaha's gut driving out a gust of air at the same time he put the pillow over his face. Pushing with both hands, he held it there until Omaha Jones stopped struggling. When Boss was sure he'd snuffed out what life was left in the man, he got off the bed, tossed the pillow onto the floor, and left the room.

The dustup downstairs had turned into a full out glass breaking brawl. Sticking close to the perimeter of the room, Boss made it to the batwing doors, ducked out, and rode away.

CHAPTER TWELVE

WHEN HATH SHOWED UP at supper time, one look at the tortured eyes of the Tisdale sisters and the gun belts tightened around their hips told him there was trouble.

"What?" he said. "What happened?"

One speaking after the other and sometimes on top of each other, they told him about the sheep and what they'd found in Hank's journal. He stayed for supper and then lingered helping them search Hank's files for a certificate of his approved patent application. They found none.

"The original is in Pettyjohn's office," Tally insisted. "I saw it when we were there. He took out the original and held it in his hand. My father's name was at the bottom of the page where he signed it."

"Are you sure it was his signature?"

A fleeting second of hesitation preceded Tally's reply. "Yes," she said. Then more decisively, "Yes, I'm sure it was his signature. I could tell by the way he forms the H in his name. He makes a little loop on it."

"Did Pettyjohn give you a copy?"

A disheartened glance bounced from one sister to the other.

"No." Tally's face crumbled. "I asked for one, but he said our father had the only copy."

"Well, one thing's certain. Without it, neither you nor your father has a valid claim to this place."

"You mean someone can come and evict us?" Ivy's tangled emotions showed on her drawn face. She was pale, eyes red-rimmed.

Hath's voice was sympathetic as he tried to soften the blow of the truth. "They can try. Or they might wait until you've completely proved it up. That way it's worth more. Scammers get more for proved up homesteads."

Ivy stared at him wide-eyed and speechless.

Exasperation sagged Tally's careworn face. She exhaled abruptly, producing a sound that signaled frustrated impatience. Then she pulled in her lips and steadied her breathing to normal in an effort to regain composure.

The three of them sat in silence a long while, held captive by private thoughts.

Ivy tried to keep the conversation going, but emotional exhaustion muddled her words and her thinking. There was no point asking the same unanswerable questions over and over. Eventually, she excused herself and retired to her room closing the door with a hard thud.

Brilliant sunshine had abandoned the sky hours ago, the remaining rosy pink sunset giving in to a greyish cast. Night followed, sliding down the mountains slowly populating the yard with shadows that moved with the breeze.

Tally lit a lamp, wrapped herself in a light shawl and went outside to sit on the front porch where she settled into a rope-bottomed rocker. Hath followed close behind and sat next to her in a porch chair held together with splints and rawhide strips. He rested a booted foot on the opposite knee and tried to think of something to say that would remove the thorny look from her face and the trouble from her life. But, of course, he couldn't do that no matter what he said.

She didn't move, didn't speak, just sat quietly staring into the distance rocking gently back and forth. The rocker squeaked with the movement. He didn't know what she was thinking, but he hoped she wasn't thinking about leaving and felt compelled to ask.

"Are you thinking about going back to Denver?"

She took a moment to answer. "Ivy wants to go back." She dipped in and out of the circle of lamplight as she rocked back and forth. Hath waited for more, apprehensive about what her next words might be.

"But there's nothing there for us anymore." She gestured with a flourish of her arm. "This is all we have now." She paused. "Besides, we have to stay here in case my father comes back."

She no longer sounded as certain of that as she had in their previous conversations. He wondered if her hope of ever seeing him again had been shattered.

Night insects chittered and croaked. Trooper and Champion whinnied in the corral. In the distance, a coyote sang. A second one howled in harmony, and soon there was a chorus as others joined in.

Hath studied Tally's lamplit profile in speculative silence for a while. The grey wool shawl hugged her shoulders, crossed in front, the edges wound around her tight fist. Muted light from the lamp did nothing to hide the anger she was stubbornly holding on to. And who could blame her? Sometimes anger generated the strength needed to solve a problem or accomplish a goal.

When he'd first met her at the livery, he could see she had something inside her. Something grittier than perseverance and more powerful than determination. He admired her tenacity in taking over the homestead. Even then he knew that if any woman could succeed, it would be her.

But now she looked so dejected he wondered if the string of obstacles culminating in the slaughter of the sheep had enfeebled that part of her.

"Don't give up," he said quietly. "Not on your father and not on the homestead. Without hope a person can die before they take their last breath. There are people all over the Rockies who have let loose of their hope. Don't be one of them."

She drew herself up straightening her spine, a look of grim resolve on her face. Even though her voice was breathy, the words she spoke were weighty with purpose.

"I don't intend to be."

Hath's thoughts traveled over scenes from his past. "My mother was one of those. After my father died, she gave up all hope in the face of poverty and trials. I think she just decided not to go on.""

Tally turned to him, the reflection of the flame from the lamp dancing in her eyes. "I'm sorry you lost your father," she whispered. "Had he been ill?"

"No. He was murdered. Shot."

At that, she stiffened. "Oh," was all she said, but he caught a flicker of something cross her expression. What was it? Offense? Anger? Fear? It was gone in an instant, and she quickly lowered her lids and looked away.

But not before he saw a secret reflected there. He stayed silent waiting for her to say more. She stayed silent, too, in the grip of some thought that washed ripples of discontent over her. They sat that way listening to the ageless symphony of night sounds. Eventually the tension in the air loosened, then dissipated. Her posture relaxed, but not the earnestness on her face.

The moon peeked through a hole in the clouds casting dim light on the yard and the outbuildings providing an adequate amount of illumination to see through the darkness without being seen in return. He dragged his gaze across the flat expanse of the yard into the near distance where a line of trees stood sentinel along the road. He was looking for something indefinable, something that didn't belong. He saw nothing and nothing moved, but that didn't mean nothing was there.

He stirred uneasily in his chair building up to a question. "Would it be all right if I stayed in the barn with Wren tonight? I'd like to help him keep watch."

Her gaze shifted back to his face. Whatever tainted memory, whatever secret thoughts held her captive had fled. A sigh of relief escaped her lips.

"Thank you, Hath. I'd appreciate it and I'm sure Ivy will sleep more soundly knowing you're here." She stood. "I'll bring extra blankets."

Before she could step away, he moved beside her. She allowed his strong arms and broad chest to provide comfort to her weary head and shoulders. But only for a moment. She delicately eased herself away.

When she returned with the blankets, he slung them over his arm, said good night, and walked his horse to the barn.

CHAPTER THIRTEEN

HATH UNSADDLED HIS HORSE and corralled him with Trooper, Champion, and Wren's horse, a long, rangy sorrel, big and powerful. The herd pricked their ears forward, and made their way over to touch noses with the newcomer, nickering softly in greeting.

Hath entered the barn carrying the blankets and his saddle. Inside, the sweet smell of straw mingled with the musky smell of animals. It was dim and shadowy and it took a moment for his eyes to adjust. Wren was propped up against pillows on a makeshift cot held together by nails and strips of buckskin. He was reading a book in the yellowish glow of a lantern, but saved the page with his finger and looked up in surprise when Hath appeared.

Hath nodded in greeting. "Hope you don't mind if I stay the night to help keep watch. In case there's more trouble."

Wren lifted his feet still crossed at the ankle, and swung his legs over the side of the cot. He mumbled something Hath couldn't make out.

"Tally said it was all right," Hath added. "You know. The women, they're scared."

This was met with silence. Hath felt the intensity of Wren's unsmiling gaze as if the Indian's eyes were piercing the middle of his chest.

Wren had revamped his corner of the barn into a small but serviceable living quarters. Canvas sheets attached to the walls kept drafts at bay. A small table next to the cot held an oil lamp, a Bible, and a few other books. Eating utensils, plates, and a cookstove were arranged on a board plank laid across two barrels. Wren's pistol, a cold, lethal beauty, was on the table next to the Bible, but still close to hand. A rifle leaned against the wall.

Wren stared stone-faced, the dark of his eyes going darker.

Hath looked around. "Mind if I take this empty stall?"

Wren didn't answer, but asked his own question. "How long you staying? For the night or…?" His voice had an edge and he spat out the words like they tasted bad. His gaze was cold.

"Not sure how long," Hath answered. "Depends on what happens during the night."

He relieved himself of his saddle, then folded two of the blankets forming them into a sleeping pad which he laid on a pile of hay taking possession of the stall. He was aware of Wren's scrutiny, watching every move with alert, distrustful eyes. Hath couldn't figure out why the Indian was so uneasy.

"Miss Tally gonna take on more men," Wren said then. "She put me in charge of hiring. I'll be boss man then."

He spoke with a particular emphasis that inspired Hath to stop what he was doing and turn around. Wren's stubborn gaze was full of meaning, as sharp and unwavering as an arrow in flight.

Is that what it is? Wren thinks I'm taking over his job?

"Congratulations. Make sure she gives you a raise." He hoped that would waylay any concern Wren might have about being forced aside.

Wren blinked, and continued watching Hath's movements.

"Miss Tally running out of money. She told me take the sheep bodies to town, sell to the mercantile. She needs money to buy more sheep."

"How many were slaughtered?"

"Not all. Only six. Mostly rams. I keep pregnant ewes and lambs in the barn at night. Because of the coyotes. I bring them in before I go to sleep."

"Good idea."

"But they got Miss Ivy's chickens. Her best layer. She wanted to win egg contest prize."

Hath shook his head. Poor Ivy. He wondered if she was going to make it. She was barely holding herself together, and if she left Tally would go, too. She wouldn't want to be alone, and she wouldn't want Ivy to be alone, either.

Hath finished setting up his sleeping pad and approached Wren's cot. Wren's wary eyes followed him every step of the way. Though they were facing each other, there was an invisible barrier between them. The Indian was unaccountably skittish.

"How soon will you have more crew?" asked Hath.

"Maybe soon. Workers coming next week to build pasture fence."

"How long will they be here?"

"Three, four days. If no rain."

"Maybe you'll find some good workers in that bunch."

Wren shook his head. "No. They move on to build fence on another spread. They travel. Miss Tally wants dependable workers who'll stick around."

The Indian seemed to be mellowing out some. Hath tried to read his face. Gone was the look like he was tasting something sour, but his expression was still dubious.

"You seen any strangers nosing around? Trespassers?"

Wren nodded. "Deserted campsite at back end of spread when I was out there looking for best grazing. Last week. Then yesterday I ran off two men."

"Who were they?"

"Dunno."

"You ever seen 'em before?"

"No."

"Were they Indians?"

"No. White men. I told them to move on. They didn't want to go. One of them had a mean-as-hell voice."

Hath tucked that information away. "What were they doing out there?"

"Just ridin'."

"Just riding?"

"Lookin' around."

Hath pondered that. Looking around? Or looking for something?

"That string of trees lining the road." Hath tipped his chin in their direction. "Maybe they should be cut down. Lots of places to hide in them. Might make the women feel safer if they had a longer view from the yard."

The Indian thought about that. "I'll ask Miss Tally tomorrow."

"She could sell the lumber to newcomers. Or keep it and you can use it to build something on the homestead. A way to make money or save money."

The Indian's eyes were working. "I'll talk to her."

"Tell her it was your idea."

The hard angles of Wren's face softened a little and the corners of his mouth quirked up into a vague semblance of a smile.

"How about we take turns keeping watch tonight?" said Hath. "That all right with you?"

Wren nodded. "You go first."

Hath shrugged. "Fine with me."

He slid his pistol out of its holster to check the cylinder. Satisfied with its load, he slid it back and went outside. He circuited the grounds keeping a keen eye on the cabin, the barn and the corral, wondering what the hell Wren was so jumpy about. Hours later when he returned to the barn for some shuteye, Wren was asleep fully dressed and booted on top of his cot.

Hath woke him up to take his turn at night watch.

CHAPTER FOURTEEN

BOSS WAS ON HIS way to get the gold. He would have gone back sooner, but he'd met a woman in Taos and hidey-holed himself up with her. Her husband was away working on the railroad, and she was afraid of the Indian raids, so she let him stay over the winter and through the spring.

She was fine and fair, and her voice was soft when she said his name with a seductive little hiss at the end. Her hair was reddish brown, soft and smooth like fox fur. She laughed a lot and was a good cook, too, so he stayed on. Why not? His horse needed shoeing and a rest, and so did he. The money and the gold would still be there. It was buried in the ground. No one would ever find it.

When her husband came riding up, Boss slipped out the back door. Now with the treasure map in his pocket, he was on his way.

Silverthorne linked to Sutton Creek over twisting roads and mountain passes traveled by bushwhackers, stagecoaches and farm wagons. The sun was warm and the air was fresh with a light breeze. It would be an easy two day ride if he used his horse well.

Two days. Two days at most, and he'd be a wealthy man on his way to California where he planned to give up his thieving ways. No more dodging, no more lying, no more running from the law. He was going to put all that behind him.

He'd done a lot of thinking about what he was going to do with the money once he got to California. Buy some land for sure. A little ranch somewhere with a small herd of cattle. Some horses. Maybe a couple of that rare breed with the long curly manes and tails. Friesians, they were called. He'd first heard about them from a horse thief in Nevada who'd been told about them by a wealthy San Francisco rancher.

Maybe he'd take in some poor orphan kids to come live on his ranch, kids with no home and no parents. Or maybe poor kids *with* parents. Just because you had parents didn't mean you weren't poor. He ought to know. His folks were hardscrabble dirt farmers who couldn't scrape together enough food to put on the table. He and his brothers were sent to an orphanage where there was plenty of food, but where they were beaten nearly every day.

Of course, he was going to need a woman beside him on a ranch like that. A wife who liked lots of kids and could take good care of them. Teach them things, like manners and book learning and God. A woman who would take care of *him,* too. He'd seen couples like that. Men and women who pledged themselves to each other for eternity. Good decent people with families. He wanted that kind of life, too. It required settling down, and that's what he planned to do.

He urged his horse into a comfortable walk. Waco was strong, well trained, and still young. When Boss estimated they'd gone about thirty miles, he set up camp in a level grassy spot well off the trail upstream from the base of a bluff. After he fixed Waco to a picket pin near a water hole in an area lush for grazing, he put the coffee on, then sat beside the fire and cleaned his pistol. The Henry was close at hand, too, just in case. This was the time of day bears and catamounts came out looking for food.

He ate a meal from the fixings he'd brought along. After he dug up the gold, he'd be eating in the dining rooms of the best hotels. Roast potatoes and a thick steak on a plate in front of him. Wine in a stemmed glass. A big slice of lemon cream pie fresh from the oven topped with whipped up cream to finish it off.

And he'd be sleeping in a bed instead of on this damp lumpy ground. He shook out his bedroll, spread his slicker over it, and topped it all with a blanket. He laid down, interlaced his fingers and rested his head in the cup of his hands. Looking up at the dark sky, he found the North star and traced an imaginary line down to the horizon. That was north. The pale silver moon was a crescent high in the sky. He connected the tips of the crescent with another imaginary line and followed it down to where it hit the ground. That was south. Whenever he slept out in the open, he always checked his bearings that way. He was a man who needed to know his place on the land.

Night birds trilled and whooped and croaked. Owls sent out their familiar ho-ho who-who calls. Insects buzzed, animals prowled, Waco snuffed and snorted. Branches scraped against each other in the wind, grass and leaves rustled. He sure was going to miss those sounds when he was sleeping in real bed.

Relaxed, at peace, and full of expectation, he closed his eyes. Soon he was asleep.

He woke at daybreak to clear sky and fresh air. Meadowlarks sang on the ground as they sought food, hawks circled the sky engaged in the same activity. He could smell wet grass and damp earth. Yawning and stretching, he breathed it all in, then took a wash in the creek. It was still a full day's ride, so he didn't tarry.

Back on the trail, sticking close to the gentle upward slope on his left, Boss again enjoyed the easy ride as Waco continued up the pass. The grade got steeper as they went, and after about an hour of travel, Boss noticed more than the normal amount of tumbled rocks strewn across the trail. He slowed Waco, and the mustang maneuvered around the trail hazards avoiding any missteps.

The pass got steeper and rockier. He rounded a bend and was stopped by a massive rockfall that completely covered the trail. It looked like a recent fall, some of the rocks were still covered with wet dirt. He looked up seeking the spot where the boulders had broken away, but didn't see it. Anxiety grew as he dismounted and looped the reins over the bough of a tree. He walked around studying the roadblock.

Some of the rocks were as big as a whiskey barrel. The gentle upward slope on his left had become a sheer slab of granite rising to the sky. A dizzying drop fell off to his right. Gone was the shallow ravine gently guiding a bubbling creek. It was now a bottomless canyon with a rushing river Boss could hear, but not see. A hundred yards below trail's edge, the splintered remains of a half-buried freight wagon and remnants of its load spilled across the ground, casualties of a previous rockslide.

His anxiety turned into a pulsing anger as he viewed the tortuous terrain that lay ahead. There was no way around the boulder barricade, and it would be impossible for the mustang to go over it. The only option was to backtrack to more level ground and bushwhack over the saddle of the mountain, the only low point he'd seen along the way.

Frustrated and swearing profusely, he hoisted himself into the saddle, turned Waco around and started back down in search of a way off the trail that would be navigable by a horse. He didn't know how long this was going to hold him up. He wasn't familiar with this mountain, didn't know what was on the other side once he topped the crest of the low point.

When he reached a gentle grade angling off the trail sloping in the right direction over the otherwise uncrossable trail, he nudged the mustang on to it. "Come on, Waco," he urged. "Go, boy. Up. Up." The path climbed steeply for a few hundred yards before leveling off in a slow ascent along the mountain face. Waco started up uncertainly, but eventually became more surefooted.

After they topped the ridge, it was treacherous and slow going through rugged forested areas where no path existed. Downed trees and fallen branches, some rotting into the soil made for treacherous travel. Limbs and ground vegetation whacked back at him as Waco pushed through. Blinding sun pressed down with the weight of an anvil. Higher elevations offered no cooling respite. Relief wouldn't come until after dark. Boss removed his hat and wiped the sweat off his forehead with his shirt sleeved arm.

The morning dragged on. He recognized none of the topography he encountered, and the farther he went the more lost he felt. Grazing was scarce and by noon with the sun directly overhead, he could tell the mustang was feeling the strain despite stops for water at ponds and small mountain lakes.

It was late afternoon when they topped the mountain col, and by then they could go no farther. Boss was relieved to see the landscape before him leveled out into a wide plateau with a run of trees indicating a creek or stream close by. Waco smelled the water and headed for it. Thunderclouds snagged on the tips of the highest mountains and stayed there.

At the water's edge, he noticed rabbit tracks. He followed them with his eyes to a thicket. Rabbit meant food, so he decided to set up camp for another night. No use going on. The western flats would be darkening when the sun went down, and there was lightning in the distance.

Best to wait until morning. By then he'd know what those thunderclouds on the mountaintop had decided to do.

He unholstered his weapon, let the horse drink, and waited until the rabbit felt safe enough to emerge from the bushes. His first shot killed it.

With Waco picketed and unsaddled, Boss gathered kindling and started a fire. He dragged some of the fallen branches over, broke them apart and added them to the flames. He set about cleaning the rabbit, and when the fire had all burned down to hot coals, he fashioned a spit from a fat twig.

While the rabbit roasted on the spit, Boss laid out his bedroll, checked the loads in his weapons, then sat on a boulder and nervously scoped out his surroundings. He'd set up camp in a sizable clearing rimmed with a stand of evergreens so thick he couldn't see daylight between them. Deep shadows loomed longer and blacker. A noise from behind made him hunch and duck. He jerked around to look. He was worried about Indians.

Dog Soldiers.

Most of the tribes had signed treaties. Except for the fearsome Cheyenne Dog Soldiers who had rejected the military's offer of land and ignored Chief Black Kettle's call for peace. Instead, they continued their resistance against white expansion into the West with savage raids against the military and innocent settlers.

Though the majority of Dog Soldier territory ranged farther north and east into Kansas, renegades and some similarly resistant Lakota often broke away into rebel bands roaming the peaceful settlements of central Colorado, so Boss was on the lookout. His sleep that night was fitful.

On day three, he trekked into a box canyon and spent an hour finding his way out constantly on the lookout for lone hostile Indians hiding in the shadows made by chapparal and mesquite. It was an eerie place, seemingly haunted by windswept spirits and phantom voices.

When he finally emerged, the clouds opened up and spit rain. He stopped and tried to make a tent out of his slicker, but a gusty swirl of wind carried it away before he could secure it. He slogged through rain and haze without it until he found shelter in a deep overhang where he spent the rest of the day and night.

The afternoon of day four brought him into the foothills. He leaned back hard in the saddle as the mustang skidded down a steep trail slipping on mud and dead vegetation. Berry bushes and saplings slapped at him and snatched at his clothes. They made it over brush and fallen logs and boulders until at last they broke onto clear ground. Topping a gentle swell of land, he rode to the precipice of a high ridge. From there he could see Sutton Creek, Bandit Bend, and the abandoned homestead.

Only it didn't look abandoned now. From his vantage point, it looked occupied and proved up considerably since the last time he'd been there. He reached in his pocket for the map.

It was still wet from the soaking he'd taken in the storm, and when he unfolded it, it came apart a little at the fold lines. He held it together on his thigh and studied it, but couldn't make sense of the crudely drawn map. He should have known better than to ask a lunkhead to draw it. Some of the pencil marks had washed away into the accumulated spills and glass rings picked up when Omaha had spread it out on a saloon table or bar top. Boss shook his head in irritation and blew an exasperated breath. No doubt Omaha had discussed the buried treasure with someone equally drunk as he was. Someone else who may be on his way to claim it.

Boss bounced his gaze back and forth from the map to the homestead below. He rested his gaze on the cabin. A lot of work had been done on it. It was no longer ramshackle. The barn stood straight and solid with fresh paint. Outbuildings looked recently built. He could pinpoint the boulder pile that looked like a praying nun, but didn't recognize anything else around it and couldn't spot the burial site.

Two women, both young, both wearing holstered gun belts were in the yard talking and target shooting bottles, but Boss was too far away to hear what they were saying. He looked around for a man. A husband, a brother, a grown son, but didn't see one.

In the far distance beyond the back of the cabin, Boss could see workmen pounding posts and stringing barb wire building a pasture fence. An Indian was clearing rocks away from a crumbling dugout. He looked inside, then piled all the rocks back one by one covering up the opening again.

Boss backed away from the edge of the ridge, his mind full of questions. He laid out his blankets, picketed Waco, and built a smokeless fire out of sight from below. He spent the rest of the night and all of the next day where he was. He wanted to familiarize himself with the activities going on down below after which he'd make a new plan.

CHAPTER FIFTEEN

*J*UST AFTER SUNUP, **BOSS** broke camp on the ridge overlooking the homestead and rode into town. Storekeepers were unlocking their doors and sweeping away the previous night's accumulation of litter from the front of their establishments. Empty liquor bottles, cigar and cigarette butts, partially eaten meals either dropped or set aside and forgotten.

Two deputies rode the near empty street rousting drunks from doorways and gutters, trying to match them up to the horses still tied at the hitching posts in front of the saloons. Another deputy collected the unclaimed horses and led them to the livery where they would be watered and fed until the owners showed up to pay for their care.

Boss kept his head down and his back turned as he stood at the Shouting Post, hoping the lawmen were too preoccupied to pay attention to him. He was looking for something specific. He knew it would be there, Wells Fargo didn't give up easily.

He found numerous Wanted Posters describing outlaws and crimes committed in Sutton Creek and the surrounding towns, even some as far away as Denver. A good number of the posters had resided on the Shouting Post so long the paper they were printed on was sun bleached and weather worn, barely readable. Over time, new wanted posters had been nailed one on top of the other, and Boss flipped through the layers one by one until he found the one he was looking for.

REWARD!
STAGECOACH ROBBERY
AT BANDIT BEND

Three masked men robbed a Wells, Fargo and Company Express Stage of payroll money and gold, as well as jewelry and valuables from four passengers. Passengers were not hurt, but a Wells, Fargo and Company guard was shot after the robbers let the stagecoach continue on its way.

All robbers were masked. Robber number one: A light skinned Mexican, long black hair, dark eyes, thin, and short. Robber number two: Light skin, broad shoulders, big belly, mean brown eyes, loud gruff voice. Robber number three: Reddish hair and beard, light skin, dark amber eyes, tall. Described by passengers as a gentleman, polite, speaks well. One of the robbers called him Boss. All three robbers were between 20 and 30 years old.

The drawings below are rough approximations as all three robbers wore masks.

A spurt of adrenaline pumped into Boss's chest, and he exhaled sharply. Wells, Fargo knew his name because Rico had said it during the holdup. He swept his eyes over the poorly drawn portraits. Representations of their faces were distorted and inaccurate, but still he worried.

Staying low, he took a quick look over his shoulder. Down the street, all three deputies were occupied with coaxing a cowboy to his feet. Boss took that moment to rip the stage robbery wanted poster off the Shouting Post and put it in his pocket. He'd burn it later. Moving slowly, not wanting to draw attention to himself, he feigned disinterest as he circled the Shouting Post browsing through the notices seeking hired help. He found one of interest and read it thoroughly. Grinning with satisfaction, he ripped that one off, too.

By then, his stomach was roiling, but the fancy meals he'd dreamed of would have to wait due to a last-minute change in his plans. On the off chance someone might recognize him from the poorly drawn poster, he avoided the saloons and eating places in the business section. Instead, he ducked into a side street and found an out of the way place that listed chuck wagon food on the menu taped to the front window. Not exactly what he had in mind, but he was hungry enough to eat leather. He went inside, sat down and ordered.

Next stop, the bathhouse, then the barber shop.

Then back to the homestead on Bandit Bend.

CHAPTER SIXTEEN

*T***ALLY DIDN'T RECOGNIZE THE** stranger riding into the yard under the afternoon sun toward the cabin. He rode straight and tall in the saddle, his upper body moving in rhythm with the horse's unhurried gait.

Standing slowly, she stepped away from the used Singer sewing machine she'd recently bought, set aside the dress she was working on for one of the town ladies, and watched him through the window as he drew near. He rode with boldness, his hat pulled low as he looked around alert to his surroundings. As alert as she was to this stranger crossing her land. Nothing definable about him especially alarmed her, but unexpected company didn't come around often.

Ivy had gone to town to distribute leaflets drumming up customers for Tally's new dressmaking business. Wren was out in the pasture completing a final check for flaws and vulnerabilities before paying and releasing the fence crew. Hath was down at the creek that bordered the claim shoring up the banks that had failed during the winter.

She was alone in the cabin. Her hand moved to her hip and touched the handle of her pistol. It was true that there had been no trespassing, no sabotage or damage to the homestead or livestock in some time, but never again would she let her guard down.

The man appeared to be assessing her spread—the barn that was now a sturdy structure, the newly built outbuildings, the recently constructed animal enclosures, the renovated cabin with windows that now had glass. Was he wondering how many rooms were inside? How many cows she owned? How many goats? Chickens? Sheep?

Or was he a Pinkerton man?

The thought tightened her chest and desiccated her mouth. She swallowed hard a couple of times in an attempt to drench her arid throat.

The stranger pulled rein in front of the porch, swung a long leg over the saddle and dismounted. She stepped back out of sight so he couldn't see her through the window though she still had a narrow view outside. He stood with the reins in his hand, looking expectant, and though he didn't appear to pose an overt threat, Tally's heart picked up its beat.

The man removed his hat, held it against his chest. "Hello?"

A Pinkerton agent wouldn't call to the house that way, but still she didn't answer.

Who *was* he?

He had weapons on his horse and at his waist making him look menacing, but his smile was wide and friendly. Nothing in his voice or tone or expression held any suggestion of ruthlessness. Still, she hesitated.

The man called again. "Miss Tally?"

Fear twitched the corner of her mouth. *He knew her name.*

He stood in the dust at the foot of the steps with a piece of paper in his hand.

Reluctantly, she moved to the door and opened it making sure he saw her own holstered weapon. Her gaze trailed over him, assessing. "What is your business here?"

The man took a step back, holding on to his smile. Cordiality shimmered in his dark coppery gold eyes.

"Howdy, ma'am. Birch Quinn's my name. You still

looking for a hired hand?"

He held up the piece of paper, and she recognized her poster asking for a worker. That's how he knew her name, and her heart slowed its frantic racing.

She swallowed hard and clasped her hands together at her waist. Releasing the breath caught in her throat, she stammered a reply.

"Y-yes. Yes, I am."

The man looked around nodding in approval, his expression pleasant. "Nice spread you got here, ma'am. I'd be mighty proud to work it. I've got experience and I'm dependable. I can do most anything from painting, building, fixing, chopping, and digging." He spoke with confidence. "And I take good care of animals."

It sounded like a puffed up version of his real story, but this man was polite and personable and clean cut, unlike some of the miscreants and undesirables she'd turned away who'd come by asking for the work. Some of the young ones looked too lazy to grow. She'd lost hope of finding someone suitable, had almost forgotten she'd posted the job.

The rider flashed another smile. "If you plan to grow oats for feed for your livestock, I'd be much obliged to take on that chore when it's time to sow the seeds."

Tally's tension released the tiniest bit. "My lead man is out back riding fence," she said, calmer now. "You're welcome to ride out and talk to him. He does the hiring. His name's Wren."

"Thank you, ma'am."

As he rode away, he looked at her and spoke over his shoulder. "You won't be sorry if he brings me on. I'm a good worker."

CHAPTER SEVENTEEN

BIRCH QUINN WAS A very good worker. The first thing Ivy did each morning was go to her window to make sure he was still there.

Tweaking aside the curtains, she peeked at him as he thumbed back his hat and strode to the storage shed near the prayer bench. He stood there, sleeves rolled to the elbows, collar open to the morning sun, hands on his hips. He seemed to spend a good bit of time at the prayer bench. Probably praying though she'd never seen him actually fold his hands or bow his head. But no matter. Everyone prayed in their own way.

He stood looking at the flowers she'd planted there, daisies, petunias, chrysanthemums just beginning to bloom. After a few moments, he went down on one knee pulled a few weeds, scrabbled around in the dirt with his hand, then stood and looked around some more.

His attention so focused, no doubt looking for something that needed doing or fixing. He did that often without being told. Not like some layabout hired hands who only did what they were told to do then waited to be told to do something else. Birch was like any ordinary man, paying as much attention to the Tisdale homestead as if it were his own.

Well, ordinary wasn't really the right word for him. In her mind, he wasn't ordinary at all. Not with those amber eyes that looked like they were trying to soak her up. His posture and attitude bore a quality that set him apart from other men. Birch was a man who seemed to be keenly aware of his surroundings, mindful of his place in any space. His beautiful eyes with dark lashes unusual on a man were vigilant, constantly moving, searching. For what, she wondered? Adventure? Was he searching for something beyond the horizon just as she was?

She wished she knew. She wished she knew more about this mysterious, intriguing man. Tally said it was important to choose a husband carefully, know a man thoroughly before marriage. Ivy intended to learn everything there was to know about Birch Quinn.

Already, she knew some things about him.

He liked his coffee black and strong. His horse's name was Waco. He took great pains with his grooming, shaved every morning, and smelled clean. Whenever she had the chance to stand close to him the scent of his soap drifted to her nostrils, and she tried to manipulate as many of those opportunities throughout the day as she could. It was relatively easy to do as he'd been working close to the barn and cabin while Wren and Hath thinned out the treeline at the road. It was good fortune that a newly arrived homesteader had offered to buy the downed timber from them and haul it away.

Ivy continued ticking off Birch's good qualities.

He was mannerly, didn't snort his food like a slopped hog. When he worked, he was methodical and precise. If he had to measure something, he did it twice, sometimes three times to be sure. He never forgot to scrape the bottoms of his boots if he had to come into the cabin to discuss something with Tally.

She wondered if he counted off her good qualities in a similar fashion. She noticed him sliding glances in her direction when she went out of her way to cross his path. From his very first day at the homestead their eyes connected as if drawn by magnets. Brazenly, she held his eye longer than what was considered polite rather than look away like a delicate shy flower.

What gave her a fluttery feeling inside was the way he looked back at her. As if he really saw her. The real her. Not the way some of the men hanging out in front of the saloons leered at her when she went to town to shop, or to attend an art class. Everyone knew the Social Center used to be a bordello, but some of the old timers never got over it and still had in mind what used to go on there.

Her wandering thoughts came back into focus when Birch stepped away from the prayer bench and opened the shed door. He went inside, and came out with the plow harness, outfitted Trooper with it then led the horse to the field where he attached the plow. By fall they'd have turnips, cauliflower, cabbage, peas. Enough for her and Tally to put up for the winter with plenty left over to sell to the general stores in town. Soon, they could begin to repay the loan from Mimi. By next summer if all went well and the weather cooperated, they'd be able to stand on their own. Tally didn't like being beholden to anyone. They'd come a long way since they arrived and though they weren't wealthy, they were far from dirt poor.

Already, Tally's new dressmaking and alterations venture was bringing in a steady stream of money from the wealthy ladies moving into Sutton Creek with their railroad executive husbands. Tally still watched every penny like it was their last, but now they both had daytime work dresses to replace the ill-fitting trousers and shirts belonging to their father they'd been forced to wear for lack of anything else.

And more good fortune had come along to sustain them. Hath was spending more time on the homestead helping out. He'd placed the day to day running of the livery into Buster's capable hands during the times he came out to the homestead. Fortunately, Wren seemed to have made peace with him. Having three hired men doing the hard work took a huge load off. Tally tried to pay Hath, but he refused to accept the money.

Gazing in the mirror over the chest of drawers, Ivy picked up her hairbrush and pulled it through her locks in long slow strokes. She paused to soften her eyes, lower her lids, and purse her lips into a pretend kiss. She wished Birch would walk over to her, take her hand or pick her up and carry her into the bedroom one of these days when Tally was in town and they could be alone in the cabin.

She could see herself standing before him while he trembled in anticipation, his hands sliding over her skin, into her hair, touching her face, her neck, his arm pulling her close. The image was so vivid she could almost feel him removing her dress, camisole and her bloomers. Something sizzled inside her just thinking about it, and her cheeks burned at the decadence of her thoughts. Even if Birch moved on, and she hoped he wouldn't, she could hold this vision to the light and enjoy it anew.

Coffee was brewing, she could smell it. Quickly, she finished dressing and pinned up her hair.

Tally was busy at the sewing machine, but the whirr of the machine stopped as Ivy filled a mug with coffee, black and strong the way Birch liked it. Tally's expression was full of words, and Ivy could see the reproach in all of them. The sound of the machine started up again as she slipped out the door ignoring her sister's frown of disapproval. Mindful not to spill coffee down her dress, Ivy strode out to stand at the edge of the field.

Birch smiled gloriously, reined Trooper to a halt, and accepted the coffee she held out to him.

"Thank you," he said. His eyes bore into hers over the rim of the mug sending a sensuous message, and something inside her swayed dangerously in response.

CHAPTER EIGHTEEN

***H**ATH ARRIVED AT THE* homestead with a message for Tally from Mimi. *Come to lunch today*, her note said. *Meet me in the hotel dining room at one o'clock.* When he handed it to her, his fingers deliberately brushed hers. She smiled at the warmth of his touch.

He returned her smile and said, "Let me know when you're ready to go. I'll hitch up the wagon for you."

Tally had already planned to go into town that day to purchase sewing supplies and dress fabric from Gallagher's. The annual Sutton Creek Founder's Day Celebration was coming up, a parade in the afternoon, a ball in the evening with music. She'd received several orders for fancy dresses from the ladies in town for the occasion. Each of them had requested skirts with scalloped hems, the latest fashion designed to show off bits of decorative petticoats embellished with lacey ruffles and embroidery.

The new prettified petticoats so popular with stylish women in the big cities had turned into a topic of heated debate in Sutton Creek. Those with a prudish bent shuddered at the idea of ornamental underclothing fearing it would lead to willful exposure, which of course it did and soon became the rage among all but the most puritanical of ladies. And because she'd accepted Hath's offer to escort her to the event, she was going to make one for herself. She had a pattern in mind that called for just the right fabric. She hoped to find it that afternoon.

Those giddy thoughts led to one that brought on a measure of anxiety. Ivy had informed her that she needed a dress for the dance, too, because she was going with Birch Quinn whether Tally liked it or not.

Tally *didn't* like it.

Second thoughts about him had found their way into her mind of late. The way he was always grinning like he knew something that she didn't. More and more she found herself uncomfortable in his presence.

Though Wren had made a civilized peace with Hath, he admitted he could barely abide Birch, but dared not let him go. With so many homesteaders moving in, and the surge of growth and development in the town proper, men seeking work had become a scarce commodity. The only unemployed were those who chose to be, so there was little hope of replacing Birch if they fired him.

Tally especially didn't like the way Ivy was completely besotted with Birch. She couldn't tear her eyes away from him. Tally had to admit he was handsome, soft-spoken, polite and respectful with both people and animals. No doubt a catch by most standards. He just wasn't a catch for Ivy. She was much too young for a man of his... Tally paused, thought for a moment trying to capture the right word in her mind.

She settled on *worldliness*. Right from the start, his gaze had drifted where it shouldn't and he looked at young Ivy the way no man should look at a women who was not his wife let alone a woman he'd just met. She was only sixteen and not of a state of mind to cope with such a man.

Almost seventeen, Ivy had shouted when Tally tried to talk to her about the age difference. But no amount of persuasion could dissuade her, and they'd argued about it. Tally dropped the subject, but just for the moment. Looking back on her own youth, Tally herself had been the scrappy one, a characteristic that mellowed out some as she matured. But Ivy? Ivy was impulsive to a fault. And stubborn.

It was a sad truth that some folks only learned valuable life lessons by suffering the consequences of their mistakes. Unfortunately, the idea of consequences wasn't a notion with which young people were familiar.

Goodness! The way Ivy mooned over him. For days after he arrived, she bubbled with enthusiasm about him and could speak of nothing else. It was Birch this and Birch that and where's Birch. All day long. When he wasn't around, she moped. Tally attempted to reprimand her for it with a mild scold, but frustration had raised her voice to volume when she didn't mean it to. Ivy lowered her lids over eyes that crackled like ice, and rudely turned away.

Exhaling an exasperated breath, Tally turned her thoughts to the day ahead, and made a shopping list. She hadn't visited with Mimi in some time and missed the niceties of polite female company. Ivy's endless sulking was draining. What Tally needed was a brief break from the demands of the homestead, and the maleness that dominated it.

When it was time to leave, she touched up her hair, pinched her cheeks and gathered her bag containing the latest collection of dress patterns she'd found in a recent issue of Godey's Lady's Book. After thanking Hath for hitching up the buckboard—relieved she didn't have to do it herself though she could have—she headed off.

It was a fulsome blue sky day. She heard the river before she saw it. Still high from the spring runoff, rushing currents falling over the rocks broke apart into glittery droplets. The midday sunshine that layered a stunning glow over the mountains also created vapor that rose from the surface of the tributary. Ghostly images drifted like windblown strands of silk through the clean, sweet-smelling air.

Champion was in high spirits. He set off at a steady pace arriving in town two dusty bumpy miles later. As usual, freight wagons bogged down just outside of town lined up to get their wares delivered. A hodge podge of new businesses fronted the street, and the ever present clatter, bang and buzz of hammer and saw filled the air. Newly constructed buildings, fences, and corrals stretched beyond the end of the street reaching into the wilderness.

Some of the business owners were moving in before the last nail was pounded, anxious to open their doors and welcome customers along with the gold coins and paper money they brought. Boardwalks had been extended at both ends where there was no road, just wheel paths in and out of town. Tally wouldn't be surprised to see the business section eventually spread a mile or more into the mountains.

She drew Champion to a halt in the empty space alongside the mercantile. The horse snorted and flicked an ear as she stepped down from the wagon and tied the reins to a post.

With plenty of time to spare before she was to meet Mimi, she turned away from Gallagher's and crossed the street to the Shouting Post. She perused the new postings without finding anything of particular interest, then idly flipped through the Wanted Posters. She'd unwittingly harbored a vague notion she might find Birch's picture on one of them, and when she found no such thing, admonished herself for allowing an uncharitable thought to take hold in the first place. There may be mischief in his eyes and he may even be a philanderer, but surely he wasn't a scoundrel.

The chiming of the bell over the door of the mercantile jangled pleasantly announcing her entrance. She was greeted by the delicious aroma of Violet Gallagher's potato peel soup, a specialty Violet cherished from a recipe she refused to share. She'd begun selling cups of it in containers that customers lined up at the door could take with them.

As usual, Pete Gallagher's smile was warm and friendly. Violet came from behind the counter to welcome her.

"Hello, Tally. What can I help you with today, my dear?"

"I've come to look at the new dress fabric that came on the freight wagon yesterday. I have several dresses to make before Founder's Day, so I need to get started."

"Happy to hear you're doing so well with your new venture. I've seen your designs on some of the ladies who come into the store. They're quite beautiful."

Tally swelled with pride. "Thank you. I'll need a variety of fabrics. Velvet, taffeta, chiffon..." Her voice trailed off uncertainly. "I'm not sure exactly what I'll need, but I have the patterns with me."

Violet clasped her hands in front of her, eyes glittering, face beaming. "You come with me," she said. "Let me show you the beautiful piece goods that just arrived from Denver. Japanese silks, brocades from Italy, linens from England..." She paused and popped her eyebrows, a one-sided smile on her face. "At least that's what the freighter told me yesterday." She laughed lightly. "Come along. I'll show you what we have and you can be the judge."

She led Tally into a small front room brightly lit by tall windows that looked out onto the busy street. Fat bolts of cloth in a variety of textures, designs and colors filled the room. Lengths of delicate lace, ruffles and ribbons of all hues dangled from rods mounted on the three walls bereft of windows. Tally touched and admired them recognizing that some of the prices offended her sense of thriftiness, but she said nothing.

"It's a bit late for alpaca, but flannel may still work for petticoats if you plan on making any," Violet offered.

The women chatted pleasantly while Tally admired the lovely fabrics, touching and stroking them, referring to the patterns in her bag, carefully making her selections. Violet rolled out the bolts of dress goods on a long wide table, passing on local news and gossip while she measured and cut according to Tally's instructions.

"Several new families have come to town. Mostly homesteaders, but railroad men and investors, too."

"Yes, I can see that," replied Tally. "It seems busier and more prosperous each time I come to town."

Her eyes rose to the window. Martin Gardner, the bank president was standing on the steps leading into the bank talking with a well-dressed man wearing a bowler hat. The man was tall and thin, his skinny neck protruding from a freshly pressed collar. Their heads tilted close together as they conversed as if afraid they might be overheard. Their stern expressions indicated a topic of conversation that bore deep importance.

Tally nodded in their direction. "I see Mr. Gardner talking to an important looking man in front of the bank. Is that one of the investors you spoke of?"

Violet finished spreading out a length of fabric on the cutting table, smoothed it with her hands, and followed Tally's gaze through the window to the other side of the street.

"Oh, no," she said picking up the scissors and bringing it to her measuring mark. "He's only here for the day. He's looking for someone. He's a Pinkerton man," she finished in a half whisper.

Tally stiffened involuntarily. "Oh?"

"Yes. He's been going door to door inquiring at all the

business establishments." Violet spoke slowly, concentrating on what she was doing so as not to make a mistake. Measure twice, cut once. She squeezed the scissors and moved them along slowly, cutting precisely across the weft of the fabric. "He was asking about someone by the name of Mrs. Jacob Spencer."

It was like the floor beneath Tally's feet vanished and she was tumbling into the void. She kept her breathing normal but only through intense concentration.

"I told him I didn't know anyone by that name." Violet glanced up. "Do you?"

Tally fought to keep her face expressionless.

"No, I don't. Did he say why he was looking for that person?" She ended her question on an up note to detour any sharpness in her tone.

"Oh, no. He was very secretive. You know how Pinkerton men are. They don't say much, they just ask a lot of questions."

Yes, Tally knew that. Questions. A lot of questions. Unrelenting questions. She made a sound of dismissal and hoped Violet didn't discern the falsity of it. "Oh, well, I'm sure it's nothing serious if he's only here for the day."

"Oh, I don't know." Distracted by the task at hand, Violet's reply was cursory. "I'd say it was something serious. Pinkerton men don't come all the way up here for minor offenses." Her tone and accompanying sniff indicated more than a whiff of moral judgment.

Tally stayed silent with studied indifference, managing to remain calm while Violet cut and measured the yards and yards of dress goods to the precise requirements. When finished, she wrapped and tied the folded dress materials into neat bundles. Pete Gallagher, chatting all the while, carried her packages to the wagon, stashed them under the bench seat, and thanked her for her business.

Back on the boardwalk, Tally drifted a slow side glance across the street. Gardner was entering the bank. The Pinkerton man was boarding the stage to Denver.

CHAPTER NINETEEN

A BUBBLE OF RELIEF burst past the barrier of anxiety in Tally's chest when the Pinkerton man took a seat after politely letting the ladies go first. She stood motionless outside the mercantile her body caught fast in a web of tension, and pretended to be interested in the window display while watching the stage's reflection in the glass. A whisper of a breeze gusted, moving a bit of hair that had come loose.

The driver cracked his whip over the horses, yawed a command, and the stage pulled away with the squeak and scrape of leather and metal. When it was out of sight, she waited for her thudding heart to slow, then headed for the hotel keeping her pace slow and measured. She needed time to calm down and catch her breath before meeting Mimi.

Mimi rose from her seat in the windowed alcove of the hotel dining room and extended both hands in greeting when Tally entered. Her sturdy stance with fine squared shoulders, and large, beautiful eyes showed her to be a woman meant for exquisite things and lovely places. What she was doing in a town like this, Tally had often wondered.

"I'm so glad you could make it."

"Thank you for inviting me." Tally managed a smile, but her nerves were still jittery. Just because the Pinkerton man had left didn't mean he wouldn't be back.

The two women touched cheeks the way ladies do in welcome, then sat across from each other at the table.

"Sorry for the last-minute invitation," Mimi said. "I hope it didn't disrupt your day."

Tally opened her napkin and spread it across her lap. "Not at all. I was coming into town today anyway. I received several orders from local ladies to make dresses for the Founder's Day dance and I had to buy piece goods and supplies."

Mimi lifted her napkin, unfolded it and put it in place. A well pleased smile appeared on her lips. "I heard you're going to the dance with Hath. How lovely."

Still flustered by the unexpected appearance the Pinkerton man, Tally composed her expression around a tight smile and nodded. Violet Gallagher's words spun in her mind. *He was asking about someone by the name of Mrs. Jacob Spencer.*

Mimi inclined her head gracefully encouraging Tally to concur. "You do think it's lovely, don't you? I know several ladies who would jump at the chance to go to the dance with him."

Tally snapped back into the conversation. She forced another smile, bigger this time, hoping it looked genuine. "Oh, yes. I'm delighted, and I'm looking forward to it, truly I am." She gave her head a little shake. "Sorry. It's just that I have a lot on my mind."

Mimi sat forward, her eyes alight with curiosity, but before Tally could say more, the waiter arrived with menus. Mimi ordered chicken and rice with sweet fried apples. Tally ordered the same. "And coffee, too, please," she added.

The waiter left, and Mimi leaned in again. Her expression softened into genuine concern as she studied Tally's face. "Oh, dear. What's troubling you? Is it Ivy?"

Tally waved her hand as if clearing the air of tangential matter. "No, Ivy's fine."

Mimi's emphatic upswept eyebrows lifted even further. "Then what is it?"

Tally moved her restless fingers to the cutlery next to her plate straightening silverware that didn't need realignment. "It's my hired man. Birch Quinn. He asked Ivy to go to the dance with him and she accepted."

"Oh?" Mimi held her inquisitive look. "And you object to that?"

"I do."

"Why?"

Tally wanted to say a dozen things to besmirch Birch's character thereby reinforcing her disapproval of him—he was a poor worker, he didn't carry his load on the homestead, he was cantankerous, deceitful, disrespectful—but none of that would be true. She hesitated, searching for words that would adequately explain her uneasy feelings about him.

"He's a fine hired hand," she began. "Hard working, intelligent, inventive. Always has good ideas about how to solve problems on the spread. And he's sinfully handsome. I can see why Ivy is attracted to him, but..." she sighed deeply. "He's much older than she is."

Mimi nodded sagely. "Ohhh, I see..." Mimi's eyes narrowed as she considered that. "Besides the age difference, what else is bothering you about him?"

Tally wasn't sure how to answer that. The bald, ugly truth was she called him a son of a bitch in her mind. She sifted through her conflicting thoughts about Birch Quinn, then executed a one shouldered shrug.

"You're right. It is more than the age difference. I have a bad feeling about him that's not going away," Tally said, finally speaking the truth of the matter.

A lengthy pause followed after which she gave her head a little shake. "I don't know how to put it into words, but I have this feeling that I've seen him somewhere before. And not in a favorable light." Her eyes met Mimi's helplessly. "But I can't conjure up a time and place where that might have been. I stopped to look at the Wanted Posters this morning thinking it might have been there."

"Was it?"

"No."

Mimi's face moved into a thoughtful expression. "Does Ivy know how you feel?"

"I spoke to her about it." Tally lowered her eyes and cringed inside as she remembered the words she spat at Ivy and the way her sister looked when they hit home. "I'm afraid I said some hurtful things to her, and she's been using a pout as a weapon on me ever since. Though, I didn't actually forbid her to go. Not that it would have made a difference. She's become quite a strong-willed girl. Always has been."

Mimi laughed lightly. "You should be glad of that. Women need to be strong willed to live out here." She sighed. "Look. You'll be at the dance, too, and you can keep an eye on her. On them," she amended with a playful grin. "But seriously, I'm sure there's nothing to worry about. Ivy's a lovely girl, pleasant natured, well mannered. Smart. And it really is a special event. Everyone will be there. It would be a shame if she missed it. Proving up a homestead is absolute drudgery. I'm sure she'd welcome some fun."

The waiter brought their food and fussily arranged the dishes on the table. The women ate in silence, but Tally was aware of Mimi's probing eyes.

"There's more, isn't there?" Mimi's tone indicated she already knew the answer to that.

Tally lowered her fork to her plate, and met Mimi's eyes directly. "Yes," she replied and unfolded the story of the slaughter of their sheep, and what she'd discovered in her father's journal. She didn't mention the Pinkerton man, though this new worry sat on her chest like a stone.

Mimi listened calmly, her brow furrowed with concern as Tally went on.

"At first I thought someone was merely playing harmless tricks. You know, trying to put a fright on two women alone. But then it got worse. And after reading my father's journal, I now think whoever was deliberately harassing him is doing the same to us, though I can't imagine why."

Mimi was silent and her face was serious as she touched her napkin to her lips and returned it to her lap. She took a moment to smooth it out with her fingers, then lifted her gaze to Tally.

"Yes, it sounds like it," she agreed. "And it may be connected to what I wanted to tell you today. Do you remember when I said I overheard two men talking in the saloon? One of them wanted to get in touch with you to pass on some information he had about your father?"

Tally nodded. "Yes. His friend talked him out of it. Threatened him, I think you said."

"I asked the bartender if he knew their names and he did."

Tally's eyes widened. "The bartender knows them?"

"No. Just their names. Frank Scott and Rudy Aldecker. Frank is the cowboy who said he wanted to talk to you. Rudy told him to mind his own business."

"Who are they? Are they still around? Do they live here?"

Mimi shook her head and shrugged. "I don't know. That's all I could find out. The bartender thought they were drifters, but I've seen the one called Frank Scott in the saloon a few times. But it's been a while."

The pinch of disappointment in Tally's chest was accompanied by a bead of hope. "I'll stop in the Land Office on my way home and talk to Pettyjohn about it. Maybe he knows them."

Mimi lifted her hand palm out signaling caution. "No. Don't."

Her words took Tally by surprise. "What?"

"Don't talk to Pettyjohn about it. Not yet."

"But why?" Urgency simmered. "Pettyjohn might be able to tell me where I can find them. They might know where my father is. And if I tell Pettyjohn my father's patent certificate is missing, he might be able to replace it. He can't have the only one. Everything is in triplicate for Washington these days."

Despite Tally's outburst, Mimi's features softened and her eyes narrowed a fraction. "I have an idea how we might get some information without involving Pettyjohn." There was a saucy dip in her voice when she said it.

"How?" Tally wanted to know, her anxiety dissipating.

A devilish smile appeared on Mimi's lips. It reminded Tally of all the times Ivy was secretly planning mischief as an impulsive twelve-year-old. That particular facial expression was never outgrown.

Mimi held on to it and widened her smile. "Let me work on it."

CHAPTER TWENTY

***T**HE WAITER BROUGHT THE* check and laid it on the table. Mimi took money from her bag and paid it. "My treat," she said and stood. "I'll walk back with you. I need to get a few things from Gallagher's, anyway. And you can show me the fabric you're going to use for the ball gowns."

The street was still busy when the women set out. Huge freight wagons rolling on steel wheels clunked and banged into town carrying the afternoon deliveries unashamedly clogging the thoroughfare and impeding passage. Burly drivers, their dark-skinned faces hardened from sun and wind during endless days of travel over perilous mountain roads ignited the air with shouts and cusses. Irascible oxen bellowed in return.

The din made conversation impossible. Talley sent a side glance over to Mimi as they made their way along the boardwalk. Deep thought showed in the set of her mouth. Her reaction at lunch had fortified Tally's reckoning. She and Ivy had good reason to worry.

She settled her wildly scampering thoughts into some sort of order. With a visit to Pettyjohn postponed, at least for now, she made a mental list of other things she needed to do.

First, she would ask Wren, Hath and Birch to listen for any gossip from freight haulers and traveling salesmen about homesteader intimidation in surrounding communities. The news they carried and gladly passed on up and down the line was usually more current and often more accurate than what was reported in newspapers.

Next, neighbors. Tally wished now she had taken the time to get to know them early on, but she'd been so occupied with day-to-day survival, and later it hadn't seemed important. Now it was imperative. Tomorrow she would ride out to surrounding homesteads and talk to them. Exchange information. Find out if they were being disturbed or threatened in a similar manner. Perhaps join forces against it.

And ammunition. She needed to check the supply cupboard. Hath and the others bought their own bullets or made them, but she'd begun supplementing their cache after the sheep beheadings. She glanced at the gun shop across the street and the two new businesses adjacent to it. Another psychic had moved in on one side, offices of the Clarkson Cattle Company occupied the space on the other. She added another task to her list. Buy more bullets.

Trooper's ears flicked forward and he nickered softly in greeting when Tally approached. She rubbed his velvety nose, took an apple from a wagon box she kept for the purpose and gave it to him.

"I'm pleased to find such fine fabric," she said to Mimi. "I was worried I wouldn't get what I wanted and end up being rushed to finish in time for the dance."

She stepped up on the wagon riser so she could reach the bundle Mr. Gallagher had placed under the seat. Oddly, she couldn't reach it. She didn't remember him pushing it back so far. Up on her tiptoes, Tally's fingertips brushed the wrapped package, and it was only by leaning in and stretching her whole body that she could get a grip on it. She pulled it out and tilted her head in curiosity.

"Something's written on it."

Mimi stepped closer to look over her shoulder. "What

is it? What does it say?"

Tally shifted the package so Mimi could read the note.

"Miss Tally. Come to the abandoned trading post at the foot of the escarpment. I have information about your father."

There was no signature, just an unreadable scrawl of initials. Apprehension swooped inside her.

"I can't make out that signature. Can you?" Tally's voice was sure and steady though her heart had picked up its beat.

"No," Mimi said. "Looks like whoever wrote that was in a hurry."

With cautious eyes, Tally tracked the stretch of land behind Gallagher's that led to an escarpment in the near distance. Its steep cliffs leveled off then rose again and joined a rise of land as if deciding to become a mountain instead.

Tally put the package back in the wagon setting it gently on the slats of the seat. "Do you know where the old trading post is?"

"Yes, but I haven't been out there in years. After the old Indian that ran it died, his daughter tried to keep it up, but she got married and then got pregnant and went back to the reservation." She lowered her gaze to Tally's booted feet. "Come on. We can walk it."

Tally's hand moved to her holster, touching it lightly as if checking to be sure it was still there. Her fingers brushed the handle of the pistol, then fell to her side.

Mimi noticed. "Is it loaded?"

"Of course."

Mimi lifted her skirt and took a derringer from a holster strapped to her thigh.

"Is yours?"

Mimi opened the chamber, then closed it and replaced the gun in the holster. "Of course."

"Let's go then."

Mimi led the way with long determined strides that flapped and fluttered her skirt and petticoats. Tally followed. Eventually the path waned, forcing them to hold up their skirts to avoid snagging them on bushes and scrub. They gave the prickly pear and hedgehog cactus an especially wide berth.

Cottonwoods up ahead meant water, and soon they were close enough to hear cascading rapids. They came to what was left of the old trading post which wasn't much. A falling down skeleton of a wooden structure with sagging shelves and a partially collapsed roof.

Mimi gazed at the dilapidated structure, her eyes filled with sadness. "In its day, it was a place for Indian artists and weavers and basket makers to show and sell their creations. Newcomers from the east bought items to send back to friends and family who prized anything made by the Indians."

Talley turned in a slow circle, her eyes scouring the terrain. The place was so still and dead she could see why the pregnant Indian girl might not have wanted to stay there. Her ears began making a check on all the little sounds around her. The wind. The rushing rapids, now at a distance, but still audible. The rachet and chirp of insects. Soaring raptures calling to each other.

"I don't see anyone."

Mimi pointed to a place part way up the slope where boulders had tumbled from the ridge above. "Let's look up there. Maybe whoever it is you're supposed to meet doesn't want to be seen."

"All right, but if no one is there, I'm going back. Something isn't right. This might be some kind of prank."

Stepping carefully, they topped a flat rocked rise. Wind speed picked up a little and their tightly bunned hair began to unravel.

Mimi stopped suddenly and threw up her hand as if she heard a noise.

Expecting to see a looming threat, Tally turned around so abruptly her skirts spun around her ankles. "What?"

Mimi's hand landed on her arm and she pointed with the other. "Look. There's..." The rest of the sentence faded into silence.

Draped like a rag doll over the fallen mess of boulders was the lifeless figure of a man. He was young, slim and wiry with a pleasant enough face except for the bloody bullet hole that spoiled his good looks.

He wore a faded red shirt with the color restored to its original by the parts that were covered with blood, some of it still oozing. His black and white cowhide vest looked new, but his boots were worn on the soles. A fine-looking bone-handled pistol had fallen from his hand. A second one was still in its holster. He wasn't breathing.

Tally's mouth turned dry as she stared, trying not to look as frightened as she felt. "Let's get out of here." She took a step to head back, but Mimi's grip on her arm tightened. Mimi's mouth moved, but no words came out.

Tally yanked her arm away. "Come on, Mimi. Let's get out of here. He's still bleeding. The killers might come on us if they're still here."

"Tally."

"What?"

"That's Frank Scott!"

CHAPTER TWENTY-ONE

*T*ALLY'S DETERMINED FOOTSTEPS THUDDED on the boards as she strode along the wooden walkway.
It had been three days since Frank Scott's body had been removed from the boulders. A bushwhacker told the sheriff that he knew Scott had a wife and son back in Wyoming and would take the dead man's belongings back to them. Tally's flush of sadness for the wife and child was overwhelmed by the disappointment burning inside her that Scott had died without revealing what he knew about Hank Tisdale's whereabouts. Today she hoped to do something about that.

She slowed her pace then stopped outside a red door with the name *Madam Simone Sinclair* painted in gold letters on it. Beneath the name was painted *Seer, Fortune Teller, Psychic*. Tally didn't believe in fortune tellers and card readers and the like, but Frank Scott had been her only link to information and he was dead now. Ordinarily, she would never have considered consulting a psychic. Would never have admitted that she'd done so. She thought them frauds and charlatans.

Coming here meant leaving Ivy alone on the homestead with Birch. She did so reluctantly, but she had no choice. Wren was out fixing the perimeter fence in the far pasture and would be there until nightfall. Hath had ridden to Denver to check on a late delivery of supplies that was already two weeks overdue. For that reason, she'd given Ivy and Birch enough work to do in the hope it would keep each of them busy until she returned.

But at least Birch was there in case of trouble. Not that she expected any. No one did. The thugs, whoever they were, would not strike in broad daylight. They were like rats, staying hidden away during the day only coming out after dark to do their dirty work.

After one last furtive look over her shoulder, she opened the door and stepped into what looked like a rich man's drawing room. She quickly closed the door behind her.

Glass beads hung from a flickering kerosene lantern. Shadows swooped and hovered over lush colorful draperies and plush pillows. A yellow ball-fringed drape gathered and tied in the middle with a ribbon hung over sheer cream colored panels that allowed only a minimum of light to enter the room through the front windows. A kaleidoscopic patterned rug covered the unpainted raw wood floor. It looked like the Persian rugs she'd seen in a Denver hotel, only this one was worn, threadbare, and well trod upon.

Candles, a tea pot, and a purple-tinted crystalline ball nestled on a black onyx holder atop a small, round, elegantly adorned table in the center of the room. Deep cushions and tufted ottomans provided seating. The abundance and richness of tapestries, swags, valances, scarves, shawls and wall hangings muffled the busyness outside.

Fabric slid against fabric, draperies swished aside and Madam Simone Sinclair appeared. She, too, was cloaked in shawls and veils. Ropes of beads around her neck clicked when she moved. So did the many bracelets on her wrists. She had small features in a delicate face, cheekbones riding high. The glow from the lamp lit her face showing deeply observant eyes, one blue and one brown. They settled thoughtfully on Tally.

"Welcome," Madam Simone said and lowered herself onto a plump ottoman. Her voice was soft and smooth like velvet.

Belatedly having second thoughts about coming here, Tally's fingers nervously fretted the corded drawstrings of her reticule. She stood uncomfortably shifting from one foot to the other.

Madam Simone studied Tally's face, her lips curved into a hint of a smile. "You're not here for money. You have a generous friend, do you not?"

Tally was taken aback. "Yes," she answered, dumbfounded, wondering how Madam Simone knew about Mimi. "I do. She's a dear friend."

"Then why have you come? A mysterious illness? A lost item? Someone is stealing from you?"

"No."

"Ah," Madam said nodding and looking pleased with herself. "You are seeking a husband."

Tally sunk onto a pile of soft cushions. "Not that, either. I fear I've spent all my love on someone else."

"But he's dead now." It wasn't a question, and the psychic's eyebrows rose when she said it.

Tally quaked inside, and she lifted her chin just a little. Her hopes of receiving mystical information about her father came tumbling down, and she pressed her lips and stiffened her spine. It hadn't occurred to her that the psychic might discern *her* sorry past. Detect *her* secret. That wasn't why she came.

"Excuse me," Tally said gathering her feet under her so she could get up and leave.

Madam held out her hand, her eyes kind and imploring. "No. Please stay. Trouble surrounds you."

After a moment's deliberation, Tally kept her seat, her spine rigid. She placed her reticule on her knees and crossed her wrists on top of it. "I'm only interested in the present, not the past."

"Ah," Madam said. "All right, then. Tell me more."

"Someone is trying to harm me and mine," Tally said with weary resignation. "My father has disappeared. And I need to know who Frank Scott is. Or was. He had information about my father, but someone killed him before he could tell me."

Madam lowered her eyes. Dark lashes fanned out over her rouged cheeks, then lifted again. "You are faced with many uncertainties."

Tally inhaled, held it briefly, then let it out in a deep sigh. "Yes. I am."

Madam's probing eyes showed intensity. "And you also have a secret of your own. A secret you have told to no one."

Tally opened her mouth to deny it, but Madam spoke first. "That's quite all right. You don't need to. Everyone has a part of themselves that isn't wholly known." She paused. "But you are in danger and you know it."

"Yes. That's why I'm here."

"Tell me about your household."

Words spilled out as Tally told her everything. About Ivy and Hath and Wren and Birch. About taking over her father's homestead, about the grisly slaughter of her sheep. About finding Frank Scott's body in the rocks.

Madam sat motionless, listening patiently without interrupting. When Tally finished, the psychic sat a moment, then picked up her crystal ball and cradled it in both palms.

"This crystal globe formerly belonged to an Egyptian Magi. It was purchased by an English Countess who gave it to me. It is made of smokey quartz and has mystical powers."

Still dubious, but immensely curious, Tally couldn't

stop herself from asking. "You can see things in there? The future?"

"Sometimes the future, sometimes the present. Unfortunately, not always in detail. But I don't converse with spirits or angels, I don't claim to speak to or call up the dead. I am a seer. I have supernatural insight. This ball shows me visions which I can interpret. I don't always know the exact meaning of what I'm seeing, but those who come to me will have complete understanding though perhaps not right away. I advise you not to ignore my revelations if their meaning is not instantly clear to you or if they seem to be extraordinary." Madam's gaze was sparkling. "Would you like me to continue?"

Despite her reservations, Tally nodded.

"What I see may not be pleasant or bring you peace. I don't control the divinations."

"I understand."

"Then I shall proceed."

Madam Simone took her eyes away from Tally, closed them, and breathed deeply in and out three times. Her lips moved, but just barely, and Tally thought she might be praying. Madam opened her eyes and stared into the crystal globe, her expression benign. She appeared to go into a trance, and sat still as a statute staring with such intensity for so long, Tally wondered for one mad moment if the psychic had been stuck dumb and turned to stone.

At last, she lifted her blue-brown gaze to Tally, and tilted her head looking like she was searching her mind for the right words to say.

"Your sister. She is audacious, yes? Bold?"

Tally scoffed. "A little foolhardy, yes." It cost her to say those words to a stranger and she immediately came to Ivy's defense. "But she's young. Ivy has ambitions."

"Yes, but she must not venture anywhere alone. And she must avoid the prayer rock."

"Ivy loves our prayer rock."

Madam ignored that and went on. "Some of the distress in your home involves gold."

"Gold?"

"And a man."

"Who?"

"I'm not sure. You have three men connected to your household."

"None of them are wealthy. They work for me. I pay them, but not in gold."

"The gold does not belong to you. Yet you have it."

Madam peered into the gazing globe and shook her head. "There is a shadow over your homestead. It's slipping away from you. Someone is..." She stopped and frowned.

"What?" Tally shifted forward on her cushions. "What do you see?" she urged, her voice thickened with urgency.

Madam swirled her finger in the air over the glass ball as if stirring a pot. "It isn't clear, but there is much trouble in your life."

"Yes, I know. That's why I'm here. Can't you tell me more?"

Madam frowned, looking perplexed. "The visions. They are bunched up. Two of the men are not who they say they are. You are being deceived, but still..."

Madam stared a while longer before speaking up again, then her gaze settled on Tally. "One of them loves you. But there are others. Another man. Other men. That is who you need protection from. That is who you should fear. They are the source of your danger. You have much to lose."

"Can't you tell me who they are?" Tally pointed to the crystal ball. "Can't you see them in there?"

"I can't see their faces, but... Frank Scott is with them somehow." She looked up. "And so is your father."

Tally's heart began to race inside her chest. "But... .but... "

Madam stopped her.

"The crystal ball does not always reveal details. It gives warnings. It is reliable, but not infallible. It is accurate, but not always in the ways of mortal comprehension."

Tally made a conscious effort to slow her breathing. "Can you tell me if my father is alive?"

Madam Simone replaced the shining orb in the cup of its onyx holder. "That is all. I can see no more. I can say no more." She spread her hands indicating she was done.

Tally waited anyway hoping for more, but it wasn't forthcoming. She sighed. "Thank you, Madam Simone."

Madam's eyes searched Tally's. "Do you have understanding of what I speak?"

Tally stood, straightened her shoulders, and laid some coins on the table next to the purple globe. "Some of it," she replied. "Not all, but enough to reaffirm a vow I've already made. No one is going to take my father's land from us." Her voice dropped to a whisper. "I'll shoot anyone who tries."

CHAPTER TWENTY-TWO

*I*T WAS UNUSUAL FOR Tally to go to town twice in the same week, but Ivy didn't spend a lot of time wondering about that. Something else was on her mind and Tally's absence would be the opportunity she needed to see it through before she thought better of it.

She'd watched Tally saddle up, then after the sound of Champion's hoofbeats faded, she gathered up the needlework and an armload of garments. Tally had asked her to hem some of the fancy dresses she'd made for the town ladies, then embellish them with silk flowers and scatterings of glass beads. The Founders Day dance was fast approaching.

It was more than a single day's work, but nevertheless Ivy sighed with put-upon exasperation and carried it all into her room where there was more daylight from the bigger window Hath and Wren put in when they built the addition. But rather than beginning her task immediately, she set the garments and trimmings aside. Instead, she picked up a pair of scissors and used them to cut lengths of lace which she then stitched to the scalloped edge of a pair of her freshly laundered pantalettes. It didn't take long, and when she finished she held the pantalettes against her body and stood in front of the mirror.

Satisfied, and feeling quite giddy, she stepped into them, then put on her second best dress over her camisole and petticoats. Unlike the shapeless daily work dress she'd just removed, her town dress snugged to the shape of her body with many black bead buttons in a row up the front. She patted and pinned a few strands of hair that had come loose then sat down and began sewing. Jittery with expectation, she turned her eyes to the window every now and then watching for Birch. He was in the barn laying down fresh bedding in the coops and pens, and catching up on projects that had fallen behind. Tally had also asked him to begin working on a second rain catchment to conserve more water for the garden and the animal water barrels.

Ivy knew the real reason for their overburdened task lists that day. It was Tally's way of keeping both her and Birch busy and occupied during the hours she would be away.

Ivy concentrated on sewing a satin bow to an aubergine gown, then using the tiniest of stitches, trimmed the low-cut bodice with burgundy beads. This time when she slid her eyes to the window, a shiver tingled up her spine.

There he was. Coming out of the barn carrying a shovel and a spade, the brim of his hat pulled low against the blazing sun. It looked like he was headed for the supply shed, but veered off and stood at the prayer rock. He leaned the spade against the prayer bench, set the tip of the shovel into the dirt and stared at the ground.

Ivy put down her sewing, stepped to the window and tweaked the curtain aside regarding him with pleasure. His head was bowed and he was looking around as if searching for something. A few minutes passed and after seeming to come to a decision, he jammed his boot on the shovel and began digging.

What was he doing, Ivy wondered. Why was he shoveling there? Blossoms were already blooming in her flower bed, and if his intention was to plant something in the precise spot he was digging, it would prohibit access to the prayer bench. So why?

Using both hands she spread the curtains wide, but as she watched her curiosity drifted away replaced by a wish that he would look over at her. Impatience propelled her to flutter the curtains in an attempt to attract his notice.

Birch caught the movement and stopped digging. Holding onto the shovel with one hand, he swept off his hat with the other and swiped his sleeve across his forehead. His smile went right to his eyes.

Helplessly caught in the moment, her heart thudding, Ivy smiled back, and their eyes locked in silent communication. His gaze lighted a fire under her clothes causing her heart to race at the intimacy of it. Boldness pumped through her veins and the heat that began at the bodice of her dress climbed up her throat all the way to her hairline.

Birch didn't look away which emboldened her further. Feeling deliciously wanton, she lifted her hand and slowly unfastened the top buttons on the front of her dress just enough to bare the tops of her breasts. She trembled, unsure what his reaction would be to her daring. When he continued to watch, she placed her hands on her breasts and slid them slowly, ever so slowly to her waist. His look was long and sensuous, full of meaning.

Her heart thundered in her ears when he set the shovel aside. His sweet gaze still locked on hers didn't waver. He didn't look away and she couldn't have even if she wanted to.

She bit the inside of her cheek suddenly unsure of the road she'd put herself on. She took a deep breath, then slowly lowered her hands and lifted her skirt and petticoats to her waist exposing her newly adorned pantalettes.

She held her pose as his gaze wandered over her. A one-sided smile appeared on his lips, and he tilted his head, his expression questioning. She widened her eyes and lowered her chin the tiniest bit sending him a nod. Birch leaned the shovel against the side of the Prayer Bench next to the spade, and walked to the cabin, his pace slow but steady.

She heard his boot on the step, his quiet knock, but she couldn't move, could only stare at the cabin door. He knocked again and she was quick to open it. There was mischief in his gaze as it wandered over her in a leisurely sweep.

Despite her previous bravado, she couldn't quite meet his eyes now that he was standing in front of her. She tried to keep her voice level, but she could hardly breathe. Her tongue was troubled. Words wouldn't come.

Finally they did.

"Come in," she said and took a step backward so he could pass.

But he didn't move. "Are you sure?" He looked like he was afraid she'd put him out like a stray dog hanging around where it didn't belong.

It was all she could do to keep her knees from giving way. It didn't escape her that she was at a crossroad. Her hand reached out and touched his cheek.

"Yes."

He crossed the threshold, and a knot tugged in her stomach. His amber eyes were mesmerizing. His hair invited a woman to tangle her fingers in it.

"I've been thinking about you," he said.

""You have?"

"Yes, but I..." He shrugged. "But I know Tally doesn't approve."

"Tally isn't here at the moment." She let the silence that followed say the rest.

He nodded, catching her meaning, but didn't step closer. "She doesn't want you to go to the dance with me."

Their bodies were almost touching. Her trembling had ceased. "Don't worry. She's not going to stop me."

Unexpectedly, her words brought on a fleeting thought. Was this really a man she wanted to become entangled with? Was she letting her imagination grow a seed of a thought into something that would never happen?

All she wanted was to get away. Away from this cabin, away from this homestead. The drudgery, the never ending, never changing day-to-day work necessary to survive. Tally said it would pay off in the end, an end that Ivy saw disappearing into a blurred horizon. She didn't want to wait. She didn't want to be the one staying up half the night making fancy gowns for wealthy ladies. She wanted to be the one wearing those gowns, and she was willing to do whatever was necessary to make that happen.

Her hand touched his hair. His hand caught hers and she felt it everywhere as he ran his thumb up and down the inside of her wrist. A shiver rippled through her and she swallowed hard.

He lifted her hand and lightly brushed his lips on the tender skin of her palm. It was a warm and chaste touch, but she soared to the heavens lost in waves of unfamiliar emotions and feelings and sensations that tumbled over and over and over again inside her.

The air in the room became heavy with anticipation.

She moved and her body pressed against his. He reached up and wound an escaped tendril of her hair around his finger, then leaned in and kissed her. His kiss quickly deepened and his arm slid around her waist. It tightened, but gently with no harsh demand in it, and she wondered how such sweetness and passion had come to her in the form of this handsome man. They moved as one to her bedroom, her shyness all gone now, a lame protest stuck lifeless in her throat. He managed all her hooks and buttons, but had trouble with the stays so she helped him, after which she surrendered her clothes garment by garment. And it was the damnedest thing, but she knew she was about to experience something mysterious and wonderful.

When it was over, she felt not at all ashamed, and realized she hadn't been told the truth about sexual pleasure. The kind of pleasure Birch had just brought upon her. She knew little to nothing about what to expect except what she'd heard the grey-haired ladies at the Social Center whisper behind their hands. They said a woman's only duty and passion should be love of home, children, and domestic duties. Desires of the body were disgraceful. It was the younger ones who said that women were just as much creatures of passion as men. But still, she didn't know it would be like *this*. Didn't know it would take her someplace she'd never been.

As she lay in exquisite delight pondering this revelation, Birch folded his arms around her and fluttered kisses down her neck.

"Ivy, honey?"
"Yes?"
"Where's the gold?"

CHAPTER TWENTY-THREE

*T*ALLY STOOD ON THE boardwalk outside the red door, her blank gaze focused on infinity as she tried to order her thoughts. She'd promised herself she wouldn't put too much stake in anything Madam Simone might tell her, yet the psychic had zeroed in on things she had no way of knowing.

Her stomach had dropped when Madam Simone referred to that nasty business in Denver, a secret that had lived its life unattached to the present. It had taken all the resolve Tally had to hold on to her composure and not let the fear show on her face while sitting in front of the gazing ball. Now, a shudder began, the rumble of dark memories trying to escape. Again, force of will headed it off, because Madam had hit upon something that had more immediate significance.

Trouble surrounds you.

It's true that any psychic might assume that was the case. Why else would anybody seek the counsel of a seer? The world was full of dark corners and jagged edges. Still, a knot slowly formed in her chest. Riding the crest of uncertainty, she let ideas buzz in her head like meddlesome wasps.

A multitude of unspecific thoughts swirled into a jumble of disconnected words leaving her no choice. She had to act on the information she possessed in order to move forward. One didn't always have the luxury of unwrapping the unknown on a moment's notice.

A wind came up and she hunched her shoulders against it. She couldn't stand there all day. She had to get home. She'd never folded under pressure, though she seemed to be out of options this time. But still. She couldn't ignore the warning in Madam Simone's words. There were men who meant to do her harm and now it was time to take control.

But the pieces weren't dropping into place forming a complete picture. Not yet. She needed more information. Her focus narrowed and she plucked an idea from the mass whirling in her head, letting it sink in before the cold lump of apprehension nudged it away. It wasn't much, just enough to relax her shoulders as though relieved of a great load. Just enough to ignite a spark under her.

She stared at the newspaper office across the street, a half-formed idea hovering just beyond her reach. She allowed her thoughts to wander and it became clear that she couldn't do it alone. Again, she scolded herself for not reaching out and getting to know her neighbors, but she'd been busy on her own homestead, her time had necessarily been spent in that small space that defined the edges of her own world.

But now she saw it as her civic duty to take a stand. If she found out that other homesteaders were being harassed and victimized like she was, the only way to defeat the aggressors was for those homesteaders to join forces.

Squinting in concentration, putting the words together in her head, she stepped off the boardwalk and crossed the street. A couple of jiggered up layabouts sprawled on the loafer's bench in front of the newspaper office were none too subtle about looking her over. She daggered them a warning with her eyes and their eyes skated away. Determination strengthening her resolve, she opened the door that said *Edwin W. Hubbard, Editor*, and went inside.

An hour later she came out with an armful of flyers summoning homesteaders to a meeting at the Social Center. She tacked one up on the sign board, then requested permission from the Gallaghers and other businesses along the main drag if she could display one in their front window. That accomplished, she headed to where she'd tethered Champion.

Afternoon clouds were moving in to cover the sun. From the look of them, they'd still be churning tomorrow. But no matter. She had to deliver the flyers to the homesteads regardless of the weather. Clutching the reins, she sighed as she settled into the saddle thinking that tomorrow would be overcast, and bad things happened mostly on cloudy days.

CHAPTER TWENTY-FOUR

YESTERDAY'S CLOUDS LINGERED THROUGH the night, then followed overhead as Tally rode through a landscape of richly varied hues muted now by lack of sunshine. The sky was heavy with unfallen rain. Black roiling billows hung low and snagged on jagged mountain tops. Not many printed flyers made it into the hands of a homesteader because she hadn't seen very many. It had been a disappointing day. She'd expected to see folks proving up claims, building fences, working their fields. Instead she saw empty land, barren spaces and dying crops. The skies promised a deluge. Good sense told her to head for home, but still she dawdled.

She already knew from her trips to town that much of the land east of the Tisdale property had been claimed. The run of proved up or partially developed homesteads had grown steadily and would soon reach the town limits.

But today she'd followed the river along the stage road heading away from town, and was disheartened to find long stretches of vacant fields with scarcely a single structure. Here and there properties nearest the water's edge were occupied and showed a few harvested fields, but many had been forsaken leaving only bare wood upright timbers of half-framed cabins and fields gone to ruin. A few had been burned early on leaving nothing but charred remains. Most of the growth and expansion stretched into the far distance, away from the river even though land nearest the natural waterway was rich with fertile soil.

The few near neighbors she encountered greeted her with faces so dejected the lines put there by hard work had been made permanent by disappointment. They accepted a flyer from her outstretched hand, glanced at it, then turned away with a thank you and a defeated nod. When asked, a few said they'd had some vandalism on their spread and hinted at receiving veiled threats, but when pressed for details wouldn't elaborate. They simply pocketed the meeting flyer and waved her farewell.

A mile downriver, she watched from the road as a family loaded their belongings into a wagon bearing a sign that announced their destination. *Going to Denver, St. Joseph, or just plain Hell.* Behind them, tattered curtains bellied out of the glassless windows of their dilapidated cabin, rippling, luffing.

The only smiles were on the faces of the newcomers she'd come upon. They seemed to support the idea of homesteaders coming together for the benefit of all, but were too busy to spend any time talking about it let alone attend a meeting. They hurriedly but politely accepted Tally's flyers and went back to work.

As a rule, homesteaders and many of the other brave souls who'd come West to the frontier—eccentrics, nonconformists, some lunatics—were of a mind to be individualists. Folks who valued their independence and were loath to be thought weak or unable to overcome adversity on their own. They believed that ownership of property was paramount to achieving the self-reliance they sought. They took pride in what belonged to them and respected what belonged to others. But they weren't joiners, and Tally's hope for a show of strength or any kind of a united front faded.

Thunder cracked and lightning fractured the clouds.

The wind picked up. Tally tucked the flyers into a saddle bag, pulled out a shawl and wrapped it around her shoulders as meager protection from the elements. She tied the ends in a knot over her chest so it wouldn't blow away. Turning Champion in the direction of home she set off at a trot. A quarter mile down the road, she tightened the reins pulling Champion to a stop when a gust of wind brought the smell of charred wood past her nostrils. Through low hanging branches whipping in the wind she saw the blackened shell of a structure she hadn't noticed when she'd passed by that morning, but now goosebumps slithered up her arms at the sound of a child crying.

The turnoff was nothing more than a small breach in the trees. She hesitated barely a moment then nudged Champion into the mouth of the overgrown lane, straining to hear past the soft thud of Champion's hoofs on the hardpack. Then she heard it again. The unmistakable sound of a child's sobs, suddenly muffled as if behind a hand or a crumpled handful of skirt. The lane faded away to a clearing thick with weeds buffeted by the wind. Birds of prey wheeled above. With her hand on her holster, she eased Champion off the path into a clearing.

What was left of a cabin that had been burned nearly to the ground hunkered on the side of a shallow rise. Behind the cabin, the outhouse door squeaked, an eerie, lonely sound. Beyond, under an overhang of sheer rock was a rounded opening in the side of the hill covered by a hang of burlap. A dugout.

Prompted by what she was certain was a child in distress, Tally dismounted and led the horse along a trail to the edge of a thicket. There she came upon a mound of rocks and dirt topping a recently dug grave. A cluster of wilting wildflowers drooped lazily out of a charred glass jar in front of a makeshift cross standing in for a headstone. She tied Champion to a low branch and a pinch of sadness took hold as she stepped closer to read the name hand carved on the cross.

A twig snapped behind her and she spun around to see a woman with venom in her eyes, a child clinging to her skirts, and a rifle in her hands held in a steady aim.

"Hold it right there," the woman croaked. She sounded parched. Either that, or her throat was so thick from crying the words were disinclined to escape.

Tally's heart skidded. "Please don't shoot." Her arms bent at the elbow, waist high, palms out as if prepared to stop a bullet.

"Who are you?"

"I'm Tally Tisdale. I'm a neighbor."

"Oh, yeah? Where's your claim?"

Tally pointed. "A couple miles that way. Adjacent to Bandit Bend."

The woman lifted her eyebrows and tilted her chin in a soft nod of recognition. "You mean the spread at Prayer Rock?"

"Yes."

"My husband bought those cut trees from you last year." The woman's eyes drifted to Tally's holster then back up to her face. "You're armed. What do you want?"

"I'm riding out to get acquainted with my neighbors. I saw your burned-out cabin and heard a child cry." Tally looked at the little girl who stared back, eyes wide with fright. Her frock was torn and caked with mud. She looked to be around three years old.

The mother took a protective half step in front of the little girl who began to cry.

"Be quiet, Anna," the mother gently scolded without taking her eyes off Tally. Then, "She's all right. We're both all right. So you can get back on your horse and get out." The woman's bottom lip quaked, but her rifle didn't waver.

Both mother and child looked dirty and tired and hungry, not all right. Thin, and their clothes hadn't seen a wash tub for weeks. The woman shifted from one foot to the other under Tally's scrutiny, her narrowed eyes returning shiny pinpoints of distrust.

Fully expecting the burn of a bullet from this angry woman's rifle, Tally spoke softly. "You look like you need help. What happened here?"

"They burned our cabin and killed my husband. What does it look like happened?"

Tally softened her voice even more. "I'm so very sorry. Who did this? And why?"

"Men. Three of 'em. They wanted our spread. Homer said no. Homer's my husband." She tipped her head toward the grave, but didn't lower the weapon. "Was. That's him there."

Tally wondered if they were the same men who were coming around her spread. The men who cut the fences. Destroyed the chicken coop. Beheaded the sheep.

The little girl pressed in closer to her mother's skirt. Tears streaked the dirt on her face as she sobbed silently, struggling with the effort to mind her mother and stay quiet.

Tally's eyes flicked to the burlap covered hole in the side of the hill. "Is that where you're living now? In the dugout?"

"Yes."

"How long?"

"Two weeks. Three."

Likely more than that, Tally guessed. "Do you have food?"

The woman didn't answer, but she didn't have to.

"You can turn your rifle away. I'm not going to hurt you or your little girl."

The woman's skeptical gaze jumped to Tally's holster

again. She tightened her grip on the rifle. "Why are you walking around with a gun?"

"Same reason as you."

The woman took her in from head to toe and back again. Her hold on the rifle relaxed but only a little. "You alone on your spread?"

"I live with my sister. Her name is Ivy. She's sixteen."

There was no response and Tally let the silence lay between them wishing she knew what the woman was thinking. The woman held her stare and hiccupped a sob. Despite glistening eyes, no tears ran down her face. Not new ones, anyway.

"You don't have to stay in that dugout," Tally said. "I can help you. You can stay with my sister and me. I'll make room for you in our cabin. You can stay until you figure things out, or as long as you need to. What's your name?"

Still holding on to the rifle but in a less threatening manner, the woman's face softened slightly and she looked like she was deciding if she should answer. "My name is Jenny Calloway," she replied. "My daughter is Anna, named after my mother." She paused then asked, "What makes you think women alone would be safe at your place?"

"We're not alone. I have two hired men who live on my claim and a friend who helps out and stays over sometimes."

Still Jenny hesitated.

"I have a garden and animals," Tally said. "We struggle sometimes, but mostly we get by. We aren't hungry. We have food and water, enough to share. And sweets for Anna," she added as if that were a sticking point.

Jenny slowly lowered her rifle and looked at Tally with sorrowful eyes. "Those men. I don't know who they were. They'd been around before, but Homer ran them off. We didn't think they'd come back. But they did."

She sniffed. "When they set the cabin on fire, Homer started shooting at them. I grabbed Anna and ran. We hid in the woods. Homer tried to hold them off, but it was no use. They killed him. But he fought to the end," she said just in case Tally was disparaging him in her mind for dying. "After that, they came looking, but couldn't find us." Her tone suggested she was gradually finding her way out of complete despair.

Tally stepped closer. "Will you come stay with us? Please."

Jenny loosened her grip on the rifle and let it pivot barrel down pointing at the ground. "It's not loaded," she said. "I ran out of bullets the same day I ran out of food."

Tally approached and put a gentle hand on Jenny's arm. "I'll help you gather your things."

Jenny nodded. "There's not much in the dugout. I couldn't get everything from the cabin. There was too much fire."

At the dugout, shored up with timbers that looked none too secure, Jenny collected their meager belongings and Tally stuffed what she could into saddle bags.

"Leave the blankets and bedding," Tally said. "I have extra. We can come back later for the rest of your things, but we need to go now. It's starting to rain. You can ride Champion and hold Anna in front of you. I'll walk with the lead."

Jenny started to object, but Tally shushed her. "It's not a problem, truly. I walk farther each day doing chores on my spread."

"Thank you." Jenny's appreciative grin didn't quite hit its mark, but Tally could tell she was relieved.

Tally untied Champion, then held Anna while Jenny mounted up, her every move shaky and painfully deliberate. When she was settled in the saddle, Tally lifted Anna toward her mother's waiting arms.

The crack and whine of a Henry rifle sent a bullet whizzing past Tally's head. Jenny let out a yelp and pitched out of the saddle, a stunned look on her face. Anna slid out of her arms, and Tally hit the ground cradling the little girl who was screaming in her ear.

Jenny moaned, so Tally knew she'd been hit. She raised her head to look for the shooter but ducked when another shot rang out. The bullet hit the ground sending dirt up in her face. Champion reared, made a terrified sound then crashed through the brush galloping away like the devil was after him. Tally, her cheek pressed to the ground, saw through tall weeds a horse and rider come out of the woods and race away.

Her heart squeezed into her throat and blocked her breathing. Thoughts she couldn't make sense of spun inside her head. She snaked her arm along the ground, her fingers reaching for Jenny. She felt something wet and sticky on Jenny's shoulder.

Anna had quieted down but she was shaking with fright. Jenny was bleeding and breathing, but not moving.

"Jenny, can you hear me?"

A word fought its way out of her mouth and ended on a groan. "Anna..."

"I've got her. She wasn't hit."

Black clouds spun and swirled. Rain began to fall with the velocity of buckshot. Tally pulled the shawl from her shoulders, wrapped it around Anna, and ran with her to the dugout.

"Stay in here," she said. "Do you hear me? Don't come out. I'm going to get your mother."

Anna responded to the hardness in Tally's voice with tight lips and quick shakes of her head.

Tally made her way through the storm to where Jenny lay moaning in pain. Trees thrashed and bent in the wind. Ashes and charred pieces from the structure fire filled the air only to be beaten down by raindrops that felt like scissor points on her skin. Heart pounding, she knelt next to Jenny. Free flowing blood from Jenny's wound mixed with the rain, and her arm was bent at an unnatural angle. Maybe broken. The skin of her face was raw and red, and she was bleeding from a gash on her head, but those injuries were the result of the fall, not the bullet, though a serious head injury could prove fatal. Her eyes were closed, but she opened them when Tally said her name.

Jenny tried to speak, but the words choked back into her throat. Tally put her lips to Jenny's ear so she could be heard over the noise of the storm.

"Can you walk? I put Anna in the dugout. Can you make it there?"

Jenny voice came out a gurgle. "I don't know."

"Try, Jenny. I'll help you, but you have to try."

Rain was now falling in sheets turning the ground into sucking mud. Tally gripped Jenny's waist. "I'm going to help you up. You'll have to lean on me. It's going to hurt, but you can't stay out here, and I can't carry you."

Jenny shrieked when Tally lifted her, but despite the pain she managed to get her feet under her. Their hair fell in wet clumps to their shoulders and hung in their faces.

"I've got you," said Tally. "Take a step."

Jenny managed to move a short distance, but her knees gave out and she slumped. Tally caught her and helped her take two more steps.

"Again," Tally said, but the word was drowned out by pounding thunder she could feel in her chest. "Try again. We're almost there," she shouted.

Step by slow painful step, they made it. Little Anna had laid out blankets into a makeshift sleeping mat. Wide eyed and terrified, she patted with her hands showing her mother where to lie down.

"Thank you, Anna," Tally said. "Good girl. Your mother

is going to be all right, but I'm going to need you to help me take care of her." The words were delivered on a certainty despite the lump in her throat. Anna's eyes were big and frightened, but she nodded.

Tally pulled Jenny's blouse away from her chest and looked at the wound.

Words wheezed from Jenny's lips. "Is it bad?"

It was, but Tally shook her head. "No, but if the bullet is still in there, we have to get it out before infection sets in." Gently she slid her hand beneath Jenny and felt for an exit wound. There was none.

Time was critical. Jenny needed a doctor and soon. Tally knew what a raging infection did to a body.

"My hired men, my sister, my friend... Someone will come looking when I don't return home," she said, but was suddenly struck with the gut-wrenching realization that they wouldn't know where to look. The dugout couldn't be seen from the road.

Swooping panic gripped her, but she kept her face immobile as she took her shawl from Anna's shoulders and wrapped it around herself. "I'll be right back."

Jenny groaned, her eyes ravaged with pain.

Anna cried out. "No. Don't go!"

She held Anna in a hug until the child calmed down. "I need to let them know where to look for us. I promise I'll come back."

Sheets of rain soaked the ground as jagged lightning cut a brilliant swath across angry grey skies. Bent against the wind and rain, Tally headed into the storm slogging through the mud. Wind whipped her skirt around her legs tripping her up making walking more difficult than it already was. But she kept going pulled along on an invisible line of determination.

At the road, she yanked off her shawl, then wove it between the branches of a low hanging evergreen and tied it securely so it wouldn't be blown away by the wind. By the time she made it back to the dugout she was shivering uncontrollably.

"Don't worry," she said, teeth chattering. "Now they'll know where to look for us."

She prayed it would be in time to save Jenny.

* * *

Tally started awake from a light surface sleep, swooping panic thudding in her chest. Someone called her name. Slowly she rose to a sitting position, then went still trying to pinpoint the sound. But no. It was only the wind hollering through the trees.

She got up and peeked outside. A full moon behind thready clouds cast grey ashy light as the night lay down in front of the oncoming day. The rain had stopped, but water pooled and ran in random rivulets across the ground. She saw no one.

Anna whimpered in her sleep. Jenny was fitful, her breathing ragged. Gently, Tally placed her hand on Jenny's forehead. Fear bubbled up as she removed her hand. Fever.

Crestfallen, she laid down again, but sleep wouldn't come. She had to get help, and her mind raced with possibilities. At daylight, she would get on the road and begin walking toward home. A neighbor might see her. Or a mule skinner, or an early stage would come along. There was help on the road, not cooped up in the dugout.

Or was there?

What if the outlaws that burned the cabin came back. The shooter might be one of them. He might still be out there. Jenny had seen their faces. They had reason to come back to kill her.

Or were those bullets meant for her and not for Jenny? The first one whined so close she felt her hair move. The second one hit the dirt in front of her face.

At the sound of distant voices the knot inside her tightened. Exhausted, unable to think clearly, her sleep deprived mind took her straight to fear, and she unholstered her weapon. At the opening, she tweaked the burlap a thin slit, just enough so she could see out.

Balls of light bobbed up the lane from the road turning into flickering lanterns as they neared. Hath and Wren entered the clearing. Ivy and Birch rode behind.

Tally stumbled outside, waving and calling. "Here! I'm here!"

When Ivy caught sight of her, she slipped off the horse and ran through the muck to throw her arms around Tally. Then Hath's arms were around her, too, pulling her close. He put his mouth to her ear and his voice cracked a little when he spoke.

"Thank God. I was afraid I wouldn't find you."

CHAPTER TWENTY-FIVE

*P*ETTYJOHN REINED HIS HORSE around to the back of the saloon and stopped behind the rolling gallows where he couldn't be seen from the street. Pale yellow rimmed the horizon to the east, but not enough to cast more than a hazy light. Saddle leather creaked and two men on horseback rode out of the shadows. They stopped facing Pettyjohn. They were Clarkson's men. Pettyjohn didn't know their names, but he knew they were on Clarkson's payroll.

The man in the fringed buckskin jacket tipped up the brim of his hat with a knuckle. "You wanted to talk to us?"

"No," said Pettyjohn. "I wanted to speak with Mister Clarkson."

"He's occupied. He sent us."

Pettyjohn didn't like having to speak to underlings, and the clipped tone of his voice indicated as much. "This is a matter of grave importance. I need to speak with him about our… arrangement."

"We'll pass your message on."

Pettyjohn's eyes flicked to the other man who sat silent, but listening intently. He had an unlit matchstick in his mouth that stuck to his lower lip. The handlebar mustache under his nose looked like it had been permanently knocked off center. Pettyjohn didn't know who he was, so ignored him and directed his comments to the man in the buckskin jacket. He kept it short and vague. The less said, the better.

"I need to discuss the terms of our agreement."

"What terms?"

The land agent sniffed and pressed his lips in annoyance. "This was supposed to be a clean and simple land deal. I only agreed to provide information. I didn't think people would die."

"Oh?" The man snickered. "What *did* you think?"

"I thought I was contributing to the economic growth of the town."

Their gazes dueled in the air. The man's was dark with a sharp edge. "Look, Pettyjohn. This is business, not an ice cream social."

"Yes, I know, but... but the women... You shot an innocent homesteader. She had a child..."

"We were aiming for the Tisdale woman..."

"But I didn't think—"

"Again, you thought wrong."

Pettyjohn let out a long breath. "Yes, it appears that way, doesn't it? Well, I'm out."

"You're out?" The man exchanged a look with his partner. "You hear that, Fritz? He says he's out."

"Yes. Please tell Mr. Clarkson," said Pettyjohn.

Fritz let his hand rest on the handle of his holstered pistol. He didn't say anything. The matchstick moved on his lip.

Unnerved by the man's stare, Pettyjohn gentled his voice and addressed them both, his liquid eyes pleading for understanding. "Please. I'm a man of stature in this town. I'm not an outlaw."

"Washington might not agree on that little point," said the man in the fringed jacket. He smirked. "For a start, I'm sure they'd be interested in your breach of confidentiality. Then there's forgery, bribery, destroying documents, interfering with government business. I could go on. Those are federal offenses and you, sir, are a federal agent."

Pettyjohn opened his mouth, but the words backed up in his throat and he had trouble getting them out. "Yes, but... but..."

"But what?" Fritz removed his pistol and drew back the hammer. The lips below the mustache tightened and the matchstick changed position again.

"Put your gun away," said the other man. "We need him. Clarkston won't be happy if you kill him."

Fritz scoffed and spat the matchstick into the dirt. "They'll send someone else. There are plenty more like him in Washington."

Cold, clammy fear gripped Pettyjohn, but he kept his composure. "Don't worry. I won't tell anyone what you've done, or what Mr. Clarkson is up to. I'm just walking away from it. Tell Clarkson he has my word."

Fritz pulled the trigger and Pettyjohn went down.

* * *

By noon, the line at the Land Office stretched half a block, newcomers waiting for it to open so they could sign patent papers and put down roots.

The man at the head of the line cupped his hands around his eyes and peered in through the glass topped door. "Nobody's in there," he shouted to the others.

"Why?" someone shouted in return.

"Dunno."

Irritated conversations commenced. There was some profanity.

The sheriff showed up, elbowed everyone aside, and attached a sign to the doorpost.

"Sorry, folks. Land Office is closed until further notice." He ignored the sighs and moans and complaints, and mounted up. Wide-eyed newcomers stared at his back as his horse trotted away.

CHAPTER TWENTY-SIX

IT WAS QUIET ON the Tisdale homestead for the first time in days. No pounding, hammering or sawing sounds punished everyone's eardrums or set their heads to throbbing. Wren was in the back pasture checking fences, a never-ending job. Tally had recently bought three more cows and it took up a lot of Wren's time chasing the ones that escaped through broken posts and torn barbed wire.

Hath had just returned from town bringing a wagon load of stock feed along with the news that Foster Goodnight Pettyjohn's dead body had been found next to the portable gallows. Tally had momentarily stilled her needle and Ivy stopped sweeping to listen to him relate the gossip and rumors surrounding Pettyjohn's murder so soon after Frank Scott had been found dead on the boulders by the old trading post. A rumor was spreading on no basis whatsoever that the murders were somehow connected, but most folks in town thought that was highly improbable.

"How in the world would a respected federal land office agent be linked in any way to an out of work saddle tramp cowboy like Frank Scott?" Hath asked with a shrug addressing no one in particular.

The three of them speculated a while speaking in low tones so as not to wake Jenny from a nap about the unlikelihood of that. Then Hath excused himself and took the supplies to the barn where Birch was conditioning saddles and checking and repairing harnesses and other tack.

Ivy finished her cleaning chores, then headed out for a few quiet moments at Prayer Rock before it was time to start the washing. Tally sat by the window while she worked so she could keep an eye on little Anna playing in the yard. Jenny, still recovering from her gunshot wound, was napping in Ivy's room much to Ivy's displeasure.

Ivy had given up her room to Jenny and Anna, and was again sharing Tally's sleeping quarters. The doctor said Jenny should get plenty of rest while she recovered and needed care until she was well enough to be up and about. Anna needed care, too, much of which fell to Ivy except for the few minutes a day she spent at Prayer Rock.

Her empathy had evaporated as fast as it had manifested when she realized that with Jenny and Anna living there, she'd never be alone, and Birch wouldn't be able to visit. But it would be uncharitable to grouse about it, so she let her protests die in her throat and consoled herself with a happier thought.

The gold.

Birch had told her about it, and she was on her way to pray he would find it, because when he did they were going to run away together. To someplace better, like Mexico or maybe California. He'd shown her the future through his eyes and it was dazzling.

She hoped it would be California. She wanted to be an actress or a singer only on a real stage in a theater not in a saloon. That was well and good for Mimi and seemed to provide her with a good living, but Ivy was a girl meant for finer things and lovely places. No, she corrected herself. She was *a woman* meant for finer things and lovely places. What was she doing *here*?

Working her father's land and hoping he returned soon, she reminded herself, but she desperately wanted to get away from the constant drudgery of her downtrodden life. Away from the unrelenting work, the animal smells, the cramped quarters, and the ever-present dust thrown up by the three times a day stage runs around Bandit Bend.

Birch said he loved her, and she said she loved him back even though she wasn't sure she did. He *was* a thief after all. A road agent. The gold didn't belong to him. He stole it. She couldn't reconcile that with how she felt about him and how he made her feel. Still, she prayed they'd find the gold because she had no intention of living like this the rest of her days.

Sitting on the bench, she bowed her head and folded her hands in her lap assuming a prayerful posture. The old woman who came around with a wagon full of books to borrow told the sisters that Prayer Rock had special powers. She said a long time ago there was a monastery on the site with nuns and monks who cared for injured travelers. A young man was brought in and cared for by a nun named Sister Ophelia. Love came to them, which was of course forbidden. Alas, they were found out, and Sister Ophelia was condemned to die.

But before she could be put to death, a terrible earthquake collapsed the walls of the monastery while she was kneeling in prayer. She was buried under the stones, and legend said she was reincarnated as Prayer Rock and could assist in delivering entreaties to the heavens.

Tally said it was preposterous, but Ivy secretly hoped it was true, and she came to pray every day that the kneeling nun would lead them to the gold. She prayed silently, but she no longer closed her eyes. Now she kept them open so she could scout the area. Birch said the gold and money box was buried somewhere around there, but the map was so poorly drawn he couldn't pinpoint the exact location. She hoped to see the shadow of a sunken place or some other unevenness in the earth that indicated something might be buried there.

Prayerful words floated through her mind by rote and she let her eyes wander. They drifted over the crude bunkhouse Hath and Wren had built next to the storage shed, so Hath had a place to sleep when he stayed over. It was small but big enough for Wren, too, although in the end he refused to move in and stayed in the barn instead. When Birch hired on, he slept in the bunkhouse.

Her gaze slid over to the shed, the neatly nailed side boards shimmed up tight to keep out weather, and the half-cut logs that served as steps to the door. It was built on sturdy stilts to keep critters out. One by one her thoughts slowly rearranged themselves until she jolted straight up with joy swooping through her, ramping up the pace of her heart. She experienced a few moments of breathlessness, but forced herself to calm down and breathe normally, because suddenly *she knew*. She knew where the gold was buried. *It was in the excavated crawl space under the shed.*

Her giddy exhilaration was swept away by the sound of galloping horses, three riders, Indians, coming around the bend leaving boils of dust behind them. They slowed when they reached the property, stopped on the road, and turned their horses to face the cabin. They sat stone still, staring.

Fear hit her in the belly and shot through her veins. She hollered, the words exploding out of her mouth. "Birch! Come quick!"

Gathering her skirt, she took off running toward Anna, but Tally flew out the front door and scooped up the child before Ivy got there. Birch and Hath hurried from the barn and followed them inside, closing and barring the door behind them. The men stood at the window looking out. Tally and Ivy moved in close, hands on hip, fingers gripping the handle of their weapons.

The Indians slowly walked their horses into the yard, and still keeping their distance, lined up on the grassy patch in front of the cabin.

"Who are they?" Ivy whispered. Her fingers dug into Birch's arm.

"I don't know," he said. "I don't think they're from around here."

Hath agreed. "I don't recognize them."

The Indians wore a mixture of tribal dress and ordinary work clothes—cotton shirts and denim pants, the usual wear of men in the West. Strings of beads and bones around their neck lay on their chest. Hoops pierced their ears. Two of the Indians were shod in animal skin moccasins, but the one in the middle wore shiny high topped riding boots. All three had long black braids. One of them, the youngest, topped his head with a flat crowned hat.

Ivy wasn't sure, but their bearing suggested they held some significance in their tribe, especially the one in the middle with the boots.

"Let's wait and see what they do," said Hath.

But they didn't do anything. They just sat silently on their horses looking at the cabin. They showed no aggression, but the expressions on their high-boned cinnamon-colored faces were somber.

Ivy went rigid when the Indian in the middle urged his horse forward a few paces then stopped at the bottom of the porch steps. He made eye contact through the window and spoke in a combination of words and sign language.

"They're Arapaho," whispered Birch.

Tally's face fell. "Oh, no." Quickly she clasped Ivy's hand and gently nudged Anna out of sight behind her skirts. Though the tribe as a whole co-existed peacefully with the homesteaders, some of the men occasionally showed their resistance in outward acts of hostility.

"Don't worry," said Birch. "I think they're friendly."

"How do you know?" Ivy's voice squeaked with alarm.

"I can understand some of their language." He looked at Hath and tipped his head in a *come along* gesture. "Let's go out to talk to them."

Trembling, Ivy drew a breath and pinched the back of Birch's shirt as if to hold him back. "No. Don't."

"It's fine. You two stay here." He waved her hand away and the men stepped out onto the porch with a nod of greeting to the Indians. Ignoring Birch's admonition to stay put, the women followed them out.

After some brief discourse between Birch and what looked to be the tribal headman, Birch interpreted.

"He said he's Chief White Eagle. The other two are his sons, Grey Fox and Angry Bear. They're looking for Angry Bear's wife. He said she ran away and his son wants her back. Wants her to come home."

Tally shrugged and looked at Ivy. "I haven't seen any unfamiliar Indian women around here. Have you?"

"No."

Birch passed the information on to the chief who responded with a scowl, then turned to the other two.

While the Indians had a lengthy exchange, the fear Ivy originally felt at first sight began to seep away, and questions played out in her mind as she watched them. The chief was a handsome man, long legged, and he sat his horse proud and tall. He spoke in a well modulated voice, and even though Ivy didn't understand everything he was saying, she suspected he spoke English well enough, but chose not to. Indians sometimes did that as an expression of resistance against the expansion of white settlements overtaking Indian land.

She especially kept her eye on the other two. They didn't involve themselves in the ongoing dialogue, but were instead looking around, their sharp dark eyes traveling over the barn, the corrals, the fields, the animals in the pens. One of them shifted in his saddle and tilted his head so he could see in through the cabin's front door which hung ajar. He noticed Ivy eyeing him, and stared her down until she looked away.

At last, the chief, sounding frustrated, said something that held a tone of finality. Birch nodded in understanding, then interpreted for the others.

"He said they came here because he was told she was here. He said his sister's husband saw her."

Tally shook her head again and widened her eyes. "Well, maybe she's somewhere in town. Has he checked the other homesteads? Tell him we'll keep watch and if we see her, we'll let her know he's looking for her."

Chief White Eagle's angry reply to that sounded like Arapaho profanity. He then raised his chin to signal he was leaving and tugged the reins to turn his horse around.

"Ask him if they're hungry," said Tally. "I have biscuits left over from breakfast they can take with them."

The chief nodded when Birch offered, and waited until Tally brought the biscuits, then the Indians left at a gallop raising a cloud of dust that followed them down the road.

When they were out of sight, Hath and Birch headed back to the barn. Tally caught Ivy's eye in a long lingering look full of meaning. An unspoken message moved between them, sent and received.

Do you think Wren...?
I don't know.
I've wondered, though...
Me, too.

Nothing more was said. Tally went back to her sewing, and Ivy went back to pray for the gold.

CHAPTER TWENTY-SEVEN

SUTTON CREEK'S FOUNDER'S DAY was established to commemorate the first gold strike in the settlement and the man who prospered from it. It came not long after the first group of settlers arrived. At the time, there were only a few dozen inhabitants living in drab shacks. Their feeble attempts at mining produced a little powdery dust that appeared to be gold but wasn't, spurring a mediocre goldrush to the area that soon petered out turning the hopefuls into go-backs.

This didn't stop a newly arrived German from making the trek up from Denver to what was then a dismal shack town to try his hand at prospecting. After a few disappointing weeks of panning nothing more than glittery pyrite, he sold his claim to another newcomer, Arthur Danford.

Within a month, Danford struck an exceptionally rich vein that made him a very wealthy man. He used some of his newfound wealth to develop the town which he named Sutton Creek after his first born son, Sutton Alexander Danford. The son grew up to be a handsome rascal and a well-known visitor to the local bordellos. Apropos of that, the Founder's Day celebration kicked off each year with an elaborate Parade of Prostitutes through the middle of town.

Current day folks in Sutton Creek were divided on the matter of the bordellos. The moral tone of the town was slowly trending toward respectability with the arrival of investors and their families, but with men still outnumbering women ten to one and opportunities for marriage meager, the Prostitute's Parade continued with a wink and a nod each year. Hath told Tally he expected it to be phased out soon as more good women took up residence, bringing along their refining influence.

Decidedly skeptical, Tally expressed her concern.

"But, Hath, I think we should skip the parade and just go for the dance. It's not something Ivy should see."

To which Hath roared with laughter and feigned incredulity. "Tally, she's almost seventeen. Do you think she doesn't now what goes on in those fancy houses up on the hill?"

Tally glanced up from kneading bread dough on the kitchen table. "Well, I'm sure she does, but..."

Still chuckling, Hath spoke up with assurances before she finished objecting.

"I promise you it won't be like the old days. The first Founder's Day celebrations saw some pretty outrageous behaviors until the town council called a halt."

Tally's hands slowed and she gave him a look that invited him to go on. "Like what?"

He pinched his lips and shook his head, refusing to go into details.

"Come on," she coaxed. "Tell me. I want to know what we might be in for."

The beginnings of a grin quirked his lips. "Well," he began, "the parlor girls weren't as refined and well behaved as they are now." He ended abruptly and looked away.

"Go on," she said, giving him her full attention, waiting.

Hath sighed, giving in. "Back then they ran footraces through the middle of town. In the nude," he finished.

Tally's eyes widened and her brows lifted. "Oh," was all she said as she tried to hide her own amused grin while she continued kneading.

Hath went on hurriedly. "But the town fathers passed a law against anything like that, so don't worry. The parade activities will be quite tame in comparison. Now it's not just the parlor house girls who march in the parade. Townsfolk and storekeepers sometimes join in, too. Trust me. Nothing salacious goes on. The girls dress as if they're going to church."

Tally divided the mound of dough in half and shaped it with her hands, then tilted her head and gave a mental shrug. She'd seen them in church and had to agree most of them looked respectable on Sunday mornings. Except for the racy French women who'd begun swarming into town looking for husbands. They wore multi-colored petticoats under ruffled skirts, audaciously displaying themselves in low cut bodices, kidskin boots adorned with tassels and bells to call attention. Many were armed with pistols or jeweled daggers partially concealed in their boot tops to keep the hell-raising cowboys in line.

She sighed. "Well, all right. If you say so."

CHAPTER TWENTY-EIGHT

*T*HE SKY HOVERED LIKE a blue silk sheet on Founder's Day morning, unusual for so late in the season. The preceding days had been warm though the nights were beginning to turn cold, and mornings were brisk despite the sunshine.

Wren watched from the barn as the two couples left for the festivities. Hath drove the wagon with Tally seated next to him, spine straight, posture excellent as usual. Ivy sat with Birch on the bench behind, trying unsuccessfully to hide their hand holding within the folds of her blue taffeta skirt. They sat with their shoulders touching, too close in Wren's opinion.

Wren couldn't quite put a finger on what it was about Birch that bothered him so. Something about him didn't sit right. He was a good worker, pleasant and friendly, maybe overly so, and hadn't put a foot wrong since he hired on. But Wren could not abide him. And it wasn't only because he was getting entirely too familiar with young Ivy.

Something was going on between the two of them, and it hadn't taken long for Tally to notice which resulted in some loud arguments between the sisters. Personal disagreements led to heated conversations, then to accusations, and eventually to questions that demanded answers. For that reason, Wren avoided getting involved, and stayed out of sight when they quarreled.

Jenny was on the mend and well enough to be up and around, but out of an abundance of caution Tally didn't want to leave her and Anna alone. Wren offered to stay behind to watch over them while tending to the homestead.

Wren shunned socializing in town whenever possible, fearing someone with a penchant for recognizing faces might start asking questions. Chief White Eagle may have decided to continue his search for his son's wife during the festivities. For Wren, visits to town were strictly business. Pick up supplies, sometimes the mail, then directly back to Bandit Bend.

Wren waited until the Tisdale sisters and the men disappeared around the bend, then mounted up and rode out to the back acreage. With so many newcomers putting down roots, more and more transients and trespassers had to be run off. If the small stones balanced on the top of the boulders covering the front of the dugout were gone or displaced, it would be a sure sign someone had been snooping around.

Then Wren would have to do something about that.

CHAPTER TWENTY-NINE

WHEN THEY REACHED TOWN, Hath reined the horse into the wagon yard at the livery to avoid the crowded street, then the four of them strolled the boardwalk stopping now and then to view goods offered for sale on tables and benches set up in front of the shops.

Ivy set her eyes on a rose stone bead necklace which Birch promptly bought for her, sending a blush of pleasure to her face. Tally admired a bejeweled hair clip, looked at the price, then put it down and moved on to a display of colored glass hatpins.

Hath stepped away and she let her gaze follow him thinking for the hundredth time how handsome he was. Lean and long legged. A smile that lit up his face. But she quickly turned away because he was looking back at her, and she didn't want him to see the longing she was hiding behind her eyes.

She coveted the shiny hatpins knowing full well she could do without. Hath returned to her side, put something in her hand and closed her fingers over it, cupping both his hands over hers.

"Here," he said. "This is for you."

Curious, she opened her hand to see the glittering hair clip she'd admired.

"Oh, thank you, but..." She offered it back to him. "I can't accept this."

"Why not?"

"Well… the price."

His eyes held hers and were exceptionally soulful—*why hadn't she noticed that before*—and now the sentiment conveyed there was laden with endearment.

"You're worth it," he said. "And I want you to have it. From me."

From me.

Tally gazed at him for a long moment overtaken more by his words than by the bauble in her hand.

He spoke before she could find words. "May I?" he asked. "May I put it in your hair?"

She was silent a moment contemplating this, then following a rush of whimsey she nodded and turned right there in the middle of the boardwalk so he could fasten the hair piece to the nest of curls at the back of her head. Passersby grinned at the affectionate gesture, and her cheeks burned under their gaze. Hath put his hands on her shoulders, gently turned her around and took a step back to admire.

"Beautiful," he said.

Warmth embraced her from the inside out, and she lowered her eyes overcome by emotion. When they resumed walking it seemed only natural to let him take her hand and tuck it possessively into the crook of his arm. She lifted her chin and let a small smile sit lightly on her lips as she walked with him.

They caught up with Ivy and Birch at the Social Center. The building, formerly a bordello built to mimic a Spanish hacienda, had a courtyard in front and black iron balconies at the windows on the second floor. Archways framed a wide inviting porch, colorful tiles were randomly mortared onto the brick façade. Potted flowers lined the walk that led to a striking oversized front door painted blue.

Chairs set up on the porch and on the lawn to accommodate parade watchers were quickly filling up. The two couples settled into back row seats as parade music rolled up the hill coming closer. Horns, fiddles, banjos, the sound of drums so resonant Tally could feel the percussions throbbing in her chest.

Boisterous miners riding their burros or stepping lively on foot came next, breaking their stride every now and then to dance a jig or toss wrapped candy to the children. Some of the miners wore gold nuggets on chains around their neck. Others carried gunny sacks filled with rocks to emulate gold nuggets. The dollar signs painted on the sacks suggested and no doubt inflated the value of their dig. Wild applause and enthusiastic cheers rose from both sides of the parade route. It was, after all, because of the miners that Sutton Creek existed at all.

The sheriff, his deputies, and volunteer firemen came next, all of them big, hefty men wearing no-nonsense expressions, dark eyes displaying authority. Behind them local dignitaries waved to the crowd as they continued the procession driving fancy wagons or riding high stepping horses. The bank president and his board of directors. Wealthy investors, senior managers and railroad executives. Ambrose Clarkson, owner of the Clarkson Cattle Company, rode a beautiful blue roan filly in the company of the newspaper editor and other important men. Tally noticed no one represented the Federal Land Office since Pettyjohn's replacement had still not arrived from Washington though his murder was still the foremost topic of town gossip along with the murder of Frank Scott.

And at last, the parlor house girls in lavishly decorated buggies pulled by prancing milky white or midnight black horses.

Tally poked Hath with her elbow and gave him a pointed look. "Did those horses come from your livery?"

Hath returned a low lidded side glance. "Buster

rented to them. They paid double."

Unable to come up with a fitting objection to that, she laughed and turned back to watch the fashionably dressed women in form fitting, high necked silk dresses. Fine frothy ribbons in every color attached to their wide brimmed hats floated behind them in the breeze. Powder and paint created a rich veneer over their faces. Black-lined eyes, lips painted bright red. Bracelets jangled on slender wrists as long nailed red-tipped fingers reached for the drinks handed to them by white-aproned bartenders who hustled along the parade route.

When the parade was over, the crowd—a colorful mixture of farmers, ranchers, miners, loggers, gunmen, lawyers, artists, preachers and shopkeepers—hurried inside where dining tables topped by flowery centerpieces courtesy of Wells Fargo had been set up around the perimeter of the ballroom.

Hath gallantly pulled Tally's chair out to seat her properly, and Birch did the same for Ivy who absolutely glowed with pleasure.

Everyone nodded and waved at friends and neighbors as they claimed a table. Hath, of course, knew nearly everyone in town, many of whom stopped by to exchange greetings and chat.

Ivy and Birch hardly took their eyes off each other the entire time. After dinner and after the tables were cleared, while the musicians gathered on a raised platform and began tuning their instruments, they nudged their chairs closer together. Tally guessed their knees were touching under the long, white tablecloth. She held her scolding tongue, and sent a disapproving scowl their way, but they avoided eye contact and continued gazing at each other like lovesick loons. Tally huffed an irritated sigh hoping that she wasn't sending a message of approval by remaining silent. Tolerance did not equate with agreement, but she wasn't going to make a scene in front of the entire town. Instead she averted her eyes to glance around the room recognizing several of the dresses she'd made. That's when she noticed the girl staring at her.

The girl was young, perhaps eighteen, thin with a rich pearly complexion wearing a fancy dress more lavish than the ones Tally had made. Her white gold hair trailed down her back in a glistening cascade, and her earrings and necklace were eye-catching but not gaudy. She sat at the Clarkson Cattle Company table. Because of her youth and striking good looks, she stood out from the rest of the jovial group, but the facial similarities—large dark eyes and wide sensuous mouth—made Tally wonder if she was related to the others seated with her.

Tally turned up the corners of her mouth in a polite smile and lifted her hand to send a gracious greeting to the girl, but quickly lowered it when she realized the girl wasn't staring at *her*. She was staring at Birch.

Birch didn't notice, absorbed as he was with the way Ivy was leaning into him whispering behind her hand, so Tally tapped his arm to get his attention.

"Do you know that woman?" Tally lifted her chin and aimed her eyes indicating the other side of the room. "There. Look behind you at the Clarkson table. The young one with the ribbons and feathers in her hair."

Birch tossed a cursory glance over his shoulder. Ivy looked, too, and so did Hath.

Birch shook his head. "No. Why?"

"She seems to know you. She's been sneaking glances at you all during dinner."

"That's Amy Beth," said Hath. "Ambrose Clarkson's youngest daughter."

This time Birch turned in his chair to get a better look. He shrugged his shoulders. "I don't know her," he said.

At that moment the young girl rose and sauntered

across the room heading for their table. Her dress was lowcut made of crisp white cambric embroidered with small pink roses. Her petticoats swished as she moved across the floor. She approached Birch and stopped.

"Hello," she said without a smile speaking directly to him. She was small with a pert face and a tiny waist. Dark lashes fanned out over startling aquamarine eyes. "Have we met?"

Birch smiled politely and stood. "No, I don't recall so."

Her eyes narrowed, suspicious and questioning. "You look familiar. I'm sure I've seen you before. I just can't recall where." The words fell from her lips like chips of ice.

"No, ma'am. I'm afraid you're mistaken."

She hesitated as if trying to read the truth behind his eyes. From the taut look on her face, Tally could tell Amy Beth was running possibilities through her mind. There was a long moment of silence during which Birch slanted a look at Ivy who was shooting arrows from her eyes at the intruder.

Still unconvinced, Amy Beth stood looking at him, her eyes locked on his face. After a long moment of doubt, she spoke. "Last year on a trip to Denver my stagecoach was robbed by a highwayman just outside of town. His eyes were the same as yours. That strange color."

A minute change in Birch's expression signaled a sharpening of attention. The corners of his mouth quivered and his smile turned into a sour grin. "No," he said, his tone hardened.

A shadow crossed his face, quickly replaced by another smile that looked almost sincere. He snorted a laugh and turned grandly to the others at the table. "It appears I have a doppelganger," he said archly. His false laughter suggested Amy Beth had just told a joke. He continued with deep sarcasm. "And apparently he's enjoying a better financial position than I, having robbed a stagecoach."

His amused chuckling ended abruptly, and he turned back to Amy Beth, tense but still grinning.

"I'm afraid my eye color is quite normal and not uncommon." He spoke fast, his voice deceptively cheerful, scorn contorting his face. "But I'm afraid you've made a mistake. I don't know you. You have me mixed up with someone else."

Just then the band struck up a European waltz, and a few couples drifted onto the dance floor. Ivy immediately stood and tugged Birch's sleeve.

"Dance with me, Birch." It was much more than a mere request.

"Of course," he said taking her hand and leading her to the dance floor leaving Amy to walk away glowering.

A deep sense of unease invaded Tally's mind adding to the anxiety already residing there. She thought she heard a lie behind Birch's words, saw one capture his face. Was she mistaken? Was she being unfairly judgmental of him? Were her suspicions baseless?

She wanted to ask Hath those questions and talk to him about what just happened, but he was deep in conversation with a neighboring rancher about the rising cost of animal feed. She steadied her breathing and watched him with waning patience hoping for a chance to politely interrupt. But their conversation went on and on, their voices beginning to drawl with drink.

She turned, startled, when a hand gripped her wrist. It was Mimi.

"Come with me," she said.

"But—" Tally shot Hath a quick glance hoping to catch his eye, but his back was turned and he was waving his arm, gesturing to make a point. Her chair scraped back with a screech when Mimi pulled her to her feet.

"Just come. I'll tell you why on the way."

CHAPTER THIRTY

THE LIVELY TEMPO OF a Texas Schottische drew more couples to the dance floor allowing Tally and Mimi to slip away without much notice.

"But where are we going?" asked Tally.

"Shhhh. Here's your shawl. I'll tell you outside." Mimi quick-stepped Tally along a corridor, their thin-soled dress boots barely making a sound on the worn wooden floorboards.

At the rear of the building an unlocked door opened onto a dirt alleyway. Dusk had thickened to night and they were thrust into darkness when they stepped outside. Though evening temperatures were still relatively mild, a sudden gust of chill wind forced them to draw in their shawls.

"Why all the secrecy? Where are we going?" Tally asked again, more insistent this time, stepping lively to keep up with Mimi.

"To the Land Office."

"But it's closed." Tally's thoughts tumbled away from her misgivings about Birch and refocused on what Mimi said. "What are we going to do? Break in?"

"We're not going to break in. I have a key." Mimi's reply was muffled in the folds of her wrap, but Tally heard her.

"Wait a minute." She slowed bringing them to a halt behind the hardware store. "Why do you have a key to the

Land Office?"

Clouds partially uncovered the moon illuminating Mimi's face. "Pettyjohn gave it to me." Her eyes darted away from Tally's and back again.

Tally frowned. "He did?"

Mimi nodded, but said nothing more by way of explanation.

Not completely sure she was understanding the implication of Mimi's words, Tally merely blinked and said a quizzical, "Oh."

"Upstairs in his rooms, I..."

"Ohhhh," Tally said again stretching out the word on a melodic breathy note as Mimi's unspoken implication surfaced on a wave of understanding. "I see."

Mimi shifted from one foot to the other and faint crow's feet rayed out from her eyes. "It... was a long time ago... I guess he forgot he gave it to me."

Tally could tell it was an embarrassing admission.

"I actually forgot I had it myself until yesterday," Mimi went on. "I found it at the bottom of my jewelry box." She stopped talking then stared anxiously at Tally waiting for her to say something.

When Tally remained silent, Mimi pulled her shawl tighter and her face softened with apology. "You're my friend. I suppose I should have told you about my... past. I'm sorry, but like I said, it was so long ago and..."

"Stop!" Tally threw up her hands and waggled them back and forth as if clearing the air of Mimi's words. "Really. No need to apologize or say any more about it. Everyone has secrets they don't share with others." She widened her eyes in understanding hoping to convey that she truly did understand, because she herself had a secrets of her own.

To get past the moment, Tally grinned devilishly and leaned in like a conspirator. "So," she said. "What are we going to do? Steal something?"

"Only if we have to," Mimi said. They resumed walking, taking care not to turn their ankles on the rocks or the dried mud ruts of wagon tracks. "I'm hoping we can get into his office to look at his papers. We might be able to find your father's original paperwork, or some hint about where he is now. Maybe we can even find a clue to who killed Frank Scott. He's the one who said he wanted to talk to you about your father. Who knows what we'll find."

Tally couldn't help but see the reasonableness of that, so using their shawls to partially hide their faces and avoid being recognized, they crossed the main street, and hurried along a side road, then cut through the open space behind a row of buildings. Foggy mist thick as a cloud descended to earth.

"Here it is." Mimi approached a door behind a long run of buildings and turned the key. The lock clicked and she opened the door, but didn't step in. With her hand on the latch, she turned to Tally.

"I hope you understand," she started to explain again. "About Pettyjohn... It was years ago, and..."

"Oh, shush," Tally said pushing past Mimi through the open door. "Are we going to do this or not? With nearly everyone in town half drunk in a saloon or at the Founder's Day Dance, this might be our only chance. Let's take advantage of it and see what we can find out."

A lantern hung on the wall just inside the door next to a rack with hooks for coats and hats. To the right, a stairway led up to another door. Shelves covered nearly every inch of wall space. It was a storage room.

Mimi took down the lantern, lit it, then turned the flame low. Document boxes with hinged tops filled the shelves. The cabinet was so full of boxes, the doors did not close all the way. Every box was marked with a handwritten label. *Homestead Lands.*

Mimi put the lantern on top of the cabinet after which they each opened boxes and browsed through the documents inside.

Tally squinted in the dim light. "I can't make heads nor tails of the coding system and abbreviations he used on these forms."

"I can't, either." Mimi replaced the document she'd been reading and returned the box to its place on the shelf.

Tally scanned and quickly replaced the documents she'd removed, but something caught her eye on the last one and she kept reading. After a moment, she looked up. "Do you know what these letters stand for? SY and RSY and CSF."

"No, but those same letters are on some of the documents I looked at, too. I have no idea what they mean."

"Could they be the initials of the person who applied for the patent? Do you know anyone with those initials?"

Mimi frowned and shook her head. "No. But I don't think they refer to a name. Pettyjohn used those same letters in other places on those forms, too. Sometimes in the margins."

"Yes, I noticed that, too." Dejected, Tally trained her gaze over the shelves and settled on the stack of document boxes on the floor lined up along the wall. "We don't have time to go through all these."

"No," Mimi agreed. She closed the top of the box she was looking through and put it back on the shelf. "Let's try Pettyjohn's desk."

Straight ahead an open doorway led into the office that fronted the boardwalk. Pettyjohn's desk faced the windows. The shades were only half drawn giving a partial view of the activities in the street.

Mimi found a pry tool in a toolbox on a shelf. Holding the lantern at knee level, she led the way to Pettyjohn's desk. Raucous laughter sounded from outside as two cowboys staggered by on the boardwalk. A spark of panic froze them in place. The cowboys passed so close to the windowpane, Tally could have reached out and touched the brims of their hats.

When the sound of their voices diminished, they stepped out of the shadows. Using the pry tool, Mimi levered open the locked desk drawers then did the same with a metal chest in a corner behind the desk.

"Let's hurry before they miss us at the dance. I'll start with the desk. You take the chest. Stay low." Mimi positioned the lantern on the floor providing a dim circle of light to work by.

Tally knelt beside the metal chest and removed bundled files while Mimi looked through the desk drawers. The only sound in the room was the dry shuffle of papers.

"I still can't figure out Pettyjohn's filing system," complained Talley.

"It doesn't seem to make sense." Mimi was seated in the chair behind the desk hunched over the drawers, fingers flying. "Some files are sorted alphabetical by name, others by number, others by date and others by those odd codes. SY, RSY and CSF."

Tally stood, put her hands behind her hips and stretched her back. "I noticed one thing, though. Quite a few of the parcels were registered in the same surname. Others were identified by a code instead of a name."

"Patents with the same claim name could mean that members of the same family chose adjoining properties," said Mimi. "That's legal, but the Homestead Act prohibits investors from scooping up huge plots of land." She shook her head, frustrated. "I wish I knew what the numbers and codes meant."

Dejected, Tally returned the files she'd searched to the chest and closed it. "I didn't find anything in my father's name or mine."

Mimi closed the desk drawers and stood. "Let's go upstairs. I think Pettyjohn kept some files in his rooms." They went up the back stairway. Mimi unlocked the door and they entered Pettyjohn's private quarters.

"Government officials live well," said Tally admiring the thick brocade window coverings. She ran her fingers over a velvet settee with matching daybed, and a sturdy walnut dining table she wished she had in the cabin. The door to the adjoining bedroom was ajar providing a view of a highboy bed covered with Indian blankets and a puffy feather quilt. A hairbrush, razor and shaving mug were neatly arranged on a porcelain tray atop a clothes chest.

Mimi went straight to the mahogany rolltop desk. The flexible sliding shutter rattled when she opened it. "Well," she whispered after a moment, sounding pleased and surprised. "Look at this!"

Tally tiptoed over. "What? What did you find?"

"A plat map! It shows how the sections and lots are divided up on the public land available for homesteading around Sutton Creek."

She unrolled the map on the dining table smoothing it out with her hands. Tally held down two of the corners to keep the stiff paper from rolling up again. Thinking out loud Mimi studied the map.

"Here's the main street through town and these are the proved up lots behind the business section." She moved her finger. "Here's where the homesteads outside the town proper begin."

Tally followed with her eyes as Mimi's hand moved on the map.

"That's strange," Tally said. "Going west beyond the town limits toward my place, it looks like most of the parcels are proved up." She paused. "Except for mine, the plots surrounding mine and everything beyond…"

She drifted off in thought.

Then she saw something else unexpected. "Look here. The original names are crossed out on some of them with someone else's name written instead."

Mimi looked where Tally had skewered her finger. "And they're all noted with those letter codes. All the parcels all the way over to…" Mimi unrolled more of the map. "Here. This big section over here where the railroad land grants begin. It's marked CFS."

"But what does CFS mean?"

"I don't know," Mimi said, deflated.

"I recognize some of the names on some of these lots. I made dresses for women with the same last names." Tally pointed out a few.

"They're married to investors and railroad executives," said Mimi. "And it looks like they have multiple parcels."

"I thought you said investors weren't allowed to acquire the land set aside for homesteading."

Mimi shrugged and looked at Tally with a helpless expression. "Sometimes the law doesn't quite work. In reality, people can do anything if they shake the right hands and make the right promises. Failing that, bribes work."

Tally looked up quickly. "Do you think Pettyjohn was accepting bribes?"

"He might have been," said Mimi, "and that might have something to do with why he was killed."

"Could be. People have been killed for less." Tally studied the map, then tapped her finger on it. "Do you know whose name this is on my father's parcel?"

Mimi peered at it. "No. I can't read Pettyjohn's writing. But it's coded RSY."

Noise from the street drifted up, and the women locked eyes. Carousers hollering and laughing. The rumble of wagons passing by. A horse whinnied.

"Let's go," said Tally.

Mimi nodded. "The map is too big to take with me. Someone will notice me carrying it." She rolled it up and put it back on the desk and closed the shutter. "I wish we had a copy of it. Maybe we can get one from Washington."

"That will take weeks, if not months."

"Unless the Department of the Interior sent a copy to the District Land Office in Denver." Mimi's eyes widened with hope.

Tally's spirits lifted. "I have friends in Denver. I'll see if someone can get one for us." She picked up the lantern and they headed for the door.

"Wait a minute," Mimi said, detouring into the bedroom. She widened the door, went down on one knee and reached under the bed for a leather pouch stuffed with papers. She pulled it out and tucked it under her shawl.

"I don't know what this is, but there might be something useful in here. I'll take it straight home, and read it tonight. Tomorrow, so we can go through it together."

"Good idea."

"But until then, let's not tell anyone what we saw here. No one. Not yet."

Tally swallowed hard and looked away. She'd come to trust Hath and was used to sharing many things with him during long conversations. Getting his ideas and input, having him help her solve problems on the homestead. Her questions always brought a dozen more from him, but almost always answers, too. Together, they came up with workable solutions. If she told him about the plat map and the codes, he might know what they mean.

"Not even Hath," Mimi added, as if reading Tally's mind. Her face was serious and her eyes glittered. "Let's wait until we know more. We need time to consider what it all means before we discuss this with anyone. We don't know who we can trust right now."

"Surely you don't think that Hath—"

"Just until tomorrow." Mini patted the leather pouch concealed in her shawl. "There might be something in here that will answer all our questions. And don't forget," she added in an undertone. "We just broke into a government office. Penalties for that are severe."

Tally opened her mouth to object further when the sound of gunfire and breaking glass from out front ended the conversation. There were laws against using airborne bottles as targets, but the rowdies felt it was an infringement on their rights to give up gunplay in the streets, so the sport continued.

Mimi locked the back door and the two of them hurried away. "Can you get back to the dance alone?" Mimi asked.

"Yes. I'll be fine. I'm not afraid." She touched the pistol at her hip.

They said good night, touched cheeks briefly in farewell, then Mimi disappeared into the darkness.

Lightning crawled the night sky above the buildings as Tally made her way back over the pebble strewn side roads. When she reached the Spanish-tiled patio of the Social Center, she heard the band playing, but the music couldn't drown out the sounds of sharp, angry voices. At the entrance to the ballroom, she was greeted by a raging brawl.

Groups of people spilled out into the corridor heading for the door. She spotted Hath right away pushing his way through, his mouth a hard line on a pained face. His fingers were around Ivy's upper arm as he hurried her away from the men pounding each other, some of them on the floor. One of the men tripped to all fours while trying to get away and his opponent took that opportunity to kick him in the ribs.

Ivy's face was red from crying, her breathe coming in sobs. Birch followed holding a blood-soaked handkerchief to his face.

"Where have you been?" Hath shouted at Tally over the uproar.

But before she could answer, Ivy pulled away from Hath's grip and flung herself into Tally's open arms.

"What happened?" Tally asked as the four of them scurried down the boardwalk to the livery.

"That girl," said Ivy, chuffing her breath and speaking between choking sobs. "Her brother..." Unable to go on Ivy's words dissolved in tears.

Tally looked at Birch for an answer, but he was still holding a bloody cloth to his mouth, so Hath explained.

"Amy Beth Clarkson. Her brother Collin came over and picked an argument with Birch. About the stagecoach robbery. Birch told Collin to shut up and..."

"And what? Collin hit him?"

Hath's words snapped out. "No. Birch swung first."

This instantly animated Ivy who raised her voice coming to Birch's defense. "He had it coming, Hath, and you know it. He said some frightful things. He said that Birch—"

"All right, all right," Tally shouted cutting her off. There was ice in her voice, but she couldn't help it. She gave Birch a murderous look, then took in a hard breath and let it out through her nose, anxiety burning inside. "Let's just get ourselves home. We can argue about who started it later."

Ghost-like mist twined through the evergreens. No one spoke on the ride home. Holding the reins with firm hands, Hath looked straight ahead, stiff jawed and stone-faced, peeved. Birch and Ivy huddled together on the back bench where after a few whispered words they remained silent. It had been a day of surprises, confusion, and tangled emotions. All Tally wanted to do when she got home was put on her nightclothes and crawl into bed.

CHAPTER THIRTY-ONE

*M*IMI DUCKED INTO THE shadows behind Gallagher's General Store clutching the document pouch, her heart pounding. She was being followed, she was sure of it. Her skin rippled with the touch of invisible eyes. Yet she saw nothing, no one.

Piano music tinkled out the wide-open doors of the saloons making it impossible to hear anything else, like the furtive sound of footsteps on dirt or the clack of stones disturbing each other. She waited a long moment, then lifted her petticoats and removed the derringer from her thigh holster. No need to check its load. It was always loaded. With her pistol in one hand and the document pouch in the other, she waited in the shadows. When she felt it was safe to go on, she stepped back into the alleyway. She hadn't gone two steps when a man with a kerchief over his face lunged forward and grabbed the pouch. As he turned to run, she pulled the trigger without aiming and sent a lucky shot into his hand. He yelped in pain and dropped the pouch, but before he could pick it up, she cocked the hammer and shot again. He clutched his side and staggered back.

Mimi snatched the pouch back and headed off across the flats through mists of fog toward the abandoned trading post hoping to reach a hiding place before the man, whoever he was, caught up to her. She ran blindly, instinctively dodging the sharp, spiny branches of woody shrubs and low-lying clumps of hedgehog cactus.

Her boot caught on a broken clump of earth painfully twisting her ankle as she sprawled in the dirt, but managed to hold on to both the pouch and the pistol scraping the skin off her knuckles in the process. She was almost to the rocky rise when she fell a second time, the forward motion sending her skidding over rocks and hard packed earth. The derringer tumbled from her hand. The leather strings enclosing the pouch snapped allowing loose sheets of paper to fall out and be carried away by the wind. Blood rose from cuts and scrapes on her legs and arms and the palm of her hands.

She wiped her hands on skirt, retrieved the derringer by the light of a half moon, and made it to a hiding place in the rocks, the same one where Frank Scott had died. There she hunkered down gasping for breath. Lights flickered from distant windows in town, but not a sound made its way over the bare stretch of ground to where she crouched trembling and in pain. Gingerly, she lifted her skirt to check the torn flesh and sticky wetness on her shins and knees. All she could do was blot up the blood with the fabric of her fancy gown. Her knee throbbed and her ankle was beginning to swell. She could stand and walk if she didn't put too much weight on her leg, but running was out of the question.

Unless he was gut shot, she knew she hadn't killed that man. Her little pocket pistol was meant to stop someone, not take a life. Chances were he wasn't even hurt all that bad. For all she knew, he could be on his way right now tracking her down while she sat shaking, trying to catch her breath, fire burning in her knee, clutching Pettyjohn's now near empty document pouch.

Slowly she rose from her hiding place, took one step and then another.

CHAPTER THIRTY-TWO

*T*HE BARN DOGS, HOBO and Buck, set up a racket and raced over to greet the wagon as it rumbled into the yard on its return from the Founder's Day Dance. Wren yelled at them to quiet down, his voice peppered with a wide assortment of salty words. Hath reined to a stop in front of the cabin and the men helped the women down. Birch stalked off without a word. Hath went to the barn to unhitch Champion, tend to the harness, and stow the wagon.

Inside the cabin it was quiet, the dogs had not roused Jenny or Anna asleep in Ivy's room. Ivy expected Tally to go straight to bed like she said she would, but instead she stomped to the cupboard, took out a bottle of whiskey, thumped it on the table and waited for Hath to come in. When he did, they huddled together in fretful conversation, their voices dropped to whispers. Tally was prickly around the tongue, her words heavy with grievance as she told him what she and Mimi had found in the Land Office. Hath spoke low and slow fluctuating between words of concern and those meant to soothe her.

In the bedroom she shared with Tally, Ivy changed into an everyday cotton dress and thick-soled boots. She wasn't able to hear all of the muffled conversation through the closed door, but she heard names. Madame Simone, Pettyjohn, Clarkson. Then something about questionable homestead allotments and coded documents. Ivy wondered briefly what that meant and if it mattered, but it was a mere eye blink in her mind, in and out before it could take hold. Its significance made little impression focused as she was on Prayer Rock where Birch was waiting.

The conversation at the table clipped off mid-sentence when she came out of the bedroom wrapped in her shawl. Anger pinched Tally's face. A worried frown replaced Hath's usually cheerful expression. Trepidation hung over the cabin like a shroud.

Ivy lit a lantern by the door saying that what happened at the dance was so disturbing only prayer could ease her troubled mind. Ordinarily Tally would have objected to her leaving the cabin so late in the night—*it was dark, it was cold, it was dangerous*—but this time she did little more than glance up and nod in response. Ivy closed the door behind her, but before it latched she heard Tally tell Hath she wanted to talk to Birch about what happened at the dance.

Ivy wanted to talk to Birch about that, too.

When Amy Beth Clarkson recognized Birch, reality rushed in like a blow to the chest and Ivy knew instantly they couldn't wait until Birch dug up the gold to leave. Amy Beth would tell her father, point a finger at Birch as the man who robbed the stage at Bandit Bend. Her father would immediately tell the sheriff if he hadn't already. Then Birch would go to prison.

The thought sucked the air from her lungs.

So they had to leave right away. Tomorrow. Tonight maybe. She was ready. She'd packed her travel bag and hidden it under a pile of blankets on the floor of the bedroom, so she could sneak out with it after everyone was asleep.

Careful of her footing in the dark and the thickening fog, she hurried to the prayer bench only to find that Birch wasn't there. She huffed an impatient breath, touched the rose beads at her neck, and sat down to wait. Automatically, her eyes went to the shed and the excavated crawl space beneath.

Of course, they could always come back for the gold, but leaving without it would be a problem. She knew where Tally hid their reserve homestead funds and could dip her hand in for some traveling money if need be. Tally would miss it eventually, but by then they'd be gone. If Birch had a little money put away they might have enough to make it as far as New Mexico or Texas. Maybe all the way to California.

A spasm of guilt gripped her. She would be leaving Tally to a drab future of drudgery on the homestead and sewing dresses for wealthy women. Women who never looked at her again after the dresses were made, and who barely made eye contact with her during the making. But she dismissed the thought with a flick of her mind. When she was set up somewhere with Birch, she would send for Tally.

But where was he?

Doubt crept in and her shoulders drooped. Had he changed his mind? Had he already left? *Was he going to ruin everything?*

Unsettled as a cat, she shifted position on the bench and struggled to tamp down her burgeoning anxiety. She'd seen through Birch's eyes a whole new life for herself. But she knew that even though she fought to keep the fire of hope burning in her mind, all the newfound certainties of her future put there by him could quickly be turned to ashes by him, as well.

A light wind blew through, sending leaves skittering across the ground. Deep shadows gathered around Prayer Rock and the bench where she sat taking deep breaths to forestall the tears of disappointment burning the back of her throat.

The barn dogs were stirred up again. She couldn't see them, but she could hear them whining, and the clink of their chains as they paced. Wren yelled at them again, then it fell quiet. He must have unchained them and taken them inside the barn. Maybe coyotes close by. Ivy's eyes darted around, and she remembered her encounter with the bear in the berry patch, hoping that now she wasn't the next meal for some night creature.

The earlier shreds of mist that drifted by like so many ghosts thickened into a mountain of fog, and she could barely see the barn or the lamplit windows of the cabin through the trees. She hated the fog. It was disorienting with no landmarks to lock eyes on and nothing to cling to. She felt imprisoned by it.

Then, the scrape of boot on stone, and a rustle that wasn't the wind. She peered through the shadows between the cabin and Prayer Rock. In what should have been a stretch of open ground something stood, black on black.

Her heart swelled with relief and she released her compacted breath. "Birch!" she whispered. "Thank God! What took you so long? We have to—"

A big man wide as a gate and holding a gun appeared out of the fog. Too late she stood and clapped her hand on her pistol.

"Don't," he said and hammered her knuckles with the butt of his weapon. The hard blow cracked tiny bones sending searing pain up her arm paralyzing her fingers.

She opened her mouth to scream, but from behind a cloth gag was jammed between her teeth and cinched around her head strangling the sound. She whimpered and cradled her agonized hand with the other. The big man in front yanked her gun out of her holster and stuck it in his belt.

Terrified, she tried to run away, but the man behind

her clamped an arm around her waist and held on stopping her. Stiffening the fingers of her good hand into a claw, she reached over her head trying to tear at his face, but couldn't reach him. In full panic, she twisted and squirmed trying to break his hold, but his grip tightened crushing her ribs.

"Stop fighting," he said. "Do what you're told and you won't get hurt."

His voice carried an accent, harsh, brusque, Germanic. She felt his breath on her ear and her stomach turned over.

A foul-smelling burlap sack was tugged over her head and pulled tight almost cutting off her air. Desperate to get away, she thrust her leg backward, kicking wildly until her booted foot connected with a leg. The man behind her grunted and cussed, and his grip loosened a little, but steely fingers yanked her back and held fast. Still she fought, her feet scrabbling for purchase in the loose dirt and stones.

Unwilling to give up, she continued to flail and kick until the man that took her gun smacked her with the back of his hand, big knuckles like sharp little pebbles against the side of her head. She jerked back and went straight down, the blow igniting bolts of lightning behind her eyes that swirled inside her head.

"She was waiting for someone," one of the men said. "We gotta get her outta here before they show up."

A rope around her middle pinned her arms to her sides. Another one looped around her ankles. The throbbing in her head kept time with the pain pulsing in her hand. Dead fear took over and she struggled but failed to stay conscious.

CHAPTER THIRTY-THREE

*T**ALLY TIPPED THE BOTTLE* over her glass again. At a nod from Hath she replenished his glass, too. Night wind buffeted the cabin. A log moved in the fireplace hissing and popping as it fell.

"Are you sure no one saw you and Mimi going into Pettyjohn's office?" Hath asked not for the first time.

"I told you. No. We were careful."

He shook his head and looked at her in bewilderment, also not for the first time. "Breaking into a government office. What were you thinking?"

"I was thinking I'd get answers to questions I wasn't getting anywhere else. Questions I maybe didn't even know to ask." She sat back in her chair, indignant but a little contrite at the same time. "It was Mimi's idea," she added, unwilling to take full responsibility for the decision, but at the same time feeling guilty about it.

"But you could go to..."

"I know, I know. Prison."

"Both of you."

She let out a long sigh.

Hath got up and stood by the window looking out into the moonlit yard. He gave his holster a hitch and let it settle back onto his hips, then turned and went to her still slumped morosely in her chair. "It's going to be all right," he said. "Don't worry."

His assurances didn't have the intended effect, because when she met his eyes she could see the doubt behind the promise. Swallowing a sob, she put her elbow on the table and rested her forehead in her palm. "I just don't want to lose my father's homestead. It meant everything to him, and if he's not..." She couldn't bring herself to say the word *dead*. "He was so proud to have an opportunity to own a piece of the American West."

Hath came around the table, went down on one knee beside her chair, and took her into his arms. Unashamedly, she slid her arms around his neck, and they held each other a long time until she pulled away.

He got up, sat across from her again, and cupped his hands around his glass as they both fell into their own thoughts.

Her mind was restless, seeking answers that kept evading her. "The more I find out and the more I think I know, the more I realize I *don't* know," she said after a while. "I'm hoping Mimi finds something in Pettyjohn's papers."

He reached across the table, lifted her hand, kissed her fingers and held on. "You might have to go down to the Denver Land Office to get your answers. And if something unscrupulous is going on here, they'll surely want to know about it. I'll go with you. You can count on me, Tally. I know you've been let down in the past, but I'll always be here for you."

She believed him. She believed that he'd always be there for her, all she had to do was let go of the past and open her heart all the way. She took in his handsome face and the strands of grey in his hair at the temples. The eyes that crinkled when he smiled, the laugh lines that showed when he laughed out loud. She'd noticed women at the Founder's Day dance outdoing each other trying to catch his eye.

Her affection for him grew stronger along with gratitude for his steadfastness. There were times when that meant the world to her, but also times when it frightened her, frightened her that it might become a controlling force.

"Thank you." Holding on to his hands taking comfort in the warmth and strength that flowed from them, she kissed his fingers in return just as he'd kissed hers.

"Madame Simone was right," she said. "About the danger. I knew that much already before I went to see her, but she confirmed it. She said there was a shadow over the homestead. She said I'm being deceived by someone. But she didn't say who or how or why."

Outside, hurried footsteps pounded up the steps and across the porch. Both Tally and Hath bounced to their feet, but before either could pull their weapon, the door burst open and Birch rushed in, his amber eyes dark, his face bunched up into a scowl.

"What?" Tally asked, startled. "What is it, Birch?"

Birch's eyes glided around the room. "Is Ivy here?" His voice was urgent and he sounded out of breath, like he'd been running.

"No. She went out to Prayer Rock." Tally noticed Ivy's shawl in Birch's hand and she pointed at it. "What's wrong?" she said sharply. "What happened?"

Words came out of his mouth with reluctance. "I... I don't know. We were supposed to ... uh... meet... at..." He stopped and took in a breath. "At the Prayer Rock, but when I got there, she was... gone." He held up the shawl. "I found this on the ground."

Tally blinked and stared at him, bewildered.

"What do you mean *gone?*" Her voice rose in exasperation, a vague sense of unease invaded her mind nudged by a whirlwind of conflicting emotions that left her breathless. "Why was she meeting you there?" She waited for him to say something.

Birch lowered his eyes as if his answer was written on the wood plank floor beneath his boots. More than a silence, a great stillness settled in the room.

Hath spoke up breaking the tension encompassing them. "All right. She must be around. Did you look for her?"

Birch nodded. "Yes, and I called for her."

"Well, she couldn't have gone far without her shawl," said Hath. "It's dark out and foggy. And cold."

Tally gripped the edge of the table to still a creeping sensation threatening to overtake her. It was almost like being smothered, like being crushed from the inside out. She took the shawl from Birch's hand. It was covered with ground in dirt. It looked stepped on.

Her eyes bored into his maintaining unflinching contact. "I asked you. Why was she meeting you?"

"We..." Birch began. "We were..."

He didn't go on. Instead, his eyes went from Tally to Hath, then back to Tally and held defiantly. Still, he said nothing.

But he didn't have to. He'd said *we*, a word that could only mean he and Ivy. Together. In a moment of startled realization, the answer came to her. She regarded him in cold silence, anger expanding her chest as she waited for him to confirm what she already suspected.

"Go on," she said, accelerating the conversation and raising its volume. "You were going to do *what,* exactly?"

Just then the bedroom door creaked open and Jenny came out closing her robe over her sleep clothes, peering at them with sleep interrupted eyes. Loose hairs dislodged from her braid hung to her shoulders in messy disarray. "What's going on? Why is everyone up?"

Tally collected herself and straightened her shoulders trying to calm herself, or at least appear that way to Jenny. She didn't want to add additional distress to her new friend. Jenny was still recovering from a gunshot wound. She was in mourning. The poor woman had lost her husband and her home.

"It's Ivy," she said keeping the dread out of her voice, unwilling to let Jenny see her alarm. "It seems she's gone out in the fog and we don't know where she is."

Jenny's eyes widened. "Oh, no…"

"But we'll find her." Tally managed to put up a brave front, somehow ridding her voice of the fear nipping at her heart. "She's probably in the barn talking to Wren or playing with the dogs and just forgot to tell us where she went. You know how she is." She turned to Hath and Birch. "Come on. Let's go ask Wren if he's seen her."

"I'll stay here in case she comes back while you're out there," said Jenny. "And since we're up anyway, I'll put coffee on."

"Yes, please." Holding her head high, Tally strode to the door taking up her shawl and lighting a lantern before opening the door.

In the barn, Wren rolled off his cot, grabbed his rifle and aimed when their boot soles stomped into the barn. He lowered it when he realized who it was. "Is everything all right?"

Tally struggled to keep her voice strong and steady, trying to convince herself there was no cause for alarm despite Ivy's dirt-streaked shawl in her hand telling her there was.

"Is Ivy here?" She flicked her eyes around the barn as if Ivy might be hiding there in the shadows.

Wren, bleary eyed, still shaking off sleepiness, shook his head. "No, why?"

When she told him, Wren immediately put down his rifle, snatched up his holster and buckled it on. "The dogs made a ruckus a while back. I went out to look around, but I didn't see anything, so I'm sure she's all right." He holstered his pistol and picked up his rifle. "But let's go take a look."

All four of them shouted out for Ivy as Tally led the way to Prayer Rock, dread in her stomach making her nauseous.

The fog was beginning to shred a little, but still they stuck close together as they made their way in the dark over uneven terrain. When they arrived, Tally raised her lantern aloft and everyone scoured the ground in the light cast by the flame. A mass of boot prints, some large, some small, churned up dirt indicating a struggle had taken place. Her stomach sank to her feet when her lantern illuminated the patch of ground surrounding the prayer bench and she tried to turn what she was seeing into something else.

Wren lifted his lantern and motioned the others to stay behind. "Stand back. I've done some tracking. Let me look around."

The others stood still as his eyes swept the ground. After a moment, he bent down, picked up a rose gold bead necklace and held it out to show the others.

"That's Ivy's." Tally's voice rose in pitch and broke on a sob.

Hath spoke up, urgent and demanding. "Let's get some lanterns and saddle up. We'll ride out to look for her."

The men instantly turned and ran for the barn. Tally lifted her skirts to follow, but Hath called to her over his shoulder. "Stay at the cabin with Jenny and Anna."

"No, I'm going with you."

Hath stopped and grasped her arm to stop her. "No. Stay. If Ivy comes back while we're gone, she's going to need you." His look was dark and full of meaning.

A burst of angry impatience rolled through her, but he was right. Overcoming her reluctance, she changed direction and ran up the path to the cabin instead.

Jenny was sitting at the table, looking troubled. "Did you find her?" she asked when Tally came in.

"No. The men are going to ride out to look for her." Tally held up the broken necklace. "This is Ivy's. Wren found it in the dirt by the prayer bench."

Jenny eyes widened, and her chest rose and fell in a long slow breath. The gaze they exchanged lasted a second too long and delivered a message that needn't be spoken. *That's not good... That's bad and could be very bad.*

She eased her arm around Tally's shoulders. "Here, why don't you sit down? I'll make you a cup of coffee."

Tally accepted the cup, but didn't sit. Instead, she stood glumly staring out the window. Within minutes she saw lantern lights bouncing through the trees, heard the men ride away talking to each other and calling for Ivy.

Time passed. The room, lit only by the fireplace, became a vast bubble of silence broken only by the occasional snap of a log. They didn't speak. Every once in a while, Tally's eyes flicked nervously toward the door expecting Ivy to come through at any moment. Foreboding was a weight in the room. Jenny looked like she was praying, head bowed, hands folded in her lap.

The dogs started up again, warning growls at an unseen threat. Jenny stirred in her chair, and Tally put her cup on the saucer with a clink. Her hand hovered over her hip, ready to grab her pistol. Something was out there. One of the men? A bear? A stranger who didn't belong?

Someone moved in the weak moonlight filtering through what was left of the fog. A figure, slightly hunched, creeping slowly from tree to bush to shadow. Coming closer.

"Lock the door," Tally whispered. "Someone's coming."

Jenny jumped out of her chair, then Tally yelled again.

"No, wait! It's Ivy!"

Gushing with relief, Tally threw the door wide, then gasped and blinked in disbelief as the figure collapsed on the porch steps.

"Mimi!" she cried. "What happened to you?"

CHAPTER THIRTY-FOUR

*T*ALLY CLEANED THE DIRT and blood from Mimi's cuts and scrapes. Her eyes scrunched up and she winced in pain, but still she insisted, "I'm all right."

"Well, you don't look all right," Tally replied and gentled her touch even more.

While Jenny was outside gathering the papers Mimi dropped when she collapsed on the porch, Tally told Mimi about Ivy and filled her in on the disturbance at the dance.

Jenny came in, squared off the fly blown pages and set them on the table in a neat pile. "I'm pretty sure I have everything from the front porch and yard."

Mimi eyed the depleted stack mournfully. "I'm sorry, but I lost some of the papers when I fell running away from that man."

Tally rinsed and wrung the washcloth then dumped the water and refilled the pan. "Do you know who it was?"

"No. It was dark, and I couldn't see him very well."

Tally took off Mimi's dirty shoes and stockings, and eased her swollen feet into a pan of water warmed over the logs in the fireplace. "There," she said. "That should make your feet feel better, at least."

Mimi let out a long sigh. "It does. Thank you."

When Tally finished tending to Mimi's wounds, she said, "Well, that's the best I can do until I get more supplies. At least I have all the raw skin covered. That should give you some relief. Doc should probably take a look at you tomorrow." She cast a discerning eye at Mimi's dirt-stained dress. "You need to change clothes, too. I have something you can wear until we can get some of your own clothes here."

"Thank you," Mimi replied. "I'll bring it back to you tomorrow."

Tally shook her head. "I don't think you should go home right away. It might be safer for you to stay here. At least for a while. Those men might be watching for you." She motioned to her bedroom. "You can sleep in there."

Tally dried Mimi's feet, then took her arm to help her stand, but Mimi shrugged her off. "I'm fine, really." She stood up on her own, but shakily, then grasped Tally's shoulder to steady herself. "It's Ivy you need to worry about. How long have the men been out looking for her?"

Tally glanced out the window. It was still pitch dark with no sign of a coming dawn. "Seems like an hour or more."

After Mimi changed clothes, Tally put the whiskey bottle away, and the three women sat at the table. She slid the pile of documents Mimi had salvaged in front of her, briefly rifled through them, then handed over pages to the other two.

Jenny looked at them uncertainly. "What are these?"

"Homestead documents. Legal papers and patent requests and approvals. Not sure what else." Tally unfolded a hand drawn map, spread it out on the table.

Jenny scanned a few of the pages in her pile then asked, "But where did you get them?"

"The Land Office." Tally briefly explained what she and Mimi had found there, and why.

"But the Land Office is still closed."

Jenny looked first at Tally and then at Mimi, and when no one responded for a longish time her brows shot up and her eyes widened. "Oh," she said in belated understanding. "You stole them?" An amused smile tilted the corner of her eyes. "Do you know you could..."

"Yes! Go to prison!" Tally and Mimi answered at the same time.

Jenny nodded and her tiny smile was quickly replaced by a dead serious expression as she began scanning pages. "All right then. What exactly are we looking for?"

Tally shook her head. "I'm not sure. Just look for anything that doesn't seem right to you as a homesteader. Anything that appears to be outside the boundaries of the Homestead Act." She looked up. "You've read it, haven't you?"

"Yes. Homer and I read it together before we applied for a patent."

"Just look for anything that seems unusual or out of line. Anything that defeats the intent of the Act. Locate your plot on one of the maps. Based on what happened to your spread, I'm guessing someone else's name is on it."

Jenny perused the map, then frowned and jammed the tip of her finger on it. "Yes! Right here." She leaned in and squinted. "Our name is crossed out. Someone wrote in another name I don't recognize."

Tally set the map in the center of the table. Heads bent, the women scanned each document then passed it around for the others to look at. Correspondence, memos, railroad land leases, formal land grants, hand drawn maps, sketches and diagrams, legal descriptions. Lists of names, some scratched out with others written in.

Questions were asked and answered, possibilities considered. They made note of questions that had no immediate answers and set them aside to be researched later. The list grew long. Worry about Ivy weighed heavily on Tally's mind making it increasingly difficult to concentrate. She passed a handful of pages to Jenny, but something caught her eye.

"Wait. Let me see that," she said. "That last page."

Jennie handed it back and Tally read it again, more slowly this time. Then she looked up at Mimi. "Remember when we wondered what those codes meant?"

Mimi stopped reading. "Yes. You found something?"

Tally nodded. "Here's the explanation. It says SY stands for Stockyard, RSY stands for Railroad Stockyard, RS means Railroad Siding, and CSF designates a Cattle Shipping Facility."

"And here," Tally continued, tapping her finger on the map. "Here's the site of the proposed Railroad Stock Yard. See? It says RSY. Notice that the homestead sites between the stock yard and the shipping facility geographically block the way preventing the herds from reaching the railroad spur and the cars that would take them to market."

Jenny and Mimi listened in silence, their expressions hardening with understanding.

"And," Tally said with emphasis as her finger traced a path on the page, "most of those designated homesteads have been acquired or are marked for acquisition by an investment company with ties to the cattleman's group or the railroad investors." She frowned and went silent, her eyes locked on the map.

"What is it?" Mimi asked.

"This railroad spur." Her shoulders sagged and she shook her head in dismay. "It's positioned for direct access from the Cattle Shipping Facility. See here? The gate from the cattle run in the shipping facility leads directly to a railroad car." Her finger traced another line on the map. "The proposed train tracks follow the river right through these homesteads, and the junction leading to the shipping facility is right here on *my* land!"

The women stared at each other, momentarily speechless as pieces of the picture clunked into place. Silence lay heavy as comprehension took hold.

Mimi's eyes narrowed in anger. "I heard some cowboys talking about plans for a huge stockyard when the railroad got built so cattle could be shipped to market, but they didn't say where." She paused, anger tightening her features. "It's the cattlemen and the investors that are taking over that land! Land speculators!"

"You mean swindlers!" said Jenny.

"Fraudsters!" said Mimi.

"Thieves!" Tally spit out the word like a bad taste in her mouth. A balloon of silence expanded in the room.

Tally never cursed out loud, ever, but in her mind she could swear like a cowboy on a cattle drive if the occasion called for it and this one surely did. She was about to verbalize the words gathering on the back of her tongue when she heard the sound of horses outside. It was still dark, but there was a faint line of illumination along the eastern horizon. Through the trees she saw the men returning in the pale light. Ivy wasn't with them.

There was tension in the set of their shoulders when they came in the door, and she greeted them with a questioning look. Hath strode directly to her and put his arm around her shoulders.

"It's too dark to continue looking," he said, speaking gently. "In the morning, Birch and I will ride out and round up some neighbors to form a search party. Wren will go to town and nail up an announcement about Ivy, and bring back volunteers to help search. If there's still time, he'll have Eddie put something in the next edition of the newspaper. The more people we have helping us search, the better the odds of finding your sister."

Tally swallowed and nodded. What else could she do?

Hath looked at the others. "Until then, let's all get some sleep."

She nodded, breath catching. "Mimi can share my room."

Birch went to the bunkhouse. Wren headed for the barn. Jenny went in with Anna who was still sleeping.

Hath offered to sleep in the cabin in case the women needed him.

"Yes, please do," Tally said wearily.

Shaking with exhaustion, distress sagging her shoulders, she picked up the blankets piled in the corner of the bedroom. Fear wrenched through her when she saw Ivy's packed travel bag. She looked away swept by the realization that Ivy would have been safer if she had run away with Birch. It was impossible for Tally to deceive herself about what was so obvious given the condition of the area surrounding the Prayer Bench. Ivy hadn't wandered off or run away. She was taken.

Tally took a moment to settle herself before putting extra logs on the fire and helping Hath make up a cot for himself.

Mimi was already asleep when Tally went in. By sheer will she forced herself to lie down. She didn't think she would sleep, but she did.

CHAPTER THIRTY-FIVE

*I*VY SWAM UP THROUGH deep layers of sleep and pain. Hammers pounded inside her head, and pain clawed at her hand. Her throat was dry and her breath so heavy she felt like she was suffocating. The bitter taste in her mouth was tinged with something sweet like cinnamon syrup, like the medicine her mother gave her when she was little and had a cough. Opening her eyes, she tried to touch her forehead to see if she had a fever, but something tugged on her arm. She turned her throbbing head to see her wrist encased in a shackle. Alarmed, she called for Tally, but little more than a whisper passed her lips. She licked them and tasted crusted blood.

Frantically, she struggled to process her surroundings. The room shifted and tilted making everything blurry. Her vision swooped away, but when it returned she saw a closed door, wide planking on the floors, walls, and ceiling. Wooden slats boarded up a window. Daylight streamed in through the cracks showing bits of blue sky. She was laying on a padded cot, and though covered by a thin blanket her feet were cold.

Where am I?

Vague memories drifted up and pictures came together in her mind. Waiting for Birch at Prayer Rock. The barn dogs endless barking. Strange men appeared out of the fog. She kicked and fought, but they hit her and tied her up. Shoved a cloth in her mouth that had the bitter tang of laudanum. That's what she was tasting on her tongue. Did she sleep? Or did she faint? She wasn't sure.

The recollection plunged her into panic. Her racing thoughts were interrupted when the soft rumble of men's voices sounded from the other side of the door. She strained to hear, but couldn't make out the words.

She cleared her dry throat and swallowed. "Who's there?" she called. "Help. Somebody please help me!"

Chair legs scraped on a wooden floor. Then footsteps coming closer. The door opened and a man came in.

She screamed.

He clamped his big hand over her mouth, and she felt the weight of his rock-hard eyes on her.

"No one can hear you outside of this cabin," he said. "No one knows you're here." His voice was deep and coarse, the same voice she'd heard in the dark. "Don't scream. It makes my partner nervous. He gets trigger happy when he's nervous. Do what you're told, and you won't get hurt."

He maintained unflinching eye contact and gave her time to let his words sink in. It was both a threat and a promise, and he tightened his hand on her face to let her know he meant business. "Can you do that? Nod if you can."

She nodded vigorously and stared at him taking in every detail of his face. Bushy eyebrows and a face like an unsuccessful prize fighter.

When he removed his hand, questions tumbled out of her.

"Where am I? Who are you? Why did you bring me here?" Her voice rasped and cracked, her words barely legible even to her.

He held up a hand to silence her, but she paid no mind.

"I want to go home."

He scowled and shook his head.

"You can't keep me here." Ice cracked in her voice, but there was little push to her protest.

"Well, we can, because we are." The way he spoke—every word cold and harsh.

Good sense asserted itself and she released her defiance. Back talk and arguing did not work with men like this. Coarse men, menacing men. Fighting the pain singing in her ribs she raised herself into a sitting position, softened her rebellious look into one of timidity, and cradled her throbbing hand in the other.

"Please," she begged. "Let me go. I want to go home."

A look of irritation tightened his mouth. He raised a finger in the air and wagged it, then made it into a finger gun. When he pointed it at her, she flinched.

He drilled her with a stare. "No. Don't ask again."

His glare frightened her. Who was this man? She'd seen him somewhere, but her frazzled mind couldn't grasp the memory flickering at the edge of her remembrance.

"Are you hungry?" he barked.

She exhaled a shaky breath and gave her chin a slow dip in the affirmative.

"Are you in pain?"

In the charged silence, another slow nod.

"Then let me tell you how this is going to work. We have food, water and coffee. I can bring you bandages and something for pain. Soap and a pan of water so you can wash your face and clean yourself up. But only if you don't scream or make trouble. Either I or my partner will be watching you at all times. You'll never be alone. Is that clear?"

Again, she acquiesced. Her eyes wide with fear locked on his.

After a pause, he said, "Do you want to go to the outhouse? You're gonna be here a while," he added with a snide flick in his voice.

A sob rose in her throat and she flashed him a look of loathing then averted her eyes. "Yes."

"I'll walk with you to the outhouse."

She recoiled. "No, no, no."

He grinned showing his ugly teeth, a humorless smile on his lips. "You can go in alone, but I'll be right outside. Don't even think of making a run for it. The road is miles away. You'll never make it." He emphasized the word *miles*. "And there are snakes," he added with an oily grin.

Tears burned her eyes, but she held them back, determined not to let him see her cry.

He clamped his hand around her upper arm and tugged her up from the cot.

"No wait!" she said when her stockinged feet touched the floor. "My boots."

"No boots. And take off your stockings."

"NO!" she objected, but he held up that big hand again. His forearms were massive and his biceps bulged.

He gave her a gouging stare then sliced his fingers across his throat in explicit warning. Reluctantly, she complied.

He guided her roughly into the other room, a bigger one with a real kitchen separated by a short length of half wall. A fireplace crackled. The cabin carried a sheen of money, not too much but some, no doubt owned by a man of means and taste. Certainly not this man nor the one hunched over the table shoveling food into his mouth.

The man at the table looked up at her through bent wire rimmed spectacles that sat lopsided on his face. Two cold black marbles peered at her through the lenses, flashing with meanness coiled and ready to spring. His sly grin was meant to intimidate her and it did.

The man tightened his grip on her arm, opened the

door and swung his arm in a mocking exaggerated gesture of presentation. "Ladies first," he said, and waved her outside. She walked lightly over warped wooden boards leading to the outhouse desperately trying to avoid splinters. Quickly she took in some details of her surroundings.

The land swept up to peaks and ridges, some rounded and gentle, some jagged and savage. Mountains in the distance looming over a long stretch of sloping ground crisscrossed by dry culverts and stream beds. A sidewinding road, the beginning and ending of which disappeared into the dips and folds of the earth. Beyond that, the sparkle of rushing river water made her think she wasn't too far from home.

At the outhouse, she stopped and speared him with a look waiting for him to step away. He did so and said, "I'll be right here waiting." Again, his words were heavy with warning.

She took her time in the outhouse, hoping to come up with a plan for escape. When she came out, he was sitting on a fallen tree with the makings of a cigarette in his hands.

While he rolled one, she tilted her head letting a loose lock of hair to veil her face and skimmed a low-lidded glance around trying to get her bearings. A brief gust of wind carried a sound to her ears, the faint but familiar sound of stagecoach wheels on hardpack. A tiny rolling cloud of dust moved in the mid-distance at the edge of her vision. She shifted her eyes to see if he noticed, but he was puffing hard, lighting up, the nippy breeze making it difficult.

She lowered her lids to conceal the glimmer of hope in her eyes. The stagecoach road was *not* many miles away. It was far, but within eyesight.

CHAPTER THIRTY-SIX

*S*OMEONE WAS RIDING INTO the yard on a burro. Hath and Birch were out with the search party. Wren went to pick up supplies. Jenny had left early that morning. Word had come that her mother in Missouri was ill, so Mimi took her and Anna to the stage boarding station.

That left Tally alone on the homestead. Someone had to feed the animals and clean the pens.

She wasn't expecting anyone, let alone a stranger riding a burro, so ducked into the barn. She leaned her shovel against a pole, picked up the rifle that was never far from hand these days, and watched from the shadows. The rider on the slow walking burro was small as a child. When he got closer Tally saw it *was* a child. Eight-year-old Wyatt, the stableboy Hath hired to help Buster at the livery. What was he doing here? She stepped out to greet him.

"Good morning, Wyatt." She lifted her hand to shade her eyes from the morning sun. "Are you looking for Hath? He's out with the search party."

"No, ma'am. It's you I need to see." He took an envelope from a stringed pouch tied to his belt and held it out to her.

"What's this?"

"Dunno, Miss Tally. A man brung it to the livery this morning. Early."

Apprehension nudged her consciousness. "Oh? Who was it?"

"Dunno, ma'am."

Curious, but also wary now, she asked, "Does Buster know you brought this?"

"Yes, ma'am. He was going to bring it himself, but got busy so asked me to."

Uneasiness stirred. "Does Buster know the man?"

A vigorous headshake bounced Wyatt's blond curls. "He said he didn't know his name. Seen him around, though."

"Did you see him? What did he look like?"

The boy shrugged. "Old. Like you."

She ignored that supposing anyone over the age of twenty probably looked ancient to an eight-year-old. "What else?"

The boy thought a minute. "Wore glasses. Broken. That thing that goes over your ear?" He demonstrated to make sure she understood. "Was gone. And he needed a bath."

"Thank you, Wyatt. You're a good boy. There are cookies in a basket on the table inside the cabin. Go on in and get one for the ride back to town. Take two," she added.

A wide smile split the boy's face. "Thank you, Miss Tally."

She slipped the envelope into the pocket of her barn apron. Something told her to wait until the boy left before opening it. When he was out of sight, she slit the flap with her finger, pulled out a single sheet of paper, and reeled.

It was a ransom note!

If you ever want to see your sister again, you'll do what I say.

Air caught in her throat. She looked ahead for a signature, but the note was unsigned.

> *We have your sister, but we want your homestead. If you ever want to see her again, you'll give us what we want. If you understand and agree, hang a milk pail on the fence post by the road. In three days, you'll find further instructions in the milk pail on how the trade will be made. If we don't see a milk pail in three days, you won't hear from us again. Or from your sister.*

She turned the page over. Nothing was written on the back.

The message froze her blood, and she fought against the meaning of the words. It was an unthinkable choice, one she couldn't possibly make. She would never give up her sister, and she'd never give up her father's homestead. A wave of helpless frustration washed over her.

What would happen to her father if he came back to find that someone else had the rights to his patent and to his land? She continue to hold on to the faint hope that he would return someday. Where would they go if they couldn't live on the homestead? She'd never go back to Denver. She couldn't.

She slumped against the barn door and put her hand to her forehead.

If only Hath were there. Abruptly, she lifted her eyes to the road, some part of her mind visualizing he and Birch returning. Of course, it wasn't so. After nearly a week with no sign of Ivy, most of the men had already gone back to their families and to their own homesteads. But Hath and Birch and a dwindling group of volunteers still went searching every day not returning until after supper. She put the note back in her pocket with a shaking hand, and continued with chores, feeling like she was unraveling from the inside out.

The blue of the afternoon still hung over the trees when Mimi arrived. Tally was inside baking bread. "Oh, Mimi," she said wiping flour from her hands.

"What happened? Have you been crying? I can tell by

your face it's something terrible."

Tally showed Mimi the note. "This."

Mimi read it and her mouth dropped open. "What are you going to do?"

"What can I do? I'm not going to let my sister die. And I can't give up this place. It belongs to my father. I'm not turning this spread over to thieves. It's all we have."

Mimi read the note again as if making sure she'd read it right the first time. "Do Hath and Birch know about this?"

Tally shook her head. "No, they aren't back yet."

Mimi put her arm around Tally in a comforting hug. "Don't worry. Let's wait and see what Hath and Birch have to say. We'll think of something."

A wagon rattled into the yard, and Tally saw Wren guide Champion to the barn, but instead of immediately unloading the goods and stabling the horse as he usually did, he jumped out of the wagon and hurried to the cabin.

The women watched in alarm as he rushed in the door. "Is Hath back yet?" he asked, his excited breath coming out in quick spurts.

"No. Why?" said Tally.

He spoke rapidly, his words tumbling out. "I think I know where Miss Ivy is."

"Where? What did you find out?"

"I asked around town if anyone heard any rumors about Miss Ivy."

"Did they?"

"No. But then I went to the reservation. Sometimes the Indians hear things. They watch and listen. Whites don't pay much attention to them. Sometimes whites talk to each other like the Indians aren't even there. That's how Indians find out white secrets."

"And did they know anything?"

"Some heard that bad men took Ivy to the mountains

and are keeping her in their hideout in Arapaho Gulch."
"Arapaho Gulch? Where's that?"
"Up the mountain in the foothills. Wilderness."
"Have you been there?" Mimi asked.
He nodded. "A long time ago. Dangerous terrain in places. Horses might not make it all the way. Steep. Trails wash out in the rains. Tumbled boulders block the way."
"Do they know who these bad men are?" asked Tally.
"They said bad men who take people's land." He paused. "They think work for Clarkson."
Tally and Mimi exchanged a look of sheer astonishment.
"Clarkson's men?"
Silence fell and Tally drifted away on a river of thought, but quickly took herself out of her pondering. "Wren, can you give me directions to Arapahoe Gulch?"
Wren hesitated. "Yah, I think so," he said wavering. "Five miles up the road to the split. You go one way to Denver. Other way to Arapaho Gulch."
She took a blank sheet of paper from a drawer and gave it to him. "Here. Draw a map." There was a swift exchange of glances as if Tally's thoughts drifted in the air to Mimi, silent, unspoken, but infinitely perceptible. They locked eyes in silent accord.
Wren laid out a rough sketch indicating landmarks, then pointed with the pencil on the paper. "Right here is the split in the road. You go this way until you reach the river. There's a crossing here. But then it's steep." He tapped the pencil. "Some old miner cabins here, mostly burned down or abandoned."
He raised his head and looked from Tally to Mimi, questions quirked his eyebrows. "You're not going there, are you?"
When they didn't answer he said, "Maybe wait for Hath and Birch. Or I'll go with you."

Tally shook her head. "No, no need. But please do something for me, will you? And hurry, all right? Saddle up two of those spare horses Hath brought from the livery. Pack blankets and ammunition. Mimi and I will be ready to ride in twenty minutes."

"Miss Tally, maybe you should wait for..."

"No. No waiting, but don't worry. If we find the hideout and Ivy is there, we'll come right back and let the men know. I promise. We just want to scout out the area so the men won't have to waste time looking for it."

Wren nodded, but with worry on his face he went out to the barn to do as she asked.

CHAPTER THIRTY-SEVEN

*I*N ANTICIPATION OF A rugged journey, Tally and Mimi dressed for the road in Hank Tisdale's old clothes. Baggy pants, flannel shirts and wide brim canvas hats. At the fork in the road, they veered right, and would have missed the trail if the horses hadn't reacted.

To accommodate the search party, extra transport was often needed, so Hath had brought horses from the livery to stable temporarily on the Tisdale homestead. Horses are social animals, have a keen sense of perception, an instinct necessary for functioning in a herd, and have a symbiotic awareness of the presence of their own species so when both horses quirked their ears at the same time on the otherwise secluded trail, Tally reined to a stop.

"Hold up. Let's check up there." She indicated a barely visible break in the trees. "The dirt's disturbed. Someone's been through recently."

A wind came up and Tally looked over her shoulder. Storm clouds snagged on a sawtooth silhouette of mountains in the distance. Mimi saw it, too, and sent Tally a questioning look.

"Just a quick look," said Tally. "If we hurry, we'll be home before the storm hits."

Riding single file, they urged their horses in and out of a gully, then up a rocky incline. The footing on the hill was loose in places, but the horses were strong and agile.

Evergreens densely packed on either side were so thick very little sky showed through. The air smelled of earth, wet leaves and pine needles.

The ground leveled off, and a quarter mile in they found themselves at the base of a steep upslope littered with boulders and broken trees. The top of the hill disappeared into a thick stand of fat spruce trees. Abandoned miner's cabins in varying degrees of decrepitude looked like they were either growing from the earth or sinking into it.

"Maybe the trail picks up this way," said Tally pointing to her left. "I'll take a look. You go around the other way. Holler if you find it."

They split up, and Tally found herself on a narrow, rutted sand trapped dirt track threading through a shallow flat-bottomed gulch. Sculpted in the dried mud were hoof prints going both ways. She dismounted, secured the reins and stepping quietly proceeded on foot keeping low, digging in the toes of her boots for purchase. Topping the steep rise she saw the roof of a cabin at the end of a narrow lane. A tongue of smoke licked its way out of the chimney.

Her breathing was troubled after the climb, so she squatted behind a bush to settle it. She wasn't sure if this was the hideout or simply the home of a recluse avoiding close neighbors. In order to get a better look, she grasped a low hanging branch, pulled herself up and planted her foot on a limb that was weathered and grey, the bark long gone.

Windy gusts swayed the trees, and she clutched another limb to steady herself so she could get a better look without losing her footing.

There was an outhouse at the edge of the clearing a good distance from the cabin reached by a wood plank walkway from the porch. Two saddled horses were tied to a hitch post in front swishing flies away with their tails confirming the cabin was occupied. Tally's heart took an extra beat when she saw one of the cabin windows boarded up from the outside.

Ivy was in there, she was sure of it.

The purple and orange tinged charcoal sky over the distant mountains now flickered with lightning. She knew from experience it would be a mistake to ignore the speed of the massing storm, and she quickly began her descent. She needed to find Hath and the search party and let them know where Ivy was.

Taking one last look at the cabin, she was surprised to see a man standing on the front porch with a rifle in the crook of his arm, his eyes scanning the ridge in her direction. Another man stepped outside drawing his pistol. He, too, was looking in her direction.

She had to get out of there quick, but she was afraid to move. She didn't know what had alerted the men, but any movement now could pinpoint her exact position.

The pistol discharged burying a bullet into the trunk of the tree above her head. She ducked and dropped to a lower branch, but the branch gave way and she fell straight down landing on her back, breath knocked from her lungs.

Winded, she lay there struggling to take in air. A man approached and loomed over her, a huge man with a large frame well overloaded. He grabbed her arm, yanked her to her feet, and threw his fist into the middle of her face. Pain radiated from her nose and blood spurted. A sickening wave of something bitter spooled out in the pit of her stomach.

His eyes traveled the length of her as he stared, dumbfounded. "You're a woman! I thought you were a man." Then, making no effort to be gentle, he hauled her to the cabin where she stumbled up the steps onto the porch.

The man with the rifle looked at her and smirked. "That's the Tisdale sister."

The man squeezing the flesh of her upper arm took another good look. "Yeah," he said and grinned. "Now we got 'em both our problem is solved." He pushed her into the cabin, opened a door, and shoved her through it. She sprawled onto the floor.

In seconds, gentle hands were on her, lovingly turning her over, a soft voice crooning her name.

"Tally? Tally, are you all right? It's me, Ivy."

When Tally's vision cleared she saw her sister's tear-stained face under a mass of tangled hair. Next to it was the thoroughly angry face of Mimi.

CHAPTER THIRTY-EIGHT

THE SEARCH PARTY BROKe up when the rain began. At first it was a gentle slow-moving rain, what the Navajo call a Female Rain, one that nurtures and brings life. But even at a gallop, Hath and Birch could not outrun it before it turned turbulent and destructive, breaking branches and toppling trees. A Male Rain.

By the time they reached the Tisdale homestead the river had overflowed its banks flooding the road and lapping at the acreage. The ravine that defined the property boundary to the west roiled with muddy water that hadn't yet topped the banks, but was severely eroding the sides. Hath feared it would breach before daybreak. They had to get the animals to safety.

Wren had already dug drainage ditches and strung a rope railing from the cabin to the barn. Hollering to be heard over the noise of the storm, he let them know he'd opened the gates at the back pasture and let the cattle loose to find their way to safety on higher ground.

"Where are the women?" Hath yelled back. "Are they all right?"

Hath wasn't sure Wren heard because he didn't answer. He was busy unlocking the sheep pens and shooing the animals toward a grassy hill.

"The goats are already gone," Wren yelled. "The fence blew down and they ran off. Now the chicken coop is flooding and the hen house is falling apart."

Thunder roared overhead. Lightning flashed like fire in the sky, rain fell in sheets.

Inside the barn, the men set to work rescuing the chickens. Hath went up the ladder to the loft and constructed a makeshift chicken coop from the spare lumber and wire stored there. Birch and Wren deposited chickens in burlap bags which they handed up to Hath. Hath released the chickens into the temporary enclosure and set out feed.

A powerful gust blew the hay loading door open wrenching one of the hinges. Rain poured in. As Hath struggled to reset the door a powerful gust of wind swept the yard and knocked the supply shed off its pilings. It landed on its side and two coyotes that had been sheltering beneath darted out. One of the rams caught sight of the coyotes, broke from the pack and ran toward the rapidly flooding ravine. Terrified, the entire flock changed direction and followed the panicked ram.

"Coyotes!" Hath yelled down to Wren and Birch. "The sheep panicked! We need to head them off before the damn fools drown themselves!"

He was frantic to save the livestock. If the goats saw the sheep, they might follow and the homestead could lose all of its animals which would be a devastating loss, one from which Tally and Ivy might never recover. With his hands on the side rails to steady himself, Hath slid down the ladder rungs on his boot soles.

The men shoved their arms into their windbreakers, secured their slickers, jumped into their saddles, and with pistols drawn headed out into wind that was blowing needle sharp raindrops sideways. Ignoring the cold, wet air hunting the gaps in his clothing, Hath took aim at one of the coyotes, pulled the trigger, and it went down. Birch took care of the other one. Dodging broken tree limbs and debris picked up by the ferocity of the winds, the men herded the sheep and sent them up into the foothills with the cattle. There they had a chance to find shelter and survive until they could be brought back after the storm. Hath knew some might be lost to falls or lightning strikes, but not all. At least he hoped not.

By now, the turbulent rains and misty air made it impossible to see more than a few feet ahead. Still, they managed to slog through the muck and mud back to the barn where they unsaddled the horses. Unsure if the barn could withstand the onslaught of the storm, they set the horses loose to seek shelter on their own. It was a risk. Not only because of flying debris and lightning, but there was the chance they'd attach themselves to one of the wild horse herds roaming the foothills, or be stolen by the Indians.

Chilled by the falling temperatures and drenched from the rain, with thunder pounding and lightning crashing around them, the men made their way to the cabin using the rope rail to guide the way. Rakes and shovels served as walking sticks.

Inside they toed off their muddy boots and shook out their rain slickers. The bread makings were on the table, batter still in the bowl.

"Where's Tally?" Hath asked again.

"She left with Miss Mimi," said Wren.

"Mimi? When? Where?"

Wren repeated the rumor about the hideout in Arapaho Gulch. "I think they went to find it, and see if Miss Ivy was there."

Hath stared at Wren in disbelief. "And you let them go?" Anger made the words come out harsh and loud.

Unruffled, Wren shrugged. "Do you think I could have stopped either Miss Tally or Miss Mimi from doing *anything* they set their minds to?"

Hath exhaled loudly through his nose and shook his

head in frustration. "Sorry. No. I don't."

He went to the window and looked out. The sky was charcoal grey as far as he could see with no sign the howling storm would let up anytime soon. The ransom note lay open on the little three-legged table under the window where Tally sat when she did the mending. Hath picked up note, read it, and felt pieces of his heart fall away.

"Where's Arapaho Gulch?" he asked glumly

Wren started to answer, but Birch interrupted. "I know where it is," he said. "I know a short cut. Storm should let up some by morning. We can ride out then."

Hath nodded, his mouth set in a hard line. "If the horses come back."

CHAPTER THIRTY-NINE

*I*VY RIPPED A CORNER off the thin cotton sheet covering the mattress and set about wiping blood from Tally's face. "Your nose is puffy, but I don't think it's broken."

Tally winced at her touch. "Feels like it is," she murmured through split lips.

"I know. I'm trying to be gentle, but one of them smashed my hand with his gun and my fingers are still stiff and sore. Do you hurt anywhere beside your nose?"

"Yes," Tally answered. "Everywhere."

The three women huddled on the cabin floor wrapped in ragged blankets while the storm raged outside. They spoke in whispers so the men in the other room couldn't hear.

Ivy finished tending to Tally, then asked, "How did you find me?"

"Wren heard a rumor in town about where you might be. The search party was already out, so Mimi and I came looking. I figured if we could find out where you were, we could alert the searchers. But we got caught."

"Do you know who those men are?" Mimi asked.

Ivy nodded. "The man that brought you here is called Fritz. The one with the rifle is Rudy. There are others. They're not here right now, but they might come back at any time. We have to get out of here. They're going to kill us. I heard them talking."

"They sent me a ransom note," said Tally. "They said if we gave up our land, they'd let you go."

"That was a lure to get you here. They hoped you'd come looking for me. They're not going to let us go. Now that you're here they can kill us both and take over our homestead without anyone standing in their way."

"Now that I know where their hideout is they won't let me live, either." Mimi's eyes flashed with anger

Ivy nodded in somber agreement. "Sometimes the other men come up here for a meeting, and they let me out to do the cooking and cleaning. I can't always hear what they're saying, but I bang the pots and pans around a lot, so they have to talk louder. They talk about their plan at night, too. I pretend to be sleeping so I can hear what they're saying."

"They're desperate," said Tally. "They don't just want our land. They *need* our land. It's pivotal to their plans for the stockyard they want to build next to the railroad. Ranchers and cattlemen from all over will bring their herds to a railroad loading facility, and our homestead sits right at the junction that will service cattle drives from every direction. We've seen the maps. There's no other way because of the mountains. Without our homestead, their whole scheme won't work. Pettyjohn was in on it, too. He falsified the necessary documents for them."

"How did you see the maps?"

Tally and Mimi took turns relating what they discovered in Pettyjohn's office.

"It's all about the cattle," Tally said. "Clarkson must be behind this."

"Fritz and Rudy do some work for Clarkson," said Ivy, "but they mentioned other people they work for, too. I didn't catch the names, but it's a group of wealthy land speculators from back east trying to get as much land out here as they can, any way they can legal or not.

"Oh, and by the way. They killed Pettyjohn, and Frank Scott, too. I heard them talking about it."

The demonic pounding of rain on the roof let up a little, but ominous black clouds still hung low threatening more. The cabin groaned in powerful winds that reared from every direction. Blowing sand ticked on the glass.

"Have you seen Birch?" Ivy's voice was a strained whisper.

Tally nodded. "When you didn't show up at Prayer Rock, he came to the cabin looking for you."

Ivy pulled in her lips between her teeth and lowered her gaze. A pained expression took over her face. "I'm sorry I lied to you, Tally. I never meant for this to happen. It's my fault we're here." Her eyes glistened, tears ready to fall.

Tally took her hand. "Don't cry, Ivy. If you want to know the truth, I blame myself. I know my disapproval drove you closer to Birch. He said you were going to run away with him, but I have this feeling there are things we don't know about him."

"You're right. There is something neither of you know about him."

Two sets of inquiring eyes locked on hers.

Ivy let out a compacted breath and her voice wavered. "He's a highwayman. He robbed the stage that comes around Bandit Bend in front of the cabin." She paused and swallowed before going on. "Then he buried some of the money and gold on our land."

Startled by this bit of news, Tally asked, "How... how do you know that?"

Ivy swiped away tears with the fingers of her good hand. "He told me," she said and sniffed. "That's when I realized the kind of man he really was. But I couldn't send him away, because he said he'd take me away from the homestead." She sighed a shuddery breath. "Even though

I didn't love Birch, even though I knew by then he wasn't the man I wanted to be with for the rest of my life, I was going to run away with him."

It was a thought that tore Tally's heart apart. "I knew about your plans," she said. "But I didn't know about the gold."

"It was before we came to Sutton Creek. No one else knows it's there. Wren built the supply shed over it."

Tally's thoughts were slow and cumbersome at these unexpected revelations. She felt unmoored to reality, not knowing what to say.

Ivy's face was a mask of misery and she gulped back a sob. "I treated you so badly and it was so unfair. I don't blame you if you hate me."

"Of course I don't hate you," Tally replied. "I know living on the homestead isn't what you anticipated for your future. I didn't mean to put you through that. You felt the burden of it every minute of every day. Proving up the homestead was harder than I thought it would be."

"And I made it all the harder because I let myself be taken in by a bad man. Even though I knew better. Even though you taught me better."

Mimi pulled her features into a sympathetic frown and took Ivy's hand.

"Look, honey, everyone's life is burdened with difficult truths. You'll realize that as you get older. We've all done things we shouldn't have. Things we're ashamed of later and wished we hadn't done. I have, too."

"You have?" Ivy looked dubious. "But you're the strongest and wisest woman I've ever known besides Tally."

Mimi nodded sagely. "It seems God doesn't always see fit to give young people wisdom until they're older. I guess he figures they have to learn a few lessons first. I know I did."

Her expression went distant with a memory. Her voice thickened and remorse laced her tone when she spoke next.

"I was only sixteen when I came to Sutton Creek with a man I thought I loved more than anything in the world. He said he loved me, too. We were supposed to be married when we got here." A faint smile appeared on her lips, but quickly disappeared as she went on.

"Turns out he wasn't the man I thought he was, either. He spent all his time and money gambling at the saloons or in the bordellos. When he ran off with one of those girls there, I was left alone with absolutely nothing. There weren't as many shops and businesses in Sutton Creek then as there are now where I could get work. But I had to support myself somehow. I went to work for the madam who ran the bordello." She shook her head dismally. "I took the place of the girl he ran off with."

Mimi held Ivy's gaze with her own and spoke with the deepest sincerity.

"I made a huge mistake coming out here with a man who was not my husband. I was merely a loose end to him. Then I was forced to make a terrible decision after he left me."

Regret made headway clouding her eyes. "I eventually made enough money that I was able to put most of it away so I could give up that life." She gave a withering smile. "None of that is exactly a secret in Sutton Creek. I guess everyone in town knows it. The old timers, anyway."

Ivy was quiet for a moment, absorbing this. Then she said, "I'm grateful Tally is so level-headed. I've never known her to make a wrong decision. We lived a nice life in Denver. She always made my safety and welfare a priority, sometimes at great sacrifice to her own. She always did the right thing. I couldn't ask for a better big sister."

Tally sat ramrod straight in solemn silence listening

to Ivy's loving words, the ravages of guilt clawing painfully at her chest making it hard to breathe.

"That's not quite true," she said. "I don't deserve your admiration. Or anyone's."

Ivy's lips parted and she stared at her, speechless.

Mimi searched Tally's face for more. "What are you talking about?"

Tally filled her lungs with air, holding it in a few seconds to calm herself.

"Look," she began. "I don't know if I'm going to make it out of here alive. But in case I don't, I have something to confess. It's something that will make you both ashamed of me, but I pray that God will still open the gates of Heaven for me when this is over. And I hope both of you can understand why I did what I did and forgive me."

"What could you have possibly done to make you say *that?*" Ivy asked, astonished.

Tally brought her hands together and laced her fingers in a knot of tension. Second thoughts were creeping in, but she swatted them away and swallowed around the words clogged up in her throat.

"Jacob didn't run away." Her voice was flat enough to slip under a door crack. "I killed him."

The silence in the small room was overpowering as her words floated in the air looking for a place to land. Ivy sucked a breath like she'd been punched in the stomach. Mimi's expressive eyes widened into a mixture of shock and curiosity.

Tally took in a deep, deep breath. When she spoke her voice thickened with emotion making the words tumble out clumsily.

"It was a Sunday night. Something I said made Jacob mad and we argued. He hit me—once, twice, three times. That's how our arguments usually ended, because I always apologized and acquiesced. But this time he didn't stop. He'd been drinking heavily all day and had lost a lot of money at the card tables." She took a moment. "I remember now that's what we fought about.

"He grabbed the fireplace poker and swung at me. Luckily, I saw it coming. If I hadn't turned my head, he would have split my face open. But it landed on the side of my head and I went down on my knees. He hit me hard enough that I was afraid he'd cracked my skull. He came at me again, but stumbled and I was able to roll out of his reach.

"Blood was running into my eyes and down the front of my dress, but I managed to get up. I reached for my bag and pulled out my pistol. It didn't scare him in the least. He laughed at me when I pointed it at him. Then he called me filthy, disgusting names." Her voice was measured and she struggled for calm. "I shot him."

Mimi visibly stiffened. Ivy opened her mouth to say something, but her voice went up in register, and all she could manage was a sorrowful, indefinable squeak.

"I shot him to make him stop laughing at me. Stop calling me those ugly names. I wanted him to stop beating me!" She took a shaky breath and let it out slowly before going on.

Ivy looked uncomfortable like she'd walked in on a stranger unexpectedly during an intimate moment. Mimi was somber, her expression set in dismay, eyes narrowed, lips clenched tight as if words were fighting to come out.

"Jacob fell back and hit his head on the hearth. I didn't know if he was dead." Tally sniffed wetly. "So I picked up the poker and made sure." Tally's heart pounded in the telling.

"I expected the neighbors to come knocking on the door, I feared they heard the gunshot. But no one did. City streets at night are just as noisy as they are here. I waited until well after midnight, then dragged him out to the barn. My head was throbbing, but I managed to get him into the carriage. Then I harnessed the horse and drove to Larimer Street where I dumped him in the alley behind one of the saloons. I took his wallet so no one would know who he was or where he lived. Then I went home, cleaned up in the bath and burned his wallet to ashes in the fireplace."

An uneasy quiet ballooned in the room and Tally could almost feel it pressing on her skin. She could tell by their expressions that she had shocked both of them beyond words.

Finally, Ivy spoke. "Father thought Jacob had abandoned you."

Tally nodded. "Yes. That's what I told everyone. No one was surprised, so they didn't ask a lot of questions. By then Jacob had a petty scandalous reputation. Just about everyone knew he was a scoundrel, so no one was suspicious. At least I didn't think so," she added. "But a Pinkerton man has been snooping around in Sutton Creek asking about me."

As Tally battled an upwelling of emotion, Mimi and Ivy scooted in close and put comforting arms around her.

"If father knew how Jacob treated you, he would have intervened and set him straight."

Tally's eyes were deep hollows. "I didn't want him to know. I was too ashamed. Father had already warned me about him. But I didn't listen."

Ivy quirked her lips, her face grim. "Just like I didn't listen to you."

"I'm not judging you, my friend," Mimi said. "After what your husband did to you? No one would blame you. In life there are no clean edges. Things overlap. You had to protect yourself."

"Don't worry," Ivy said with emphasis. "No one else will ever know. It's over."

Through the cracks between the boards covering the window Tally could see the darkening of evening coming on. She tried to still her chaotic thoughts and wrench her mind away from the emotional seesaw she'd been on to focus on the immediacy of their situation.

"We have to think about how we're going to get out of here." She paused. "And if we do, I'm going to turn myself in."

Mimi protested. "You'll do no such thing," she said giving Tally a hard stare, daring her to disagree. "You had to protect yourself. No one is going to know what we just talked about." The finality of her words grew stronger accompanied by Ivy's decisive nods.

A long pensive silence stretched out until Ivy's eyebrows shot up. "I have an idea how we can get out of here," she said.

Expectant gazes lit up.

"Tomorrow Rudy goes into town for supplies. That leaves us alone with Fritz. I'm not sure I could have escaped by myself," she said. "But with the two of you here we have a better chance of getting away."

Mimi piffed a hard breath and gave her head a shake. "What, are you crazy? The three of us together couldn't overpower that man. He's big as a buffalo!"

"Yes," Ivy said. "But he's blind as a bat without his glasses."

CHAPTER FORTY

THROUGH THE SLITS BETWEEN the boards covering the window, Tally watched the afternoon sky open up blue, bright and warm. The rain was done for now, the most threatening clouds had mostly moved away. Ivy's plan had weighed so heavily on her mind sleep had barely visited her in the night.

Though skeptical, she couldn't put aside the thought there was a chance Ivy's idea was a good one. Tally wasn't a particularly spontaneous person, preferring to mull things over for a time weighing the potential downfalls and dead ends. In the end, despite her misgivings she agreed to what Ivy had proposed. Mimi, quick-thinking and courageous, could surely be counted on, everything she did, she did with passion, and as for Ivy, she was young, strong and fearless, so it would be a mistake to underestimate her. Life often demanded you do things you wouldn't normally do in exchange for survival.

She steeled herself, yearning for her own younger days. The plan Ivy proposed just might work. It was control she needed now, calculated unbending control.

Her gaze sharpened at the sound of horses. "Riders coming this way."

Ivy approached to peer over her shoulder.

"Who are they?" Tally asked.

"The rest of the gang. Looks like they're here for a meeting." Ivy released a breathy sigh and gave her head a dreary shake. "Probably about us."

The three riders dismounted, hitched their horses to the rail then tramped toward the porch.

"Look," Mimi whispered. "One of them has his hand wrapped in a bandage."

"He seems to be limping a little, too," Tally added. "And he's holding his side like he's been hurt."

The men came up the steps and over the threshold into the cabin, their deportment all business. Disgruntled greetings were exchanged with Rudy and Fritz. Their voices rumbled in a hushed but urgent sounding conversation amply punctuated with salty language.

The women leaned in to hear through the door, but jumped back when the lock released and the door swung open. Rudy stepped in, his face as hard and colorless as a cement block.

He pointed at Ivy and his words snapped out like whips in the air. "You. Get out here and fix some grub."

Next he pointed at Mimi. "Get a bucket and mop and clean this place up."

Then he glared at Tally and spoke in his weasily voice.

"Go out feed and water the horses." A sneer rearranged the muscles of his face when his severe gaze unsettled her. "But don't think you're gonna ride away or nuthin'." He gestured with his chin at the visitors and his lips moved in an ugly grin showing ugly teeth. "Remember, we got your little sister in here with us."

Tally's chest jumped with her heartbeat, but she managed to keep her expression neutral, because what he was sending her to do was a blessing in disguise. It would give her a chance to commit the landscape to memory, help to get her bearings, figure out in which direction was home.

Thick tendrils of hair had come unpinned in the night and she allowed them to veil her low-lidded eyes as she scanned the room she'd been dragged through the previous day. It was a large room, but the men took up a lot of its space as they sprawled legs akimbo in chairs around the distressed pine table.

She gave each one a quick glance before averting her eyes. A square faced man with close cropped hair. The other one had a nose too prominent for his cheeky face. The sharp-eyed man next to him with the bandaged hand lifted his lip in a sneer and glowered at her. She didn't know their names, but remembered seeing them among the idlers taking up space on the boardwalks in front of the saloons many an afternoon.

Ivy, at the stove, busily cracked eggs into a frying pan. Mimi had a mop and bucket in hand, and was reaching for a can of cleaning powder on a shelf over the sink.

The man with the bandaged hand stared at Mimi.

"Hey," he called out to her. "Hey, you." The tone of his voice cut deep with spite and malice. "Ain't you the bitch that shot me in the alley on Founders Day?"

Mimi ignored him, but fear rippled through Tally. She steeled herself and slowed her step, but the man didn't say anything else, though his eyes drilled into Mimi watching her every move.

As Tally stepped out onto the porch, she spotted her boots in the corner where they'd been tossed after they were yanked off her feet. Mimi's and Ivy's, too. Their pistols were nowhere to be seen, the men had probably taken possession of them, but a rifle looking like the one Fritz had brandished leaned against the wall next to the door.

Outside, the ground was soft but not muddy, drying quickly in the sun helped along by the high altitude aridity. Tally deliberately took her time with the horses so she could scope out the surrounding area.

The back wall of the cabin was built up against a steep, rock strewn rise of earth. No back door, just roof high windows. In front, the ground rolled in a gentle downward slope to a forest in the distance so thick she couldn't see daylight between the trees. Clusters of evergreens huddled here and there in the clearing. High mountains heaped and stacked one upon the other in the distance. No sign of the stage road Ivy said was down there, but hopefully she'd remember in which direction it lay.

Split logs were piled on the porch positioned within easy reach of the door along with smaller cuts of brushwood some small enough for kindling. She swiveled her eyes to a heap of wood sheltered on the lee side of the cabin away from the wind, then ran her gaze and let it rest on the murky rainwater splashing and swirling in the ravine beneath the boardwalk bridge leading to the outhouse.

Ivy's plan *could* work.

But it wouldn't be easy. They'd have to make their way home on foot. She didn't see her horse or Mimi's. They must have both run back to their home stables, at least she hoped they did. Then she pictured Hath's worried face when they arrived saddled but riderless. He must be having the most dreadful imaginings, his emotions in chaos.

The cabin door swung open emitting the rich aroma of fresh brewed coffee, and the sound of Ivy banging pots and pans and dishes as she prepared and served the meal. Mimi swept dirt and debris out of the cabin and off the porch. She furtively scoured the tree line, then met Tally's eyes in a swift sideways glance as she shook out throw rugs.

Back inside, chores completed, the men's meal ended, whiskey bottles on the table, Rudy returned the women to confinement with a pan of leftovers for their meal. Cigarette smoke seeped in under the door from the main room. The men spoke at length in measured tones, but an argument eventually raised the volume.

Tally put her ear to the door. After a bitter laugh that sounded like a bark, someone's short fuse fizzled to life igniting a river of cussing. Someone's fist slammed the table and angry words flew. Chair legs scraped the floor and a chair toppled over with a clatter. Boot soles pounded on the floor as the men took their argument outside. They weren't arguing about what to do with the women, that had already been decided. The disagreement was about how and when.

"You have until tomorrow. Just get it done," the square faced man hissed angrily before all three gang members galloped away.

Rudy and Fritz watched them leave. After a whispered exchange, Rudy saddled up, reined around and rode off to town. When he was gone, Fritz shuffled back inside bringing with him brooding silence.

The women exchanged frightened looks.

Through the door came the scritch of a match and the smell of Fritz's freshly lit cigarette. Liquor slurped out of a bottle and splashed into a glass.

"We have to do it now," Ivy whispered. Her words hung in the air as she waited for a response.

Anxiety tightened Tally's nerves, but she instantly swept away any lingering remnants of indecision and focused on what had to be done. Without hesitation she and Mimi both nodded agreement.

Tally's body vibrated with tension and anticipation. Mimi's eyes glittered wide and bright with urgency. Ivy slowed her breathing, held out her arms and bowed her head. They joined hands and fell into silent prayer. When the prayer ended, they took their positions and held them until Ivy dipped her head in a grim nod and said, "Now."

Mimi began coughing loudly, gagging and gasping at the same time. She put her hand to her mouth as though physically choking back something that was pushing its way out.

Ivy pounded on the door with both fists. "Help! Fritz, help! Open the door! Mimi's sick! She's throwing up her breakfast!"

The door opened with a jerk. Fritz hurried in pulling his pistol, then drew up short, glaring at them through watery eyes.

Ivy pointed. "Mimi needs to go to the outhouse."

Mimi looked up. Her crinkled face beet red, eyes tearing, bits of food on her lips, spittle dripping.

Fritz's eyes flashed with indecision, and he muttered something through tight lips that sounded like cussing.

"Hurry," Ivy pleaded. "You need to get her to the outhouse before she... you know." She gestured to the floor with her hand.

Fritz, his expression overcome with revulsion wrapped his big hand around Mimi's arm, pulled her to the door and pushed her through. "Move!"

At that same moment, Tally put her hand on her stomach, hunched her shoulders and began retching, summoning up the most painful face. "I don't feel well, either," she moaned. "It must be something we ate." She cupped both hands over her mouth, dry convulsions bent her double.

"Please," she pleaded, her voice muffled by her clasped hands. "I need the outhouse. Now!" Her moaning grew loud and more wretched.

Fritz made an explosive huff of air with his lips, and spread-eagled his hand on Mimi's back to hurry her along.

"Get that one outta here," he shouted over his shoulder. "If she makes a mess on the floor, you're cleaning it up!"

Tally, leaning on Ivy's shoulder, fell in behind Fritz and Mimi who still limped a little, favoring the ankle she'd twisted when she was captured. On the porch they slowed just enough for Tally to grab a thick cut stick of brushwood and conceal it behind her back. Together they stepped along the stone trail, sharp points digging into the soles of their bare feet.

Halfway over the footbridge spanning the rampaging gulley, Mimi faked a stumble on a warped board and fell heavily against Fritz her hands grasping the front of his vest. Taken off guard, her weight threw him off balance and he staggered. Before he could fully recover, Ivy stepped forward, hooked her foot around his ankle and yanked hard.

Fritz teetered and pitched forward, but didn't go down. Arms flailing, he lurched to the side struggling to stay vertical, but before he could get his feet under him Ivy and Tally each rammed a foot into the back of his knees buckling his legs. He grunted and cursed, letting his pistol slip out of his hand as he instinctively reached for the railing. Mimi elbowed his face, and with only one earpiece to hold his spectacles in place they flew off and dropped into the water.

Fritz went down with a thud. He quickly rolled over, but before he could get his big feet under his enormous bulk, Mimi scooped up his pistol and pointed it at him.

"Stay down or I'll shoot!"

Fritz stopped midrise and fell back on his haunches. Disoriented by the fall and unsettled at the loss of his glasses, he frantically patted his hands on the planks in search of them, but froze when she cocked back the hammer. He turned his head toward the sound, his eyes two vacant holes in his face, unfocused, absorbing nothing.

"Take off your boots," Mimi ordered, her voice low and mean as the devil.

Unable to focus and baffled by the turn of events, he didn't move.

"Take 'em off, I said, and throw them off the bridge!"

A storm massed over his face and he opened his mouth to object, but froze when she shouted, "Now!"

Stripped of power without the benefit of full sight and the loss of his gun, he reluctantly toed off his boots. Tally kicked each one off the bridge into the water below where they landed with a splash then swirled away downstream.

"Now your trousers," Mimi said.

"My trou..." he said uncertainly, his bleary eyes hard on her. "No."

Mimi pulled the trigger and Fritz recoiled as a bullet whizzed by.

"Take 'em off now! Or we'll take 'em off for you." Mimi grinned. "It won't be the first time I've helped a gent remove his britches."

When he made no move, Tally gripped the chunk of brushwood with both hands, hefted it over her shoulder and feigned a swing at his head, deliberately missing.

His hands flew up in defense. "No, don't."

"Then do what she said. Take off your pants."

He hunched his shoulders and ducked when she again threatened with her improvised weapon. Tally wasn't sure how much he could actually see or if he could make out who was speaking. From the way he squinted and jerked his eyes around she guessed he saw nothing more than blurry silhouettes.

Still seated on his buttocks, Fritz rocked his weight from one side to the other pulling his pants down over his fleshy hips, then off completely.

"In the water," said Mimi. "Do it now."

Cussing mightily, he tossed his pants over the edge and they, too, churned away.

That done, Mimi bashed his head with the butt of the pistol. His eyes rolled up and he fell flat. "Let's go! He won't be out long," she said, and they took off running.

In the cabin they scrambled into their boots, quickly laced them up then headed for the door. Ivy snatched up Fritz's rifle on the way out. But all three stopped in their tracks at the sight of Fritz heading for the cabin on wobbly legs. Blood ran down the side of his head, and he waved his arms in front of him as if feeling his way like the half blind man he was. He stopped every few steps to turn in place in an attempt to get his bearings.

"He's not sure where we are," whispered Tally. Her eyes flew to a path that began at the edge of the clearing then turned out of sight into a stand of aspens. She jerked her chin. "Let's head that way. I don't think he can see well enough to find us once we're in the trees. Hurry. We have to get to the road before dark."

They made a dash for the path taking a wide berth around Fritz who had fallen and was now so dazed and disoriented he no longer posed a threat. But Ivy broke away and veered off in his direction. He lay on the ground face up, dazed and disoriented, too weak to even lift his mammoth bulk into a sitting position. Ivy stood over him and touched the muzzle of the rifle against his forehead.

Tally watched stupefied, and in a voice freighted with dread called out to her. "Ivy! Don't!" She made a move to intervene, but Mimi stopped her.

"Wait. Let her do what she has to do. Lord only knows what they did to her before we got here."

Ivy turned the muzzle of the rifle skyward, then leaned over and reached for his arm. Dazed and weak as he was, he saw or sensed her movement. With one final burst of energy he lashed out at her with claw-like fingers, but his energy melted away, and his arms fell to his side.

She stared at him as he lay motionless. "You broke my fingers," she said. "My hand will never be the same. It's ugly now and it aches constantly. My fingers are so crooked I'll never be able to fold them in prayer or stroke the fine hairs of my baby's head."

His unseeing eyes pleaded with hers. When he spoke, his lips barely moved. "Please. I don't want to die."

"Oh, I'm not going to kill you," she said.

Then she took a breath, raised her right foot and stomped down as hard as she could, the heel of her boot slamming into his hands. She pounded away at his knuckles and fingers over and over and over again as he howled in agony. Up, down, then up again and down again unmercifully until every bone was crushed and broken.

Then she gathered her skirts, and walked to where Tally and Mimi waited, her steps sure and steady along the way.

"Let's get out of here," she said. "I want to go home."

Unsure in which direction the road lay, they scrambled over loose rocks and convoluted dips and ridges, up rocky inclines and in and out of gullies stopping frequently to wait for Ivy to catch up, who unlike Tally and Mimi was wearing a skirt. Side blown wind lashed the trees against each other, and Tally nervously looked up watching for rain, not trusting the cloudless sky.

A misty grey vapor smudged the air quickening an early twilight. Stringy clouds slowed and gathered overhead. Ivy frowned at them as if they had been hounding her all her life.

"Let's hurry," said Tally. "There are some old miner sheds up ahead. We can shelter there."

The haze thickened and began to spit just as the shacks came into view. The women took refuge in the least dilapidated one, but Ivy objected. "We can't stay here. Rudy will be coming back with supplies."

Mimi shook her head. "He won't ride all this way back, especially not in the rain. No doubt he'll spend the day in a saloon, then lay up in one of the bordellos for the night. He'll be in no condition to ride back until late tomorrow.

We'll be home well before that and have plenty of time to talk to Sheriff Cupman. She checked the sky. "The rain won't last. It's only a drizzle. It should end by daybreak."

Nevertheless, they kept their conversations to a minimum, speaking only in hushed tones.

"Even after we make it to the main road, we'll have a long way to go," said Ivy.

"I'm sure we'll be able to hitch a ride with one of the farmers. After all this rain they're sure to be out and about rounding up their livestock or going to town to stock up on supplies," said Tally.

"First thing I'm going to do when I get home is write to Washington and report Clarkson's gang of land grabbers," Tally said. "They can't get away with this. I'll bet hundreds of Americans are cheated out of their land by crooks and con men like them."

Ivy pondered this a moment, then said, "I wonder how many women have patents in their own name."

"I wonder how many women know how to go about getting one," said Mimi.

"Probably not many," Ivy put in. "And there's no one to teach them the intricacies of completing all that legal paperwork."

"Why don't we teach them?" said Tally. "We could hold classes at the Social Center for widows and single women who come to town alone. Help them get the paperwork and fill it out. Write up a list of supplies they'll need to get started. Give them tips and tricks to avoid some of the mistakes we made."

"That would have helped us a lot when we first got here," said Ivy. "We could tell them what happened to us and what we experienced. Help them protect themselves so it doesn't happen to them."

"Washington doesn't want this land out here to sit idle, they want it developed," added Tally, excitement building. "Maybe we could even get funding to help women get started. Help with the basics. You know, tools and seeds."

Enthusiastic at the prospect of starting up such a venture, they talked and exchanged ideas late into the night.

Finally Tally stifled a yawn and tamped down her excitement at the prospect of their new venture. "We should get some sleep," she said. "Because tomorrow, ladies, we are going home." They settled in as best they could, taking turns staying awake with the rifle close at hand while the night wind rattled the door.

By morning, sunshine turned lowering clouds and everything else the color of tangerines proving Mimi's weather prediction to be accurate. Once out of the pine forest, they reached the T in the road, and from there knew their way back. The homestead was still a good distance away, but a neighboring farmer driving his team over the partially washed-out roads recognized them immediately and reined to a halt.

"Hey," said Thaddeus Morgan. "Aren't you the ladies everyone's been looking for?"

"Yes, can you give us a lift to Bandit Bend?" said Tally.

"Sure, hop in. Hath is sure gonna be happy to see you. I don't think he's slept a complete hour since he formed the search party."

Around the last curve, the views opened up, and Tally's heart thumped at the sight of an oncoming wagon, Wren holding the reins, Hath seated next to him. As they neared, Thaddeus reined his team to a halt and Wren pulled up alongside. Hath's easy smile spread across his face and his boots hit the ground before Champion was able to bring the wagon to a complete stop.

Words filled the air as all three women talked at once eager to relate the events of their captivity. Along with a flurry of hugs, joyful greetings, a few tears of relief, and promises of retribution to the land grabber gang, Hath and Wren assisted the women into their wagon and headed home.

When Wren turned up the trail into the yard, Ivy went silent, her eyes shining with unshed tears. Tally put a comforting arm around her and held her in a sisterly hug.

"Don't cry, Ivy. We're home now. We're safe."

Ivy stared at a mountain of loose dirt near the Prayer Rock and the hole under the supply shed from which it came. "Where's Birch?" she asked, a tremble in her voice.

Hath cleared his throat before answering. "He's gone, Ivy. I'm sorry, but he's gone."

CHAPTER FORTY-ONE

*I*VY STOOD IN THE middle of the road at the apex of the bend looking into the distance.

"Here they come," she called out to the others gathered along the roadside in front of the homestead. Tally and Hath and Mimi. Wren was there, and Buster from the livery. The Gallaghers from the mercantile, dozens of other storekeepers, and homesteaders. Further back off the road, dining room staff from the Sutton Creek hotel were setting up tables with food and drinks. Whiskey, beer, coffee, and fruit juices for the children. The mood was jubilant.

Ivy shaded her eyes from the sun and stood on her tiptoes. "I can see one of the prisoner wagons. The Marshall's bringing them now."

The entire town had eagerly awaited this day, this moment.

When Tally, Ivy and Mimi told Sheriff Cupman how Clarkson Cattle Company colluded with the railroad land speculators, he immediately ordered his two deputies to form a citizen posse with men from the homesteads to track down Rudy and Fritz and the others.

Then he marched across the street, deputized three burly bullwhackers unloading their wagons, and the four of them stomped into the Clarkson Cattle Company, handcuffed Clarkson in front of his employees, then marched him through town to the jail.

Within a month, the volunteer posse had located and brought the crooks back to Sutton Creek, but it was only a temporary hold. The jailhouse was small. No more than four prisoners could be held there at one time. The others had to be locked in the basement of the hardware store and in the mercantile storage barn. All were guarded around the clock by armed volunteers. But more secure facilities were needed, and quickly. Cupman requested transport wagons to take the prisoners to Fort Garland where they'd be held in a military prison until a judge arrived to hold trials.

When word spread that a jail on wheels was headed to Sutton Creek, most of the town laggards and troublemakers hightailed it out. But the homesteaders and families planned a day of celebration.

"I see them. I see someone coming," Ivy told the waiting crowd. Onlookers stirred and moved into the road stretching and craning their necks to get a better look.

A dust cloud rose from the roadbed as riders came around the bend motioning with their hats. "Clear the road! Prisoner transport! Move away! Stand back."

The caravan followed. First came two chuck wagons, trailed by a supply wagon filled with wagon parts and other essentials. Cigar smoke drifted from the wagon carrying additional deputies and marshals in case they were needed. All of them were just as rough and tough as the worst criminals. A remuda followed, extra horses for the teamsters, lawmen and guards.

When the transport wagons came into view, Ivy lifted her skirts and shouldered her way through the crowd to lock arms with Tally and Mimi. The procession slowed as it rounded the bend, and low level anger rippled through the gathering becoming more animated as folks got a look at the handcuffed prisoners in waist chains attached to the wagon floor. Whoops and catcalls, jeers and cheers filled the air as town folks mocked and taunted the prisoners, calling them out with ridicule.

"Crooks!"

"Thieves!"

"You thought you were so smart, didn't ya?"

"Don't show your face in this town again!"

"Good luck at Fort Garland! The military's waitin' for ya!"

"And a hanging judge, too."

Some of the prisoners responded by rattling their chains, cussing back, and spitting through the bars in defiance, their faces marked by deep grooves twisted in anger. Others stared into space with blank eyes, looking defeated, seeming to accept their fate.

Wives and mothers and grandmothers looked on, their faces tight with reproach as they wrapped protective arms around their children.

Fritz and Rudy in the second transport glared at Mimi and the Tisdale sisters as it passed. The women had moved to the edge of the roadbed to make sure they would be seen by their tormentors. They didn't speak or acknowledge the men in any way. Except for Ivy who looked them in the eye and screwed her lips into a satisfied smirk.

When the caravan disappeared from view a momentary hush fell over the crowd like a huge sigh of relief. It was quickly replaced by bursts of laughter, giggles and guffaws. Glasses and bottles clinked as the hotel staff passed out plates of food, and poured whiskey, beer and coffee. Goodfellow toasts made the rounds. The men shook hands, clapped each other's back, and drank. The women exchanged neighborly hugs, then gathered at Prayer Rock to send up prayers of gratitude.

"At last. They're gone," Tally said with a note of finality. "Thank the Lord."

"There are still some out there," Mimi replied sounding like the wise woman she was.

"That's all right," Tally replied. "We'll be ready for them."

Ivy was scanning the grounds. When she found what she was looking for she turned to Tally and Mimi.

"Will you excuse me, please?" she said, not even trying to dim the twinkle in her eye. "I see Buster over there standing all by himself." An impish smile twerked her lips as she stepped away. "I think I'll go over and say hello."

CHAPTER FORTY-TWO

THE NEXT DAY, A lone Arapaho elder, frail and grey-haired rode an old roan colored mustang slowly into the yard, the edge of her shawl and the hem of her gingham skirt fluttering in the wind. The door squawked noisily when Tally stepped out on the porch to greet her.

"Good morning, *beesnenitee*." She'd had made a point of learning a few Arapaho words since the Tribal Chief had come looking for his son's wife.

The elder nodded, then lightly touched the tips of her fingers to her chest and pointed to her eyes. She folded her arms into a cradle. *"Notoone,"* she said*, "notoone."*

The elder's gestures told Tally the old woman was looking for something or someone, but Tally didn't understand the word *notoone*. Out of the corner of her eye she saw Wren walking over from the supply shed. He approached and greeted the elder in their native language, bringing a smile to the old woman lips. She reached her hand out to him and he took it in both of his after which they stood close in quiet conversation.

Tally didn't understand a single word they were saying, but their expressions told the story. They knew each other well. Perhaps they were family. She stood quietly and waited for them to finish. When they did, Wren put his arm around the elder's shoulders and spoke to Tally.

"This is my mother, Singing Star Woman."

"Oh." Tally nodded and smiled in greeting, then

turned back to Wren. "She said she's looking for someone."

"Yes, ma'am. She's looking for her daughter." He paused and took a deep breath. "That's me," he said quietly. "I'm her daughter."

"But you…" Tally began then stopped and waited for Wren's explanation.

"Yes," said Wren with a slow nod. "I am her daughter by birth. But I am a Two Spirit Person."

Tally wasn't totally surprised to hear this. She and Ivy had both wondered, but she remained silent without question or judgment letting Wren speak.

"That means I am both man and woman. Those who are like me in the tribes are valued."

Tally smiled. "I do know that, Wren. But I didn't realize that when the Tribal Chief came here with the others, he was looking for you."

"I didn't want you to know. I was afraid you would send me away. Now it's time I must tell you the truth. I am married to the Chief's son. I ran away because my husband did not honor the Two Spirits in me. He was cruel. He was unkind."

Tally's heart stirred inside her. "Oh, Wren, I'm so sorry."

"But I must go back now. My mother tells me she is sick, she needs me. She says my husband has promised to not be unkind if I return."

Disappointed, but swept with joy to see a family reunited, Tally graciously replied. "Wren, I will miss you greatly. You've helped us so much and I appreciate it more than I can say." She gestured with her arms, spreading them wide to take in the entire homestead. "I couldn't have done all this without you. You're always welcome to come back. Your husband, too. Does he need work?"

"Thank you, Miss Tally. I will be grateful for the work.

My husband, too. But for now, I must take care of my mother before she Walks On."

"I understand. But please know my door is always open to you."

"Thank you, Miss Tally. But there's something else I must tell you now that it is safe. Now that Birch is gone."

"What's that?"

Wren smiled, eyes glowing with something akin to delight and mischief. "When Hath returns, go out to the dugout in the back pasture. He knows where it is. Ask him to remove the boulders sealing the entrance. There's something inside for you. It's what Birch was looking for when he dug up the ground around Prayer Rock. What he was looking for when he came here."

CHAPTER FORTY-THREE

One year later

HANK TISDALE WALKED OUT of jail a free man. Not because he wasn't guilty, but because the three cell jail in the tiny town of Paradise, Colorado burned down and put the sheriff and the only deputy out of a job.

But the truth of it was, Hank didn't actually rob a bank. He just tried to.

Desperate for money to finish proving up his homestead, and fortified by an overabundance of liquid courage, he did try to rob that bank. But right after he stumbled in that day, pulled his gun and handed the teller a note that said *give me all your cash and gold* it was at that exact same moment the sheriff came in behind him to make a deposit.

Hank was arrested on the spot.

Now he was in a stagecoach happy to be on his way back to Sutton Creek, and happy, too, that the clothes he'd worn into the bank that fateful day still fit. The sheriff's wife prepared meals for the prisoners, and she was a darn good cook. If there was anything to be grateful for it was that he had eaten well. But his horse was gone, sold off by the sheriff to pay for his keep.

He'd worried constantly about his homestead long empty miles away. Had his cabin burned down? Or been blown apart in a harsh winter storm?

He'd been able to keep up on the news somewhat, and had heard from some of the over imbibed cowpokes sleeping off a drunk in one of the adjacent cells about land grabbers and swindlers chasing off homesteaders and stealing patents. Was he going to find out someone had taken over his spread?

Or did Clarkson own it now since Hank hadn't come up with the money?

He'd worried about his daughters, too, and surely they'd worried about him when his letters stopped arriving. The sheriff had assured him that a Pinkerton man would be sent to Sutton Creek to notify his daughters of his incarceration, but the man they'd sent couldn't locate them.

"Whoa!" The driver slowed the team then called out to Hank. "You're almost home, sir. We're comin' to Bandit Bend. Mind you be quick steppin' out. Don't want to get robbed here."

Hank craned his neck to look out the window. The stagecoach swayed and jolted as the driver brought the team to a halt.

Eager to be home, Hank opened the door and jumped out brushing road dust off his clothes. His heart sank as he surveyed his spread.

The trees that bordered the road were gone now and he could see freshly painted fences and healthy-looking livestock enclosed behind sturdy fences and fine-looking corrals. No longer falling down, the barn had been rebuilt, reroofed and painted bright red. A porch had recently been added to the cabin. Lace curtains hung in the windows.

Someone was living there.

Dejected, he walked slowly into the yard, but slowed when a man came out of the barn. The man shaded his eyes with his hand and watched Hank approach. A stern-faced woman came out of the cabin, put her hands on her hips and watched, too. She was heavy with child, a baby soon to be born. As he drew closer, he saw her light brown hair was parted in the middle and braided. Silver rings glittered in her ears. Closer still, he saw her expression soften and a smile brighten her face as she opened her arms in greeting.

"Ivy!" she called over her shoulder. "Hurry! Father's home!"

Her eyes swelled with tears, but she swiped them away with the back of her hand, then took Hank by the arm.

"Come with me, Father," she said. "I'd like you to meet my husband, Hath, the father of your first grandchild."

CHAPTER FORTY-FOUR

Four Years Later

BIRCH QUINN HAD A new, but hard-won life. He had a new name, too. Cole Harper.

As Birch, he'd dug under the supply shed his last night on the Tisdale homestead, but hadn't found the loot he'd buried there. Angry and defeated, he didn't see that he had any other choice but to run off.

As Cole Harper, he hightailed it out of Sutton Creek and stayed on the move drifting from town to town always on the lookout for a stranger staring at him too long, standing too close, or starting an unnecessary conversation. When he'd lost the last of his hired hand money at a card table, he robbed a few stages, and hid out in the mountains.

When he acquired enough cash, he headed for Poncha Springs to pay a visit to Rico's widow Clarita. He found her still working at the trading post. She told him she only worked parttime now, because her father had died and left her a small, rundown ranch, but when Rico never returned, she had no one to help her run it.

Clarita was beautiful and pleasant natured, and Birch was no man's fool. He told her his name was Cole Harper, and immediately took advantage of an opportunity. He talked her into letting him move in with her to help take care of the ranch. Despite the hard work, he cherished the quiet, the comfort, and the isolation of the spread, as well as Clarita's cooking.

They now had a son named Ethan, and another child on the way. The arrangement had worked out so well for them both, they planned to get married the next time the traveling preacher came through Poncha Springs. Birch didn't let his mind focus on the past. Too much bad history. None of which Clarita was aware. Birch firmly believed that ignorance of the past helped a marriage and a homelife survive.

It was while sitting on his porch in a rocking chair reading a book to three-year-old Ethan, that he saw a man on horseback ride on to the property. He rode slowly through the hardy wild grass fronting the cabin. There was nothing threatening about him, yet Birch put down the book and said, "Go inside, son."

Ethan, who Birch was proud to say was a chip off the old block, resisted.

"No," said the little boy. "I want the rest of the story."

"Later." Birch lifted Ethan off his lap careful to keep concern out of his voice and his eyes. "I promise. Now go inside and see what Momma is cooking up for supper."

Ethan pushed his lower lip out in a pout. The screen door squeaked open and slammed shut as he reluctantly went inside to his mother. Clarita's voice drifted out the door. "Come along, Ethan. It's time for a nap."

Birch kept his gaze steady into the far distance. Snow topped summits with splotches in the recesses that the sun couldn't touch were barely visible through a blue haze. The ranch was so remote no one ever came calling and wayward strangers rarely wandered in.

This stranger sat strong and straight in the saddle which lessened Birch's apprehension allowing him to release some of his unease over the intrusion. Still, he didn't like strangers coming around.

Questions buzzed around in his head. *Do I know this man? Is he lost?* Something about him nudged Birch's mind in a halfway familiar direction, and his attention shifted from curious to unease. He momentarily fought against an urge to flee.

The rider stopped a short distance away from the porch, not too close and not too far, just close enough to be heard. He removed his hat, pulled a cloth from his pocket and wiped his neck and forehead. "Afternoon," he said, pleasant enough in greeting.

His eyes laid heavily on Birch, but his voice had a smile in it, so Birch stopped his hand from drifting to his holster. "Howdy, stranger. You need something to eat? Water for your horse?"

Why else would a stranger come trespassing on private property way out here? He looked vaguely familiar and Birch stirred his mind trying to figure out who this man was and why he would come on to his property with a rifle in the crook of his arm.

The man returned his gaze for six long seconds. "Howdy, Birch."

No one called him that anymore, and instant recognition hit Birch like a foot in the stomach. It was the Wells Fargo guard he'd shot on Bandit Bend. Stunned, words escaped him.

"How did you find me?" he asked finally.

The man's eyebrows arched at the question and he gave Birch a dumbshit look, then shook his head in weary amusement.

"You might as well have left a trail of breadcrumbs," he replied in mock reproach. "Your eye color gave you away. Everyone remembered it."

Birch took a slow deep breath and waited while the man ticked off names.

"The stagecoach passengers you robbed described

your eyes. Wells Fargo put their description on a wanted poster. The stableman in San Miguel where you broke Rico out of jail then left him to die on the trail. The bartender at Silverton Inn where you killed Omaha. Hath and Wren at the Tisdale homestead, the Tisdale sisters—"

"Well, you wasted your time!" Birch interrupted gruffly. "I don't have the loot."

"I know. The Indian on the Tisdale property found where you buried it and hid in the dugout in the back pasture. The sisters turned it over to the authorities and Wells Fargo gave them a nice reward. Enough so they could prove up their homestead, register the deed. They own that place free and clear now with a little extra in their bank account."

To Birch, this was a gut wrench after all the work he did for them to now not have a share.

The Wells Fargo detective went on.

"They were issued a couple of adjoining patents and are using their extra money to prove them up, too. Got themselves quite a spread now." He grinned. "Those girls are quite the go-getters. Them and that other one, Mimi. The three of them started a document business helping other women with the paperwork so they can acquire homesteads of their own."

Birch's flight response ramped up again, his eyes jumped around as if trying to find an escape route. But he held steady. He was used to talking his way out of trouble, and wondered if there was a chance of that now. After a beat of silence, he spoke up.

"So what are ya gonna do? Arrest me? I've got a wife and kid now I have to take care of. Another one on the way. You gonna leave a widow and two babies out here all alone to fend for themselves?"

The man squinted and looked like he was debating the question. "No, I'm not going to arrest you," he answered, smirking as he talked. "I'm a part time doctor now. I'm here to administer an elixir."

That was unexpected, and Birch tilted his head as if he hadn't heard right. "Oh, really? What's that?"

"A .44 Henry cure for stagecoach robbery fever."

It took Birch a few seconds to catch up with what the man said. When it did, his hand flew to his holster, but too late. The guard's Winchester discharged with a deafening roar burying a bullet in Birch's chest.

Birch jerked back, stumbled, and swayed on his feet. The pain was staggering. He moaned, spasmed, then loose-limbed went down.

The screen door screeched open. With effort he turned his head toward the sound and saw Clarita step out onto the porch gazing at him with cold, slitted eyes. For the first time, she looked like, what she was, a harlot's daughter. A breeze danced in fluttering the WANTED DEAD OR ALIVE poster in her hand. His name was on it.

The detective slid his rifle into a scabbard. "Wells Fargo will issue your reward next week," he told her. "An agent will bring it out personally."

"Thank you, Agent Mathias," she replied.

"Have a good day, ma'am." Mathias tipped his hat, reined his horse around, and rode away.

AUTHOR NOTE

Women needed guts to live in the Old West. Early Hollywood movies rarely acknowledged that, often portraying Western and Frontier women as weak willed and frivolous, utterly unable to care for themselves, or get along at all without a man.

Women in the Old West faced unbelievable hardship and sacrifice. Wild animals, hostile Indians, rainstorms, floods, insects, bandits, disease and death all in an unfamiliar, unforgiving land.

Women were lured by the Homestead Act that allowed anyone twenty-one years of age or older—*regardless of gender*—to own land in their own name. Adventurous women headed West, but others did so for a variety of reasons. Boredom, love of the outdoors, curiosity. Some packed up belongings and headed West because they simply wanted to get away. Some wanted to escape, others needed to hide. Some did it with husbands or fathers, but some did it on their own. Some left husbands to do it on their own. Historians say that 12 percent of early homesteaders were single women.

They shot bears and snakes, and menacing intruders. They built cabins and dugouts, pushed plows, planted crops, fed and cared for animals. They chopped off toes while splitting wood with an ax, froze their fingers or broke an arm caring for livestock. They dug graves for their children and still found a way to go on. Because there was no turning back.

Some women made it and some didn't. I wrote this book to honor them all.

ACKNOWLEDGEMENTS

It isn't entirely true that writing is a solitary endeavor. All authors need someone. Advance readers, editors, critique groups. And because authors can't know *everything*, they often seek out experts and researchers. Even if authors do their own research, there is always someone at the other end of that, too—librarians, museum curators, historians, or someone with particular knowledge about a specific topic.

I've been fortunate to have wonderful people like that on my team during the writing of this book, so let me thank them all again.

First, a big thanks to Geoff Habiger and Artemesia Publishing for acknowledging the value of a book calling attention to the contributions of courageous women in the progress and development of this great country. Thank you also for your keen eye as the story unfolded.

Miriam Kleiman, Public Affairs Specialist at the U.S. National Archives answered all my questions with patience and good humor without ever sounding too busy which I know she was. She had a mountain of information on the tip of her tongue, and knew just where to look or where to direct me to dig deeper for the information I needed.

Greg Bradsher, Senior Archivist at the National Archives and Records Administration, was a joy to speak to and provided me enough information and historical perspective to fill a dozen books. He knows everything there is to know about the Homestead Act of 1862, and about homesteading and land ownership in the American West which helped me with the authenticity of my story. On a side note, I was interested to know that Mr. Bradsher worked with the Monuments Men team that located and restored artwork stolen by the Nazis during World War II. He was also a consultant on the set of the movie "Monument Men" released in 2014.

A million thanks to author Lena Jo McCoy, my irreplaceable critique partner and first reader whose thoughts, comments, and knowledge of farms, ranching and domestic animal care was incredibly valuable to me during the writing of this book. She is also astute at picking up subtle contradictions and inconsistencies in a draft manuscript.

Special thanks to Wade Weber, Educational Director at the Scottsdale Arizona Western Museum; James Muhn, Author, Archivist, and American West Land Law Historian; the staff at the Homestead National Monument in Beatrice, Nebraska; and the Summit County Historical Society in Dillon, Colorado that has collected a wealth of information on homesteading in that state.

And thanks to my daughter Barbara Bowman for reading pages as I wrote them, and also for being my roadie at book signings and other author events.

- C. C. Harrison

ABOUT THE AUTHOR

C. C. Harrison is an award-winning author of contemporary suspense and American West fiction. She knew she was going to be a writer when she received her first grade library card. Since then her novels have been honored both regionally and nationally.

"I write books about ordinary women who find themselves facing danger because of someone else's mistake, but sometimes their own. They're courageous women who find a way to overcome fear and adversity to do what needs to be done." Harrison can be found in the desert, the mountains, or some far flung corner of the Southwest.